IF THE
DEAD
COULD
SPEAK

By Tim Mahoney

Other books by this author:
The Resurrection of John Dillinger
Dead Messenger
Dead Like Lazarus
Dead a Long Time
Secret Partners
Jack's Boy
Ghost Patrol
We're Not Here
Halloran's World War

ISBN: 9780990897408

This book is dedicated to those whose advice helped it along the way: To Alison M. and to the core members of the Minnesota Writers Guild: John R., Karl, Miranda, John P., Pam, Don, Kate, John H., Tricia and Morris. May they all have good luck on their literary journeys.

NOTE

This novel is based closely on the true gangster history of the Public Enemies era. The crimes in this story actually occurred, much as described, in the spring and summer of 1932.

Rose Perry and Sadie Carmacher met the fate described in this book. So did Arthur Dunlop. The characters whom the reader will meet, and who went on to shoot their way into the history books, committed the crimes described in this story, and many others. Underworld masterminds Harry Sawyer and Jack Peifer are presented here much as history knew them.

During the early 1930s, Saint Paul was described as "the poison spot of American crime," on the floor of the U.S. Senate. Since the turn of the century, the city had been home to a protection racket that allowed criminals to purchase immunity from prosecution. Aided by a profoundly corrupt police department, gangsters based in Saint Paul roamed the Midwest, pulling off bank robberies, kidnappings and murders. Most of the notorious criminals of the Public Enemies era had connections to Saint Paul's underworld.

CHAPTER ONE

March, 1932

Papa Alt liked it cold. He could buy trainloads of coal, but his mansion was so chilly, his servants dressed like they were ice skating. His butler, in leather gloves and topcoat, escorted me through a parlor of Persian rugs and potted ferns and into Papa's den.

Papa Alt wore a white shirt, cufflinks removed, sleeves rolled up, collar open. His den was teak, decorated in Great White Trophy Hunter, with antlered buck heads and monster muskies.

"Don't sit, Powers," he said, "you won't be here so long."

I played humble and removed my fedora.

Papa Alt looked me over as if I were one of his trotting horses.

He had sparse white hair, blue eyes, a hearty complexion and had reached his 60s in athletic trim. The Germans got a bad rap because of the War. Papa Alt was no scowling Hun. He was known for his smile, his outbursts of civic generosity. He negotiated honorably with trade unions, and a job with Alt was a job for life, complete with Thanksgiving turkey.

But Papa was not smiling this morning.

"You were recommended as discreet," he said. "If so, that would be a miracle in this town. I am in need of information. It concerns two gangster molls. They are gossiping in the taverns."

I stood hat in hand. There was nowhere to lay it, except for

Papa Alt's oak desk.

He said: "These women are said to be girlfriends of a machine-gun gang. I wish to know about these gangsters, and why they traveled here."

He fiddled with a meerschaum pipe, then began to fill it from a glass beaker of tobacco.

"We need our vices, Powers." As he filled the pipe pinch by pinch he said: "Their names are Rose Perry and Sadie Carmacher. They arrived from Duluth, and they frequent the Green Lantern. Can you have a report for me in a few days?"

"Certainly," I said.

He lit the pipe with a gold lighter. Exhaling blue smoke he said: "Excellent."

The butler, afraid I might snatch something, escorted me out. I stood on the porch, pulling on leather gloves and rewrapping my scarf. Across a snowy street stood Altwasser Soft Drinks. There were medieval towns in Germany, I imagined, that resembled this brewery, with its stout brick buildings, turrets and cobblestone streets. It had been Huntz Brewery until 1921, when that family, ruined by Prohibition, sold to Otto "Papa" Alt.

At the time, Papa was a money-lender. He bought the brewery for dimes on the dollar. Soon Altwasser Ale, trucked in barrels at night, was poured at speakeasies all over the Northwest.

Papa was now the wealthiest bootlegger between Chicago and Seattle. I assumed he hired me because of the Lindbergh Baby Kidnapping, a case two weeks old and unsolved. Papa Alt had three adult children and four grandkids. Just in the last few months, kidnappers had struck two wealthy Saint Paul families. Rich men on Summit Hill were hiring guards, and locking down their mansions.

I drove my rickety black Ford home, not fool enough to try parking downtown. I took the streetcar to Royal Cigars on Robert Street. They didn't sell many cigars there, and smart guys knocked at the back door. If the doorman recognized you, he let you in to a smoky room. Through the haze you'd see clerks scurrying in front of a blackboard. It listed handwritten details of races at Hialeah, Hawthorne, Belmont and Pimlico. I can sit for hours with the Racing Form, picking off a winner here and there, but not today. It was a much better bet working for Papa Alt.

If I impressed Papa Alt, maybe I too, could have a job for life.

The guy I wanted was Pat Reilly, who sat, Lucky Strike in lips, behind his tellers cage. Pat was a little guy with blond, greasy hair combed straight back. He had crooked, rotten teeth. He was just a dumb kid, really, the worst horse player I knew. He worked two jobs to support losing habits.

"Pa-drake," I said.

"Don't pull that Irish shit on me."

Pat sold bet slips all day. He drank highballs to kill the pain of working.

I said: "Something tells me you haven't backed a winner all day."

"Pick a longshot at Hialeah, will ya Mickey?"

"Patrick I don't have the time. Here's five bucks to pry your mouth open."

He palmed the fiver I passed under the cage.

"Two dames," I said. "Hit town from Duluth."

"I don't know nothing, but ignorance costs five bucks apiece."

I slipped him another bill. The price was extravagant, but it was smart to keep Pat happy.

He said: "You're talking about Indian Rose and what's her name, right?"

"Rose Perry."

"Maybe that's her real name. The man you want to see is Tommy Filben."

"That's ten bucks worth of information?"

Pat snapped his nicotine-yellowed fingers.

"Sadie," he said, "that's the other one."

"What does Tommy have to do with them?"

"They called from Duluth, looking for money."

"How does Tommy know two Duluth girls?"

"Beats me," said Pat.

"What about these girls?"

"They drink hard."

"What else?"

"Staying at the Hotel Saint Paul, blowing cash."

"I heard they've got the lowdown on certain gangsters."

"Shut up," said Pat. "People who talk don't say nothing because ..." he shook out a fresh Lucky, " ... Chief Ryan's got the biggest ears in town."

He tapped that Lucky on his wrist to settle the tobacco. "Not even the nuns could cram nothing through my thick Irish skull," he said.

"Don't give me that Irish crap. These girls came here with a tommygun gang. Who are they? What do they want here?"

"I plead ignorance."

Impatient, I drummed my fingers on his counter. "Don't gamble that ten bucks, Pat. Put it toward rent."

He sputtered. "Jeesh. Rent. Don't remind me."

I called on Tommy Filben at his radio shop, but as usual, it was closed. The doorman at the Hotel Saint Paul was new on the job, and had no information to sell regarding two females, one of them an Indian. I chatted up cabbies, but they must have been driving blind.

So I walked toward home. I stopped for a Coney dog at the
Gopher Tavern, then wasted two cents each on the Dispatch and
the Daily News. I dropped a penny a tip into the thick wool
mittens of Blind Benny at the newsstand. It was a long winter, and
I pitied Benny, standing on street corners when he should have
been rocking his grandkids in front of a roaring fireplace.

I climbed the hill to my apartment and on weary legs mounted
four flights of stairs. When I opened the door, Snowflake was
turning in circles. Hula Girl popped up, paws against my overcoat.

Hula Girl had two missing teeth, which gave her a goofy snarl.
She snapped her jaws demanding dinner. Snowflake retreated to his
bowl and simply waited. From the electric refrigerator I retrieved a
mash of cooked German sausage. I portioned crumbled meat into
two cereal bowls, and mixed in Kellogg's Corn Flakes. I don't
know why I bothered to mix it, since the dogs scarfed it up, as
indiscriminate as snow plows. I set the bowls down as Hula Girl
squealed in delight. Snowflake, silent as a monk, spread his legs and
gobbled.

Snowflake could have been a show-dog, a cream-white German
Spitz of high pedigree. Hula Girl was a mutt, a Border Collie mixed
with something smaller. She had white at the tip of her paws and
splashed on her chest, but was otherwise black. Neither topped
thirty pounds on their fattest day. Both had been left to me because
where my wife went, no dog could follow.

I threw my coat over the couch and sat to look over my city. I
paid good money for this apartment, and in return got shiny oak
floors, plenty of steam heat, modern appliances and wonderful
views. Looking out the parlor windows I saw the speakeasies, dice
parlors, bordellos, horse wires, pool halls, bowling alleys, hotels, all
jammed into the crazy Seven Corners. That intersection was
clogged with streetcars, lurching trucks, honking autos, and the
occasional horse-drawn wagon. Out the kitchen windows, my view

was the magnificent Cathedral of Saint Paul. Its massive copper dome and its cross pointed at a cloudy Heaven.

I made myself a chocolate milk and settled down to read the funnies. Snowflake and Hula Girl lay beside me like living bookends. I turned the radio to WCCO and was disappointed to hear the musical mush of Guy Lombardo.

It seemed I had lucked into a simple but lucrative job. It was no mystery why Papa Alt had chosen me: I was known around town as a messenger with connections. Papa and I also had a friend in common, a certain Irish priest.

No question, Papa Alt was in on The Deal. Everybody in town knew The Deal. It had been in place since I was a boy. The Deal was simple: Pay off the cops, commit your crimes outside of Saint Paul, and you'll never get spanked by Dame Justice.

Under The Deal, Papa Alt's bank and family would be safe from gangsters. But maybe Papa Alt was worried that a gang from Duluth wouldn't honor The Deal.

With the chocolate milk, my dogs, comforting thoughts and bland music, I fell into a deep, dreamless nap.

Until the phone rang.

"It's Reilly," he said, and hung up.

These guys didn't talk on the phone.

I wrapped up in fedora and overcoat, threw a handful of peanuts to distract my dogs, and drove my Model A down the hill. It was a frosty dark March evening, and the car slipped over steel trolley rails all the way to the Loop. I found lucky parking at the police station, which occupies a city block, and looks like a combination train depot and Greek temple. I walked around the corner to The Green Lantern and knocked at the back door. An eye appeared at the peephole. Bess let me in. I handed her my hat and coat and walked for the bar.

These Duluth women might as well have been sitting under a

neon arrow. One was a chubby Indian. The other was a skinny white girl with stringy hair. They sat in the dark corner near the coat room. A short guy in a blue suit and straw hat was apprising them of his personal virtues. I stepped in between him and the girls.

This guy rocked back and tilted his hat, like he wanted to fight. Pat Reilly stepped up behind the bar, damp towel over his shoulder. In the horse parlor, he was just another loser. At the Green Lantern, he was head bartender.

Pat told the guy: "Rico, beat it, will ya."

The guy looked at Reilly and then at me.

"Go on, I'll buy you a drink," I told the guy.

"Go fuck yourself," Rico said, and turned away.

"What are you ladies drinking?" I asked the Indian.

She sputtered. "Ladies?"

"You talking to us?" said the white girl.

She was drinking a gin fizz. The Indian woman rattled a tumbler of ice cubes. The white girl had one eye focused, the other lazy, fixed to the side.

"You're turning down a free drink?" I asked her.

"Never," she said.

Out of her purse she pulled what looked like a lipstick tube, but turned out to be a cigarette lighter. Removing its red cap, she lit a Chesterfield, then crumpled the empty pack.

"Just being a wise ass. Name's Sadie."

She shook my hand, her grip cold and bony.

"Double gin fizz," Sadie said. "Rose is whiskey rocks."

Rose tried to hide an impish grin. She was a lovely woman, with dark skin, short clean hair, and a gold crucifix dangling into her cleavage.

"Rose is this, Rose is that," said Rose, "everybody's talking about Rose, but nobody really knows anything about Rose."

"Rose is bitter," whispered Sadie.

"Men are whores," said Rose. She looked at me, a flash of lively brown eyes. "Did you know that, stranger? Men can be whores too."

"What did I do?" I said as Reilly laid drinks for them and a ginger ale for me.

"Men talk right over you," Rose said, "like you weren't there."

"I'm Michael," I said. "You're new in town, right?"

Rose said: "Go away, Michael, before you get hurt."

Sadie, a gleam in her good eye, shook her head. I took that to mean Rose was sometimes a burden.

"Yeah, we're new in town," said Sadie. "What you got?"

"Passwords," I said.

"Oh," muttered Rose. "You're one of those." She sipped whiskey. "I'm so tired of big shots. Just once I'd like to meet an ordinary fellow."

"I know my way around town, that's all."

"We're waiting for someone," Sadie said, and blew smoke toward the whiskey bottles on the back bar. Her skinny legs dangled off the stool and she kicked the chrome rungs with her leather boots. "Otherwise we could be friendly."

Rose shook her head and muttered: "Nope."

"We'll be here tomorrow night too," said Sadie. "Rose will be in a better mood, won't you Rosie?"

"I haven't had dinner," I said. "I know a great place on the Levee."

"What's the Levee?"

"The Italian neighborhood."

"Great place to get knifed, I'll bet," said Rose.

"Aw, it's okay," I said. "If you know your way around."

"I could go for spaghetti and meatballs," said Sadie.

"Forget it," said Rose.

Sadie picked up her bright green purse.

"See you back at the room," she told Rose, and inspected me with her good eye. "Italian," she said.

As I was helping Sadie into her coat I saw that little guy, Rico, glaring at me. I beckoned Reilly over.

"Patrick," I said. "Who's the guy?"

"Rico? Don't worry," Reilly said. "If you were in trouble, you'd never know it."

I drove Sadie across town, through the tunnel, down the riverbank, toward the Levee.

"Heater in this thing work?" she asked.

"Nope."

"What's your racket, tough guy?"

I swiped at frosty windows with a stolen hotel towel.

"This and that," I said.

"Huh," she said. "When am I going to meet a man with a profession?"

"I do okay," I said.

We arrived at Martinucci's, a brick place with a glassy front, the striped awning rolled back, the family name spelled in gold on the windows.

"They serve wine?" Sadie asked. "I can't eat Italian without wine."

We sat at a table covered in checkered cloth. With her lipstick-tube lighter, Sadie lit the candle in the Chianti bottle. The menu was scribbled on a chalk board. Sadie rubbed her hands for warmth as she read it.

"You know this joint," she said, "what's your favorite?"

"Lasagna with white sauce."

"What the hell is in white sauce?"

"I don't know exactly."

Her lips turned down in disapproval. I noticed, here in decent light, her drawn-in eyebrows and wrinkled forehead. She might have been twenty-five, she might have been forty-five. She had bad skin, sharp features and dirty hair. I could sense a lifetime of rejection, boys making fun of her lazy eye, as the pretty girls got all the attention. Surgeons can fix a lazy eye nowadays. But nobody had ever taken care of this girl. Sadie the dropout, Sadie the homely outcast.

I kind of liked her.

"So," I said. "Duluth."

"Fuck Duluth," she said. "You ever spent a winter in Duluth? It's worse than here, a hundred times worse than here. You married?"

"Not anymore."

"Nothing gold can stay," she said.

"What's that?"

"Robert Frost. The poet? Nothing lasts for shit, is what he's saying. Only he says it like a poet."

One of the Martinucci's teenaged girls took our orders and delivered Sadie's wine. As a concession to the 18th Amendment, it was served in a coffee mug. Sadie drank hard, cup to her cracked lips.

I asked: "How did you meet Rose?"

"That's a story. Two weeks, that's all I've known her." She brushed at her scraggly hair. "At first she don't have much to say. But once you crack the shell, she's a good egg."

Sadie wore no jewelry. If she owned furs, she would have worn them on such a bitter night. Her cheap cotton dress wouldn't have fended off a molecule of Duluth's winter. She shivered in her Navy pea jacket, the kind that costs a buck at any war surplus store.

"Running out of cash," she said. "Hard to find work. Maybe we'll hit Chicago."

"What kind of work you do?"

"Anything, Mister. Desperate times. You name it, I do it."

The candle flame flickered as a party of four, heavy with spaghetti, made an exit.

Sadie twirled her fork on the tabletop. "You got a cigarette?"

"I smoke a pipe," I said.

"Cheapskates smoke a pipe," she said.

She turned to look for the cigarette machine but just then our plates arrived, along with a basket of warm bread and a cruet of olive oil. Sadie twirled the spaghetti around her fork and sucked it down. The meatballs, almost the size of baseballs, she sliced and gulped. My dogs were more ravenous, but not by much. Sadie stuffed half the bread into her pocketbook.

I was pretty sure I knew her profession, so I didn't push it. Duluth is a port city, lousy with Great Lakes sailors.

"Why Saint Paul?" I asked.

"Oh, Rose got connections. I don't know a soul. I'm just hanging on."

Her hands shook. She lay down her fork and spoon.

"You wouldn't have twenty bucks for a girl, would you?"

She covered my hands with her own, thin and cold, her nail polish chipped. "I mean as a loan," she said. "Until I get on my feet."

I began to suspect that a nasty Yen Shee habit accounted for her pale complexion and shaky hands.

"Rose don't eat, see, that's it, she drinks," Sadie said. "I never met anybody like her, could eat nothing and gain weight. I eat all the time, and no gain. I'm always cold. I'm always hungry. Can you figure that? You ever been to Florida?"

"No."

"Me neither. Twenty bucks, Mister?"

Twenty bucks was a week's pay at a bottom job, and you'd be

lucky to get that right now, a bottom job. The meal was 35 cents, the wine 15 cents. That I could afford. But twenty bucks? That was close to half of Papa Alt's fee.

"I don't have that kind of cash."

"I thought you were doing okay?" She mopped tomato sauce with buttered bread.

I said: "You're not a gangster's girl, are you?"

"I ain't a girl at all."

"A lot of rumors floating around ," I said. "A gang of machine-gun bandits, maybe from Duluth. They blew into town, snatch racket, I figure, looking to take a local swell. It's a five dollar rumor, anybody can provide details."

Sadie swallowed. "I'm respectable."

"Five bucks," I said, "Is five bucks. Ten plates of spaghetti, ten glasses of wine."

"Mister I don't know who you are, but if you can spare five bucks, I've got five dollars worth of happy for you. I just need the money pretty bad."

"I'm more interested in rumors."

She drained her wine cup. "Are you driving me home, or am I walking through snow?"

At the Hotel Saint Paul, I signed in for a $6 room under my alias, P. M. Powell. Sadie waited in the marble lobby, at the golden elevator, returning the hotel dick's stink-eye glare.

"Punk," she said as the elevator doors closed, the dick staring at her still.

When I turned the key in room 422, Sadie stepped in and said: "Hey, it's hot in here."

"I thought you were cold," I said.

"Well I'm hot all of a sudden."

I cracked open a frosty window, letting in the night air, and the noises of autos and streetcars. She hung her Navy pea coat in the closet and shed her pink blouse. For the first time I saw her as sexy. She had smooth shoulders and a narrow, girlish waist.

"Michael, right? Michael, are we drinking?"

I bumped into the writing desk, picked up the phone and ordered Canadian and set ups.

She sat on the bed, hands in her lap, staring out the window. Up on Cathedral Hill, the lights of many mansions twinkled. A spotlight shone on the Cathedral's copper dome and giant cross.

"See, it's…" she slipped off her brassiere and lay back. Her breasts flattened out to almost nothing. She kicked off her salt-stained boots.

"Are you one of those talkers," she said, "or do you get it over with?"

"I'm a romantic," I said. "So I've been told." I lay my suit jacket atop my overcoat on a plush red chair.

"Go ahead," she said. "Tell me your life story."

I loosened my red-and-gold striped tie, looked into the mirror, saw myself. Do we ever get used to that stranger?

"My wife dumped me," I said.

"High school sweetheart, I suppose. You're not going to make me take my own skirt off, are you?"

I knelt at the bed, unbuttoned her gray skirt, pulled it off, leaving her in panties and stockings.

I folded her skirt on top of my suit jacket.

"I met her in a tavern on Staten Island," I said. "I was a soldier, she was in nursing school. A college girl, imagine that. She was a gorgeous natural blonde, could have roped any guy in the place, but she took me home."

I unbuttoned my starched white shirt.

"You ain't horrible looking," Sadie said. "I could have gone for you myself."

I lay down beside Sadie, both of us crossways on the bed. "I gave her everything I had," I said, "but it wasn't enough."

"All I hear is sad stories," said Sadie. "I'm the Cleopatra of sad."

A discreet tap at the door roused me from the bed. I tipped the bellman $1 and wheeled in a narrow cart. It held a sweating silver ice bucket, two highball glasses, a bottle of Hamm's ginger ale and a flask of dark liquor. It might have been genuine Canadian, or might have been cheap boot.

"So," I said, and used silver tongs to drop ice in each highball glass, "that's how I got to be me. How did you get to be you?"

She sat up, her naked back against the dark headboard, her stockinged legs sprawled on wool covers.

"Girls leave home sooner or later," she said. "Me, I was seventeen."

She reached for the night-table, fished in her green leather purse.

"What do you need in there?"

"My lighter."

She dropped the purse. "I left it at the restaurant. I'll get it tomorrow. They're open Sundays, right?"

I came up with a book of Green Lantern matches. I struck the match and I will never forget the illusion, Sadie's face aflame as I held the fire to the end of her cigarette.

We gulped our drinks. She rattled ice cubes in that glass and said, "I can't be all night, you know."

I rolled the stockings off her skinny legs, and she lifted her hips to allow me to slip off her panties. I dropped my trousers and underwear and lay beside her, naked to naked.

She grasped my man thing in her cold bony hand and said, "Plumbing works. So that wasn't your problem."

"Problem?"

"Yeah, why she left you."

I kissed her greasy lips.

"Most men don't kiss my kind," she said. She had been holding a Trojan in one closed fist, and now she rolled it onto me.

I held her close, smelling hair gel and cigarette and wine and cheap booze and garlic tomato sauce and underneath it all, that woman scent all men crave, our mothers, the divine aroma, the first one we ever knew, the most powerful smell on Earth.

I stroked her stringy greasy hair, looked at her, bad eye and good eye.

"Are you ready?" asked Sadie.

She reached down and stroked herself wet. She was a business woman after all.

"Okay, hop in," she said.

I slipped in. She wasn't my Peggy but it didn't matter.

"Umf," said Sadie.

"Am I hurting you?"

"It's okay now," said Sadie.

We did that primitive thing slowly until we pumped up a rhythm that had us both grunting. My sensations were real, but I suspected Sadie of professional fakery. I rolled off her, hobbled to the bathroom and washed up. When I emerged, she was already in stocking and panties, standing at the drink cart, mixing a knockout punch in a glass.

"Five dollars?" I said, standing there naked.

It is always bad to negotiate naked.

"You know how much I need dough, don't you?" she said.

"Ten, then," I said. I pulled a t-shirt over my chest, reached for my wallet and said, "And ten more for information about your gangster boyfriend."

"If I had a gangster boyfriend, would I be here with you?"

She swirled her drink.

"See a girl like me needs a protector. On account of all the vicious bastards. I had a mug in Duluth, but he punked me out. Because I'm used up, I ain't a girl anymore. Rose said somebody would look out for me here."

"I hear there's a gang of kidnappers come to town."

"Kidnappers?" said Sadie. "I'd turn them in if I knew. Kidnappers, like the ones stole the Lindbergh baby? Who could be so heartless as to steal a child?"

"Summit 5-3-2-1. Call me if you hear anything."

"Thanks for dinner," she said and kissed me on the cheek. "You're a sport. I'll see you around town."

I felt a tug of heartbreak watching her, skinny and ragged, out of place in swanky hotel. I like women, I'm a sucker for women, I need women, I admit it. It's not the glamorous women who appeal to me, but the ordinary ones, the humble, the downcast, the nobodies.

Sadie Nobody walked down the bright corridor toward the golden elevators. She flashed me a sweet smile.

The elevator arrived with a bing.

A big red arrow lit, and pointed down.

CHAPTER TWO

That night I dreamed of winter in Hell. The Devil was Frosty the Snowman, with a bloody knife instead of a carrot as his nose. His Assistant Demons wore parkas, icy face masks and glowing red gloves. Carrying torches, they stalked happy families, who were sledding innocent down a snowy hill. I shouted to warn the children: Flee! Flee!

I woke up coughing.

Flee?

My feet were like ice blocks as I shuffled to the kitchen for a glass of water. Hula Girl left the bed too, and hopped on the table at the city-side windows. I had tacked a carpet remnant on the table, with space for both dogs. It was a magnet for black and white fur.

As predicted on the radio, a blizzard roared in from the Dakotas. The wind rattled the building and blew a whirling confusion of flakes past the windows. I spotted a fiery glow on the Mississippi docks. It was a small fire but reflected all over the frosty window panes. I stumbled into the bathroom for aspirin. Hula Girl watched the fire, and I fell back into bed, where Snowflake's legs scrabbled in a rabbit-chasing dream.

There was something keeping me awake, something that didn't mesh. I appreciated Papa Alt's generosity. Fifty bucks a week, that was well above blue-collar wages. But he'd told me that Sadie and Rose had arrived in town with a machine-gun gang. And Pat Reilly said the women had begged Tom Filben for money. Would Sadie and Rose have been reduced to begging if their boyfriends were high-rolling gangsters?

What did Papa Alt really want? Perhaps he feared kidnapping, or a brewery shakedown, but there was another possibility. Maybe Papa Alt feared that this new, brazen gang would say to hell with The Deal and hold up his bank. His son runs the bank and his youngest daughter works there too. Maybe Papa Alt's nightmare was his children lying bloody on the floor as robbers raked the bank with tommygun fire.

Papa Alt had deep connections to the police. That's what enabled him to keep his brewery open. So why didn't he ask the cops for information about these two stray women?

I faded to sleep, puzzling over Papa Alt's motivation. It was just past dawn when I awoke again. Was I dreaming, or was some maniac pounding on my apartment door?

The dogs were in full barking panic. When my bare feet touched the cold floor I realized it was no dream. My heart pounded as the maniac thumped the door.

As the dogs leaped snarling at the door, I opened it on the safety chain and saw a tough, familiar face. I sighed, unsnapped the chain, flung open the door and said:

"Kick the door in, why don't you?"

"Next time I will," said the Bulldog.

He wore an open trench coat over a beautiful gray pinstriped suit, red handkerchief in the breast pocket. Bulldog McMullen dressed as swell as a railroad executive. But he was no gentleman, not with his shifty wise-guy face, his swollen hands, his broken nose, his disjointed cheekbones. McMullen had turned cop after some palooka had KO'd his dream of prize-fight glory.

Snowflake backed away barking. Hula Girl planted her paws and growled.

I said: "Good morning to you too, Bulldog."

"Inspector wants you," he said.

"The Inspector's out of bed before noon?"

McMullen stood aside. "Move it, will you? We don't get paid by the hour."

"All right, all right," I said, and retreated to the bedroom for fresh trousers and a shirt. "Will this be a formal occasion? Jackets for gentlemen? Or tie and tails?"

The dogs kept their snarling distance from McMullen. I emerged to find him at my dining table, leafing through the Dispatch.

"The ads are the best thing in that rag," I said. "Shortheimer's is having a sale on pork chops, in case you're wondering what's for dinner."

McMullen grunted. "I see she left you the furniture."

Both dogs understood the command "Stay here." Snowflake drooped his fluffy white head. Hula Girl snorted and leaped onto the couch to sulk. I threw peanuts for them and closed the door. Detective McMullen followed me downstairs and opened the door of his beat-up Dodge.

"Something's burning," I said, getting in. "Wiring's shot in this jalopy. City ought to do better by you boys."

"City's going to miss the April payroll," said McMullen. "That's what I hear."

The blizzard had passed, behind it a blast of bitter cold. The windshield wiper only worked on the driver's side, so my view was a gray tunnel of frost. Bulldog nipped from his silver flask as we waited for a cop to wave us through the car-and-trolley snarl at Seven Corners.

"So, give me a hint?" I asked.

"No dice," said McMullen.

He drove to the Upper Landing, a concrete dock built in the steamboat era. It was abandoned to Italian mom-and-pops once the railroads made it useless. On the dock, an ambulance and squad cars were parked around the black-burnt wreck of a car.

The smell of burnt wiring was so strong, I expected flames to shoot out from under the hood.

Uniformed coppers scrambled around the dock. I paid no attention to these guys, flunkies for the all-powerful detective division. Talking beside the burned car were Doc Ingerson, long and lanky, and Inspector James Crumley. He was a flabby mountain of a man who, immune to cold weather, wore a seersucker suit year round.

Doc's minions, three bundled-up med students, were wrestling a form out of the passenger seat of that burned car. When I got out of the Bulldog's car, I nearly gagged from the stench. It smelled like somebody had burned a thousand cheap hot dogs over a gasoline and rubber fire. The charred thing the med students extracted was stiff in the sitting position. It took a moment for me to realize it was a blackened corpse. This one joined its mate, already on a gurney, covered in a white sheet. Doc Ingerson, hidden inside a parka, wrote on a clipboard.

Crumley retreated to the squad car, devouring a fried-egg sandwich on Italian bread.

The burned car's tires had melted, its windows popped.

"Man," I said, looking at the blackened corpses. "If the dead could speak."

"If the dead could speak," growled Crumley, "they would shut the hell up."

I plopped into the rear seat of the frigid squad car. Crumley gagged down the sandwich, licked his fingers, and from the dashboard snatched a paper cup of coffee.

"Jimbo," I said. "What do you need me for? The snow's going to ruin my good shoes."

"You ain't got no good shoes," said Crumley.

He wiped his buttery fingers on his trouser legs.

I looked again at the corpses, and wondered if they were children, or had been reduced to child size by a very hot fire.

"Who got burned up?" I asked.

"I'm the one asks the questions, now."

Crumley sipped coffee.

"So ask before I get pneumonia."

"What was you doing in the Green Lantern last night?"

"Having a drink."

"Way I hear it you're off the booze."

"What if I am?"

"Then you got no business in the Lantern."

I shrugged.

"I got all day," Crumley said. "We could sit here chatting until the sun goes cold."

I looked over my shoulder. The two corpses were about to be loaded into the snow-coated meat wagon. Now I remembered my hellish frozen dreams.

"Oh we know who they are," Crumley said. "Don't you worry about that."

He thumbed a notebook that almost disappeared in his meaty hands.

"Notorious, them two," he said. "Notorious in Duluth."

That word, *Duluth,* hit me like an electric shock. I looked back to see the meat wagon's door closing and Doc Ingerson slinking toward his car.

"Margaret Rose," said Crumley. "Aka Margaret Perry, aka Rose Perry. Last known address, Duluth workhouse. Sadie Carmacher aka Marjorie Schwartz. Last known address, Duluth workhouse.

Last seen with," he searched me with bloodshot eyes, "a divorced bum from Saint Paul."

Two firemen used long poles to poke around in the burned car.

"Sadie...?" I muttered.

Crumley dabbed his lips with a white handkerchief.

"I guess you said your fond goodbyes last night," Crumley said.

"Somebody burned those girls up?" I said. When I was a kid, a punk named Swede had thrown a rock and hit me in the head. That's what it felt like now.

"Congratulations, genius," Crumley said. "Hey, I been here two hours. It ain't news to me."

"Burned alive?" I croaked.

He shrugged. "Ask the Doc. I ain't got no medical degree now, like them fellas at the University."

He choked on coffee. "This divorced bum, he left with the Jewish girl, oh, it must have been close to nine o'clock."

"Crumley..."

"Don't throw this mess in my lap now, you can clear it up."

I watched the meat wagon take all that was left of Sadie and Rose uphill toward the morgue. *That can't be the end, not like that,* I thought, but I said to Crumley:

"I took her to Martinucci's."

"Yeah and then?"

"Dropped her at the Saint Paul."

I focused on his fat face, hoping he would just let me go.

"Ain't that sweet," he said. "Date night. And what time did Cinderella get home?"

"I don't know. Eleven. Before eleven."

"Then a flaming kiss good night?"

I flushed with anger.

"Crumley you cannot think, even in that twisted mind of yours, that I set these two poor girls on fire. Tell me you don't think that,

Jim. What kind of monster would do that?"

"Oh, take it easy, Powers, I ain't judge and jury."

"When did the Indian girl leave the Lantern?"

"That's police business, now."

"With who?" I asked.

It was like I could hear Sadie's voice: *A girl like me needs a protector.*

"That kind of information ain't free," said Crumley. "You know we gotta pay our sources, now."

"You can't hold me on this, Jim."

"Sure I can."

"You've got no evidence."

Bulldog McMullen slipped behind the wheel.

Crumley barked: "We can hold him, can't we Bulldog?"

McMullen glanced back at me.

"Nah, I don't want to book him. He's a pain in the ass. He'll bring DeCourcy down on our necks. Anything worse than a lawyer it's a French lawyer. How do you say lawyer in French?"

"La Scumbag," said Crumley.

"Jimbo," the Bulldog said, "we been here all morning. It's Sunday. It's a holy day of obligation. Let's go home."

"Bulldog just saved your skin," Crumley told me. "How you going to thank him?"

"I uh…."

"He'll plead poverty, now," predicted Crumley.

"Pint of Canadian next time I see you," said Bulldog.

"Getting off cheap," said Crumley.

"Make it a fifth," said Bulldog.

"Can we give you a ride to your domicile?" said Crumley.

"Where'd you learn to talk so nice?" the Bulldog asked Crumley

"Finishing school," said Crumley.

"Shit, let him get a cab," said the Bulldog.

"I'm afraid my partner has declined to be your chauffeur," said Crumley.

"Out," said the Bulldog. "Before we run you in."

I emerged from the squad car stunned by how fast all this had happened. A few hours ago, Sadie was devouring her last meal not fifty yards from here, and then in a hot hotel room I had my arms around her, two warm bodies on a frozen night.

I glanced up there, at the green-striped awning of Martinucci's, and saw a young woman in a black coat. She was my downstairs neighbor. I crunched through a snow bank to join her. She was shivering.

"Janie," I said, "What are you doing out here?"

"I don't know," she said. "Maybe they figure it's dead females, so it belongs on the Society Page. Or maybe it's because Thornton sets aside Sundays for his hangovers."

Janie was of average height, strong build, chubby and a bit boyish, twenty two years old, with red hair cut plain and hanging straight. Her pale freckled face might as well have been stamped: Made in Holland.

Her photographer drove by in a car that said DAILY NEWS in gold script on its door. He snapped a flash photo of the burned car.

"What do you know about this?" Janie demanded.

I shrugged. I didn't want this kid involved in my lousy world. "Nothing," I said. "But don't worry, Crumley and the Bulldog are on the case."

"Crumley won't tell a girl reporter anything."

I watched the meat wagon turn the corner, leaving tracks in the snow.

"You evaded my question," Janie said. "What do you have to do with this thing?"

"Me, why nothing, I'm out for my morning constitutional."

"Oh sure, a snowbound stroll along the industrial Mississippi. Where's your dogs if you're out for a walk? Come on, save me a trip to the morgue. Doc Ingerson gives me the creeps."

"You'll owe me, right?"

"Powers!" she said.

"Two prostitutes. Crumley knows their names. You'd better get them from him, official, they've got aliases. They were at the Lantern last night. Reilly was tending bar. He'll tell you I left with the skinny one. Don't believe him."

"Powers, you're old enough to know better. Looking for love at the Lantern? That's like panning for gold in a sewer."

She cocked her head. "Seriously, you took this woman home?"

"We had a drink, a plate of spaghetti, that's it. I felt sorry for her. She was hungry."

"Oh, you felt sorry for her."

I sighed.

"You're holding something back," Janie said, and bit her lips. "I shouldn't press, maybe you're embarrassed. Divorced guy looking for company. I understand."

"At least you didn't call me a bum."

"What?"

"Never mind."

"What was her name?"

"Sadie."

"Sadie that's all?"

"Carmacher." I spelled the name for Janie. "New in town. She traces back to Duluth. That's all I know about her. Well, okay, she was broke and desperate. I had the feeling she was looking for something good to happen here in Saint Paul."

"What makes you say that?"

"Hunch," I said.

"Well," Janie said. Her hands were encased in red wool gloves.

She pulled a skinny reporter's notebook from her purse. "I'll turn this in and go back to my society weddings. Thornton will pick it up with the cops. He drinks with them and the gangsters too."

I said: "How did Crumley know who the girls were? That's what I can't figure out. Everything in that car burnt up, and yet Crumley knows their names. Crumley, who couldn't find a pig in a barnyard, suddenly he's Dick Tracy."

"He's omniscient," said Janie.

"And benevolent."

"I can't stand how these cops get away with it," Janie said. "I could never be a police reporter. Never! I don't know how Thornton does it."

"Janie," I said, "the muck goes deeper, much deeper, than your newspaper heroes know."

"Okay, handsome, fill me in."

That "handsome" was ironic and hurt my pride. I was at least a decade too old to be handsome to Janie.

"Crumley's got powerful friends," I said, "otherwise he'd be in Leavenworth. That's what makes it so hard to operate in this town, you never know who's backing who. And no, you can't quote me in the Daily News."

I didn't know how much to tell this nice Wisconsin farm kid about Saint Paul. After twelve years of Prohibition, the whole town stank of booze money. There was no authority, only chaos, greed and dark dealing. There were honest Saint Paul cops, but any arrests they made could be nullified by Chief Ryan or Jim Crumley. Even murderers could buy "protection policies" that kept them free to roam the streets. The only criminals who went to jail were those who were too dumb or too broke to pay off.

That was The Deal.

Even the county sheriff and prosecutor were in on The Deal. Not all the judges were crooked, but cases could be steered to the ones in cahoots. The governor, who styled himself a man of the people, had floated into office on a tide of bootleg cash. Federal liquor agents rotated in from Washington, and soon were paying off mortgages and sending their children to elite colleges.

I sometimes thought God had abandoned Saint Paul, and left that Cathedral as a cheap memento.

"Come on, Powers," Janie said. "Tell me something I can print."

"Observers with knowledge of the underworld said the victims were prostitutes, recently arrived from Duluth."

"Prostitutes, that figures."

"There's nothing wrong with prostitutes," I said, "don't get moral on me, Janie."

"Sure okay, Duluth prostitutes, thanks," said Janie, and scribbled in her notebook. "That's something to print, at least. Anonymous source, better than nothing."

Janie covered her red hair with a hood.

"See you around, Powers," she said. She tucked her purse under her arm like a football, and hunched off into the blowing snow.

CHAPTER THREE

Saint Paul was a city of deception. "Soft drink parlors" peddled beer and bad whiskey. Behind false fronts, "cigar stores" ran dice games and horse wires. Any house with an over-size garage belonged to a bootlegger. Yen Shee dens posed as a chop suey dives. Barber shops were clip joints in more ways than one, shilling for the numbers racket. The city's busiest beauty salon ran a back stairway for sporting girls.

Front doors were for rubes. Smart guys knocked at the rear. Many of St. Paul's crooks were right guys, some of the cops brutal criminals. Filben's Emerald Radio shop fit right in: it hadn't sold a radio since RCA met Victor.

Filben's radios sat in the display window surrounded by dusty purple velvet. Some were big consoles, some table models, all were tagged with outrageous prices.

Tom Filben figured on two counts. Count one: according to Pat Reilly, the girls, desperate in Duluth, had called him begging for cash. Count two: Sadie and Rose were burnt in a gangster's car, or so I assumed.

Filben made his money on gangster vehicles, registered under names he considered hilarious. When a car or truck was registered to Arthur Gallery or Benjamin Dover, you could be sure it was a Filben deal. Gangsters and bootleggers paid cash for these vehicles, but Filben held the paperwork as if it were a credit deal.

Any vehicle impounded by police, therefore, could be reclaimed by Filben's Saint City Finance. Filben would return said vehicles to the bootleggers for a fee. Bank robbers soon realized the advantage of this scheme. At any bank robbery between Detroit and Kansas City, the transportation was likely provided by Saint City Finance.

I walked down a slushy alley between brick buildings and knocked at Filben's garage. The corrugated steel door rose as if by magic. Behind it stood Tom Filben in white sport jacket, checked trousers, and white patent leather shoes.

"Just installed," Filben said.

He flicked a toggle switch and the door descended. "Ordered two for my home garage. They really work."

"Until you get electrocuted."

"Michael me boy, join the electric century. Why, the day is coming when we sit in easy chairs and push buttons to get things done."

Filben was an average size guy of 40 years. Normally, his complexion was pale like a Dublin fog, but today he was sunburned. He stumped around with a cane ever since a bootlegger, feeling he was overcharged, had taught him a knee-buckling lesson. Filben poked me with the cane.

"Had breakfast?"

He fetched his overcoat while I looked around his dingy warehouse. It was a hospital for wounded slot machines. They lay on the concrete floor, or on wooden benches, the hopeless cases piled in pyramids.

"Lowry or Talk?" he asked.

"Oh, the Talk."

Minnesota doesn't have its own climate, it borrows from Canada or Mexico. Today the wind was from Guadalajara, and we walked crowded downtown streets, with snow pushed into melting piles, the weather almost balmy. When we passed Blind Benny's stand, I bought a Daily News and tucked it under my arm. A stalled streetcar was beleaguered by honking cars, and a uniformed cop, worse than useless, chatted with the streetcar conductor.

"I think we're done with snow this year," Filben said.

"How's Mrs. Filben?"

"I tell you," said Filben, "I wish I was female. The woman never did an honest day's work in her life."

That would describe Tom as well, but I declined to point that out, and opened the Town Talk's door. The Talk was an exception to the Saint Paul rule. It really was a restaurant, and not a front for criminal activity. Although the way they overcooked eggs might have been a crime.

Opal showed us to a dark corner table near the kitchen. After she walked off to fetch our coffees, I said: "You're looking mighty tan, Tommy."

"Cuba," Filben said. "Land of opportunity. They have gamblers, we have slot machines, so…"

"How are the beaches?"

"Beaches? What beaches? Havana's got no beaches. It's the busiest little city I ever saw. Nobody's got time for the beach, they're busy making deals. Those people are hustlers, let me tell you."

"So Christopher Columbus Filben conquers the Caribbean."

He unfolded the Daily News. "No word from the Lindbergh kidnappers, I see."

That evasion wasn't going to work.

"Tom," I said. "The burned car."

"Oh." He fumbled in his pocket for rimless eyeglasses. "The two girls. Who were they, does it say?"

"It doesn't say," I said. "That way, they sell you another paper tomorrow, with the names in it."

"Boy are you cynical."

"I was a newsman, before the War."

Opal delivered white mugs of coffee. Mine was blank, his said TOMMY in bright red.

"Adam and Eve on a raft," I said.

"The usual," said Tom.

He watched Opal rush away. Her skirt was hitched up to show leg.

"She's available," observed Tom.

"Let's talk about these other girls. The burned ones."

Filben popped up. "Got to see a man about a horse."

He stumped off, supporting that bruised knee with the cane. I read the Daily News, its stories so fresh they inked your fingers.

Janie's story had been put through the re-write wringer. It ran under the byline of Kevin "Goggles" Thornton, police reporter. I learned only two facts: The women were shot before their bodies were torched. And the burned car was a Buick. It was strange and chilling to read about this woman whom I knew, briefly, as skinny hungry Sadie. Over her bowl of spaghetti, I remembered, her hands had shaken. Had she sensed it was her last meal? Sadie's ghost, I could almost see her now, staring in through the Town Talk's windows. I shook my head to chase off her hungry ghost, and the awful scene at the docks, the burned bodies, the vile smell. This city had been coddling gangsters for thirty years. Unsolved murders by the hundreds were written into the Book of Saint Paul's Dead.

For distraction, I turned newspaper pages. To sports, no baseball yet. To the comics, no laughs today. Opal set down poached eggs for me and dry toast for Filben.

She poured more coffee. "When are these snow mounds going to melt?" she asked.

"Fourth of July," I said.

"Ain't you the optimist?"

"Did Filben get lost?" I asked.

"I wish he would," she said.

She had curly black hair, blue eyes, thick pouty lips. She was cute, young enough to be in high school, but old enough to be a dropout. A kid like this, you hope something good happens to keep her from getting sucked into the trade.

"Opal," I said, "you know over on Robert Street there's the Carlson Academy. They teach shorthand and typing."

"So?"

"It's an honest trade," I said.

"I'm making okay here."

"As long as you can put up with guys like me and Tommy."

She raised her penciled eyebrows. "He's an ass grabber."

As she shot off to the kitchen, Filben stumped over, damp overcoat draped on his arm.

"Going somewhere?" I said. "Eat your toast."

"I'm afraid I overindulged last night with the Jameson's."

"You and everybody else in this joint."

"I think I'll go home."

I engaged his evasive blue eyes.

"Tom," I said. "A word. Seriously now." I tapped the newspaper. "These girls. They were shot in the head and burned."

Filben's lips quivered.

"In a Buick," I said. "That wouldn't happen to be one your cars?"

"I don't know 'em."

He stumped toward the door. I left a buck and change for Opal and ran after him, out to Wabasha Street, into the crowd, and up onto a streetcar. I dropped a nickel into the fare box and pushed through the standees, grabbing strap after strap like a monkey. Filben hobbled off at the next stop and slithered through the revolving doors of the Golden Rule Department Store.

I charged down the perfume aisles toward the elevators. A girl in blue-and gold uniform accepted me as the lone passenger and closed the door.

She pulled the brass lever and as we ascended I said: "Fella in here, white coat, uses a cane?"

"Must have took the escalators," she said. "I seen him in Mens."

She opened the door on floor three and there stood Filben, choosing an umbrella. I tapped him on the shoulder and said, "The black one goes with your outfit."

"Powers, what do you want from me?"

I had a certain reputation around town, from my days of guarding booze in the freight yards. I'm not the toughest guy in Saint Paul, but Filben, after that knee-bashing, had gone shaky. I stepped up face to face with him.

"The girls in the Buick, Tommy, why did they come to town?"

Filben snatched an umbrella and I bullied him toward the open elevator. I bumped him in. Breathing heavy, he ignored me as we descended. I pulled out a buck and palmed it to the operator.

"Stop between floors," I said.

She looked at me, puzzled.

"Go ahead," I gave her another buck. "Stop between floors."

She threw the brass lever and the elevator stopped with a jerk.

"I wish to converse with this gentleman," I told her.

"Sure," she said, "but make it snappy."

"Filben, the girls."

Either Filben was sweating or melted snow was dripping down his sunburned forehead.

"I don't know," he said.

"I was told they called you."

"Called me? Who told you that?"

"One of my guys."

Filben gulped. "I get nervous in tight spaces," he said.

"We'll be moving as soon as I get an answer."

"Okay, maybe they called the house, and maybe my brother answered. If it happened at all, I don't know where they got my name. I'm in the phone book, you know."

"They asked for money."

Filben raised his hands in a prayerful position.

"I didn't know these girls, Mick."

"Three hundred thousand people in Saint Paul, and they just happened to pick you out of the phone book."

"All right," Filben said, and cast a worried look at the elevator girl. "Let's have a civil conversation, okay? On the ground floor."

I gave the operator the nod.

Filben and I walked through the Golden Rule's revolving doors and stood in the alcove at the streetcar stop. The store dick burst out, red-faced, dressed in cheap rumpled suit. He sure didn't shop for clothes at the Golden Rule. He hassled Tommy about the umbrella. I palmed him two bucks and said: "That ought to cover it," and he went away.

"So give it to me, Filben."

"I did a favor for a guy, years ago. His wife remembered me."

"Keep going."

"The wife got arrested in Duluth a few months back. She called me when they let her out."

"Why not call her husband?"

"Stillwater," he said.

"Okay, the husband's in prison so the wife calls you. This is Rose we're talking about, right? What does she want?"

"Look, I didn't talk to her. I swear on the Blessed Virgin. She called the house, Jim answered, she asked for fifty bucks, Jim hung up. That's everything."

"Her husband was?"

Filben sputtered. "In the rackets."

"Duluth or Saint Paul?"

"There are things called highways nowadays. People go back and forth."

"Tommy," I said, "you should see a doctor. I hear the knee has a tendency to flare up."

"Look," Filben said. "Rose's husband. Denver Mint. Okay? That's all I'm saying."

"Denver Mint. Federal, right? Why isn't he in Leavenworth?"

Filben shook his head. "He got nailed for another job. Unrelated. Nobody did time for the Denver Mint."

"And the favor you did for this guy?"

"Long ago. I connected him to somebody for a modest fee."

"He needed to launder money from the Denver Mint?"

"I never said that," Filben insisted.

"Tommy," I said. "You should wear boots so you can wade through the crap you're spewing. What gang were these girls connected with?"

"No gang," said Filben. "They were drifting prostitutes. And the car that burned? Wasn't one of mine."

I let him go and wandered the streets, thinking. Neither Sadie nor Rose owned a car, or they would have driven from Duluth. They had arrived broke and by train. Why would somebody burn them up in a new, expensive Buick? Where did that car come from? If Filben hadn't given the girls money, where did they get the cash to splurge at a luxe hotel?

I walked to the police station, waltzed past the intake desk and climbed the back stairs to the third floor.

Two years ago, when Big Joe Ryan made chief, he scrambled the department like a bowl of eggs. Big Ryan's enemies got midnight shifts at the Margaret Street or Rondo stations. His pals were named to the Purity Squad. Speakeasies either paid off Purity or got the axe. Crumley and the Bulldog were turned loose from the

Homicide squad, and helped smash up speakeasies, busting the bad booze and loading the good bottles into a paddy wagon. These raids often made the front page of the Daily News. The editors never realized they were providing free advertising for the police shakedown racket.

Or maybe they did realize. I never made it past legman in the news game. All I did was chase sirens and call rewrite. I don't know what goes on in the publisher's boardroom. I was yanked out of the news business by Uncle Sam. After discharge, I joined a million other veterans looking for work. When Prohibition was voted in, I finally found a way to make a good living.

Sergeant Billy McAmbly was one of the few cops who was too proud to put his hand out. I attended Sacred Heart with Billy, where he was first-string catcher during our trophy run. His picture is still there, in the hallways of the Sacred Heart, along with that trophy. McAmbly had gone from high school into the police force, and had been an honest beat cop until Big Joe Ryan became chief. Then Billy was demoted. They stuck him in Bertillion because he declined to play Big Ryan's game.

I walked back to the drafting table where Billy was hunched under a spotlight. The table was scattered with paper scraps, photos, razor-knives and glue pots.

"Mickey," said McAmbly.

He shut that spotlight off, reached to the floor for a bottle of beer. McAmbly, just over forty now, was a heavy black-Irishman, with dark-and-gray curly hair. His red face was bloated with drink, blood vessels snapped off like broken dreams. His police tunic bulged at the brass buttons. He set the beer bottle on the drafting table and said: "Still off the booze?"

"More or less."

"What kind of Irishman are you?"

He flipped through a stack of blank Bertillion cards.

"Ah, that's why I drink," he said. "Instead of catching bank robbers, they've got me up here making baseball cards. Let me make one for you?"

"Billy, I've no desire to be notorious."

I picked up a card. On its front was two photos, full face and profile, of a mean-looking bastard wearing a flat cap. Tommy Carroll. Yes, another Irishman. Minneapolis belonged to shady Lutheran bankers and Jewish gangsters. On our side of the river, it was the Irish in charge, with a few Bohemian Catholics thrown in.

On the back of the card, McAmbly had written in parochial school script: Armed robbery, scar left cheek.

I said: "Billy, the Burned Ladies."

"Prostitutes, I heard."

"Their Buick. What came in on it?"

"How the hell do I know?"

"Billy, you *are* the identification unit. How's your mother, by the way?"

"Still complaining," he said, walking off. "How's your aunt Doris?"

I studied a corkboard pinned with Bertillion cards. I recognized a few faces, but new crooks arrived every day. Every train that steamed into Union Depot delivered gangsters who were at risk in their hometowns, but safe in Saint Paul, as long as they paid off the cops via the Green Lantern tavern.

McAmbly stumbled back to the drafting table, swigged from his beer bottle.

"Stolen," he said. "That Buick, stolen."

"From who?"

"How close do you read the papers?"

"I never miss Maggie and Jiggs."

"Late January. Over in Hudson? Bandits held up the whole town. The Buick disappeared then. Brand new, right out of the dealer's garage. Never seen again until it caught fire on the Levee."

"Plates?"

"Removed. Not registered in Minnesota or Wisconsin either."

"Big holdup over in Hudson?"

"Didn't you read about it?"

"What's one more holdup?"

"You and the Chief have something in common," he said.

"What's that?"

"It's hard to find anybody who gives a shit. But I do." He sighed. "My kids have to grow up in this town."

CHAPTER FOUR

The Cathedral's altars were draped in Lenten purple. I sidled up to Janie. It was hard to miss her. The Cathedral's stone interior was huge, the mourners few. Janie had applied a blush that made her cheeks glow. Her red hair was stuffed underneath a broad-brimmed black hat. Black blouse, gray skirt and nylon stockings completed her funeral outfit. She held the hymnal and her lips moved along with the organ music, but nobody really sang in this last forlorn tribute to Margaret "Rose" Perry.

An old, thick-built Indian woman in a wine-purple shawl kneeled muttering in the front pew. A young thin Indian man in black trousers and white shirt sat beside her, his arm around a grim boy of maybe ten years. At the other end of the pew fidgeted Jack Peifer and Violet Nordquist.

Jack ran the Hollyhocks, a swank casino-speakeasy out in the mansion district. He was also the grand master of prostitutes, and a contender for chief gangster of Saint Paul.

Jack had a twenty-year head start on Violet. He was built soft for easy living. She was that thin Scandinavian beauty you see everywhere in the Twin Cities. But unlike most of them, she made money modeling. If you wanted to see her in the scanty, you could check the lingerie ads in the Daily News.

As sunlight streamed glorious through stained-glass windows, Father Mack approached the coffin, holding an incense burner. He was an Irish giant. The altar boys who flanked him seemed like toddlers. In the Cathedral's shadowy alcoves lurked a few gawkers. The Burned Ladies had achieved sensational Page One play in all three dailies, complete with pictures of the torched Buick. The gawkers were hoping to witness a gangster funeral, or maybe even a shootout.

But the only sound that disturbed the Cathedral's silence was the tick tick tick of the incense burner against its golden chain. The aroma and smoke of frankincense floated above Rose's coffin.

Janie and I, and Jack and Violet, followed the Indian family as they wheeled the casket toward the side doors, which burst open on a chilly spring day. The young Indian man needed the help of two funeral home guys, Father Mack, Jack, myself and Sam Tanaka to muscle the coffin into the hearse. Jack dusted his hands when he let the coffin go, hustled back into the Cathedral to fetch his hat.

"Strange," Violet said. "Isn't it?"

Rose's family clambered into the hearse.

"These Catholic rules," said Violet. "Ladies must wear hats in church. Men are forbidden to. Odd. Does it make sense to you?"

"Thirteen years of Catholic school," I said. "The rules of the Church make perfect sense to me."

She shot me a quizzical look.

"I'm kidding," I said. "Nobody knows what the rules are anymore."

Away drove the hearse. Jack emerged from the Cathedral, a beautiful gray fedora set over his greasy hair. Between his cashmere and Violet's furs, they were a fashion show.

"Should we go in one car?" he asked.

"I'm nervous when Jack drives," Violet said as we piled into Jack's Packard. "We adore Sam's driving."

Sam Tanaka and I pretended we didn't know each other. He pressed the Packard's electric starter.

I slid into the front seat alongside Sam and Janie. Jack and Violet settled in the rear seat. Jack tapped me on the shoulder.

"My wife doesn't trust my driving," said Jack. "How do you like that?"

"I love you darling," cooed Violet. "But you're a terrible driver."

The Packard sputtered.

"Sam, I asked you to change the son-of-a-bitching spark plugs," Jack said.

Sam did not defend himself.

Violet shut her eyes.

"Sorry, darling," Jack said, and to Janie he explained: "The foul language. My wife dislikes it."

"Excuse me," said Janie, "I didn't know you two were married."

"Oh, we're not, darling," said Violet. "My Jack is sentimental."

Violet focused on Janie. "None of this, I trust, will appear in the Daily News. In this town we count as celebrities, I know. But I would hate to see our names linked to this vile crime. We're simply performing an act of Christian charity."

"I'm the Women's Page," said Janie. "I'm weddings, not funerals."

"That's very nice, dear," said Violet.

Why a Cathedral funeral for a drifter from Duluth? And why was the city's top pimp-gangster in attendance? I wasn't dumb enough to interrogate Jack Peifer, especially not with Violet along for the ride. But I did know that Father Mack was Jack's friend, and gangland's favorite priest. Father Mack was a tough guy who preached that there were no saints, only sinners. That notion endeared him to gangsters. I assumed that Jack had arranged the Cathedral Mass, and had shown up in person, as a signal to his prostitutes that, even in death, he would not neglect them.

It was a shaky theory but it was all I had.

The charred remains of Rose Perry were buried on a hillside looking over Fort Snelling, where the Minnesota River rushes into the Mississippi. From this knoll, the river cliffs, the rushing water, the spring landscape would be a pleasing sight, if you weren't here for a burial. Even so, it's a prettier cemetery than the one at the Fort, the War dead buried, already forgotten, in regimented rows.

When we pulled in we'd passed a battered Dodge squad car that contained two cops. After we rolled the casket to the graveside, Father Mack in purple stole uttered Latin prayers. I drifted back to that Dodge.

Bulldog sat in the driver's seat. Crumley couldn't fit behind the steering wheel. He weighed down the passenger side.

"Inspector," I said. "Let me guess. You were expecting the killers to show up gloating at the funeral."

"You should have been a detective," said Crumley.

"We could use another smart ass on the force," agreed the Bulldog.

My fingers played a drum-beat on the window sill.

"So, you boys got any good leads?"

"We got any good leads, Jim?"

"Nope," said Crumley.

"Just another double-murder-incineration in Saint Paul," I said.

Crumley rolled up the window.

Bulldog pitched a burning cigarette into the just-green grass, and he too rolled up his window in a puff of smoke.

I walked back to the gravesite as the young Indian man performed the solemn duty with shovel and dirt. Peifer palmed Father Mack the customary tip. The mother's lips were trembling, and the little boy hid behind her, clinging. I said to the man who I assumed to be Rose's brother: "Sorry for your loss."

"Who are you to be sorry for us?" he said. "Please don't bother our family."

On the drive away from the cemetery, we passed a dark Studebaker parked among bare trees. It was only a glance, but I could have sworn there were two men inside, and one of them was Swede Fanlund. I got a flesh-crawling feeling, and looked out the Packard's rectangular back window.

"What?" asked Janie.

"Guy I knew in high school," I said. "The Swede. He wasn't exactly a scholar. It's just odd that he's parked out here, middle of nowhere. The Swede has been blessedly absent from our fair city for years."

"Excuse me," interrupted Jack. "But we insist."

"Pardon me?"

"We shan't drop you at the streetcar stop," said Violet. "That would be uncivilized. Sam will drive you two all the way home."

"Swede Fanlund," I said to Janie. "Couldn't be. Why the hell would he be back in town?"

We made light talk until the Packard pulled up at our apartment building. I wondered if I had only imagined seeing Swede Fanlund. I used to have nightmares about him, but that was back in high school. Maybe it wasn't the Swede in that Studebaker, but some big ugly stranger, pulled over to read a road map.

I invited Janie up for coffee. She liked my view. I had first met her downstairs, on the day she moved into the dark, damp basement.

"Where are your dogs?" Janie asked.

"Little Elmer," I said. "Walks 'em now. He takes them to the Capitol lawn, where they render their opinions of our elected officials."

Janie made a sour face.

"So," I spooned coffee and set the percolator on the stove burner, "now you've met the famous Jack Peifer. What do you think?"

"Eh," said Janie. She doffed that black funeral hat and shook free her curly locks. "He's too old for the beauty queen. What's he got?"

"Money."

"Oh is that all?" said Janie. "How boring. You're not going to smoke your pipe, are you?"

"No."

"Because in the newsroom, I'm choking on fumes all day."

She stepped to the windows that looked over the city.

"Your rent must be fantastic," she said.

"I get along," I said.

"I'd love to know how," she said.

"Wouldn't you, though?"

"Tell me," Janie said, "why does queen Violet insist that her husband can't drive the car?"

I shrugged.

"She's neurotic," guessed Janie. "About her face. He's reckless. He drinks and drives. I've heard he's been in several drunken car crashes. She's afraid a car crash will scar her lovely face. It's not like she's in Vogue or anything. She's just, you know, Miss Minnesota Milk Maid. Who does she think she is? Myrna Loy?"

She locked me in with her eyes.

"Come on," she said. "What's the deal, what am I missing?"

"Deal?"

"Jack Peifer, owner of the swankiest joint in town, pays for the funeral of a Duluth jailbird."

"Pays for the funeral?"

"Yes, the whole thing. My source was Father McCarthy."

"Peifer paid for Rose's funeral?"

"Are you deaf?"

"No," I said. "Just slow of hearing."

Now it was my turn to stare at the busy little city of Saint Paul. Traffic and streetcars weaved around Seven Corners, like spiders on wheels, weaving, weaving, weaving.

Janie lifted the percolator off the stove. She set two white cups and saucers on the checkerboard tablecloth and poured steaming coffee. I opened a box of chocolate-covered biscuits. A shop downtown imported them from Ireland. They made good packing around the smuggled Jameson's.

I spread the biscuits on a plate.

"Why bury her here?" I wondered. "I'm curious to find out."

"I already know," said Janie. "I asked the priest. Rose's brother, he lives in Minneapolis. The mother's moving down eventually."

She bit into a biscuit.

"Jack Peifer," I said, "for your information, Miss Vetter, is the boss of gambling and prostitution. His crosstown rival Harry Sawyer is in charge of everything else."

"Such as?"

"Planning bank robberies, laundering money, fencing jewelry, and selling police protection policies. They've got it divided up. It keeps the peace. Jack's in charge of this, Harry's in charge of that."

Janie said deliberately, as if I were a slow-witted child: "But Rose … was from … Duluth."

"You never know how far the web spreads. And Rose's friend Sadie was a prostitute for sure."

"How do you know?"

"I, well, she kind of caught me in a moment of weakness."

"Oh, Powers."

"She was desperate to be, ah, cared for."

"It wasn't a financial transaction?"

"It was."

"How much?"

"Five dollars."

Janie sputtered. "My daily wage exactly."

"Plus tip," I said.

"I knew I was in the wrong profession."

"Sadie was searching for something," I said, "you could sense it. She was searching for warmth in a cold, cold world. And the poor kid was from Duluth, coldest city in the world."

I met Janie's skeptical gaze with one word: "Duluth."

"What about it?"

"I'm not supposed to show my face in that town again."

"According to whom?"

"The sheriff. But I called around, I know a few guys. Sadie was born in Poland, her parents made the trek, she grew up in Hibbing."

"Iron ore mining?"

"Yep. Parents were Jewish. They weren't miners, they ran a dry goods store. Sadie's mother cursed me in Polish. I think it was Polish. Then she slammed the phone. So I called the brother, pretended to be a Saint Paul cop."

"You lied."

"Truth doesn't pay."

"The truth," Janie said, "will set you free."

"Or set you on fire, like Sadie and Rose."

"Go on, cynic. Sadie's brother ..."

"The brother told me Sadie had been disowned by the parents. She had run away to Duluth five or six years back, rarely retuning to Hibbing. The father banned her from the home. The parents didn't know how she was making a living in Duluth. Sadie claimed to be selling perfume at a department store."

"Her connection to Saint Paul?"

"I can't figure it."

"Okay," Janie said, "so Sadie gets busted for hustling in Duluth, and meets Rose in the workhouse."

"But why was Rose in the workhouse?

"Ask the sheriff in Duluth."

"Janie, I can't phone the sheriff in Duluth."

"Right."

"Ever," I said. "But he might talk to a young female newshound who's desperate for a story."

"I'm hardly desperate, Powers. Even if I came up with the story, Major Hoople would say 'nice work, little girl' and hand my notes to Thornton."

Janie bit into a chocolate biscuit, chewed it over.

"So Sadie," she said, "is the scorned daughter of a merchant family, a social outcast, selling her favors to Great Lakes sailors. She meets Rose in the workhouse. They had a plan. One of them knew Tommy Filben well enough to ask him for money. You say he refused them but they bought tickets to Saint Paul anyway, which means..."

"They got the money. Probably from the whore master, and potential employer, Jack Peifer."

"What was the girls' next move?"

"Don't know, can't guess."

I held back on the possible Denver Mint connection. One, I wasn't certain what it meant. Two, I didn't want to drop Janie into the quicksand of Saint Paul.

"Jack wanted them for his stable of prostitutes," guessed Janie.

"Makes sense," I said. "But I don't know about Jack as a murder suspect. Alive, the girls were assets. Dead, they couldn't earn him a dime."

"Why the flames?" said Janie. "They were already dead. Why risk setting the fire? What kind of message was that, and to whom?"

"I don't know," I said. "They're going to bury Sadie in Duluth, her family, but..."

"Why? Why can't you be seen in Duluth?"

"It had to do with cops and booze. A guy can get in trouble up there. They don't honor The Deal."

Janie stood and took in the Cathedral view, hands behind her back.

"It's something isn't it?" I said. "That Cathedral? If that magnificent thing was in a European city, it would be surrounded by tour buses. But here it sits in dreary Saint Paul, a thousand miles from the nearest tourist."

"It's inspiring," said Janie. "Don't you find it inspiring?"

"I'm not a good Catholic anymore," I said. "I skip all the Holy Days of Obligation. But when I look at the Cathedral, I want to believe."

Janie bit her lips.

"Well," she said, "I've got a wedding page to fill up." She grabbed that black hat and made a move for the door.

"Go get 'em kid," I said,. When the door closed, I muttered: "and if you know what's good for you ..."

But does anyone really know what's good for them?

I stood pondering mysteries, smoking my pipe, looking over the city. After a few minutes a Yellow Cab pulled up and honked, and Janie ran out and slipped into it. It seemed an extravagance, a cub reporter taking a taxi to work, with a nickel streetcar only a few steps away. But I just mixed that in with all the other mysteries, and smoked my pipe down to the bottom.

CHAPTER FIVE

So I drove toward the Saint Croix River on a lovely spring afternoon in my jalopy, which had been carelessly bolted together by the minions of Henry Ford. A few good side jobs, and maybe I could see Filben about financing a Studebaker or some well-constructed car.

As I crossed the Route Twelve Bridge I had the impulse to speed on until I reached a certain little white farmhouse in the Wisconsin woods. Before he died, Uncle Joe had split five winters worth of firewood and stored it in the barn in Eagle River, his gift to posterity. That would include me. Someday. But Eagle River was a long drive, and the farm didn't belong to me yet. I took a left turn into the Village of Hudson.

I pulled into Carlson Buick, a garage of white painted cinderblocks. The garage was surrounded by autos, each with a huge fluttering price tag. Wanting to avoid a sales pitch, I used the back entrance.

Inside the garage was a greasy office, a calendar pinned to its door. It displayed the days of June 1931 and depicted a woman at a French carnival. She had blond curly hair, wore a revealing white dress, stretched out one sexy leg. I knocked on the door and a dog went into a frenzy.

Someone in that office shouted, "Fritz!" followed by the noise of a wrestling match. Finally the door was opened by an older fellow restraining a snarling German Shepherd.

The fellow muscled the dog out the garage door, and chained him at a doghouse underneath a winter-bare oak tree. This fellow had white hair, blue eyes, pale skin, and a kindly expression. He shook my hand.

"Name's Marty Schure," he said. "Been waiting on you."

"You have?"

"Pilgrim Insurance?"

"I'm afraid not."

His kindly expression soured. "What are you, some kind of newspaper man?"

"No."

"Well, you look like a nosy newspaper man."

"I'm an investigator."

"Well you can go to hell, waking me up in the middle of the day. I suppose you want to know about the robbery. I've told every got-damned idiot in this town about the robbery. I don't see why I have to tell you."

"Mr. Schure, would it be possible to buy you breakfast?"

"Breakfast? I eat pie for breakfast."

"A slice of pie then."

"There's good pie in this town. It's the only good thing left in this got-damned town since they ruined it."

"Since who ruined it? The gangsters?"

"The got-damned Communists," he said.

The café was two blocks away, and as we walked the streets of this tidy, prosperous village, Marty Schure pointed out the sights.

"They busted into the clothing store," he said as we passed it, "with an axe. The got-damned fools got inside there, but they couldn't open the safe. Bunch of got-damn amateurs if you ask me."

"How many?"

He held up four gnarled fingers.

"Three o'clock in the got-damn morning. See the first thing they did was ambush Randall. Took his gun right off him. Randall don't talk about it. Randall's embarrassed. It sapped the manhood right out of him."

"Randall is the…"

"Town constable. He's thinking of retiring now. Sapped the manhood right out of him, those boys did."

"So the robbers were young."

"You're got-damn right they were. Then the drugstore," he said as we passed that. "Forced the back door, knocked the combination right off that cheap safe, took money, took drugs. Randall could tell you but he don't like to talk about it.

"Now the bank, they couldn't get in there. They threatened Randall, put a gun to his head. They said wake up the banker and have him open up. Three in the morning, can you imagine? Wake up the banker? They wanted to steal every got-damn thing in town. Well, Randall wouldn't do it. He said there's a time lock on the vault, you fools. God himself couldn't open the vault before 8:30.

"They knew what they were doing, I'll tell you that. When they busted into the grocery, the burglar alarm sounded, and they ran right to it and cut the wires."

We turned in to Sophie's Blue River Café, where Marty acknowledged every diner before we sat in the corner. Sophie herself delivered coffee and apple pie. That was automatic for Marty, and I said, "Me too. I'll have the same."

On the other side of the window, jacketed figures passed on the windy main street as Marty sipped coffee.

"The things they took. Steak. Furs. Clothing. Medicine. Cash from the tills, but not so much as they'd hoped for. Candy bars. Candy bars! Then they came back to me. And this one, a skinny fellow with creepy eyes says to me, "How'd you like to survive this.

old man?"

He divided his pie with a knife.

"I said I would be pleased to survive it."

"Then lock up your dog," this gangster says, "before I shoot him."

"So I put Fritz in my room, and he barked and barked. See Fritz don't bite he only barks. The creepy punk said: 'See that blue Buick? I want that one.' "

My pie and coffee were delivered.

"You on expense account?" asked Marty.

"Oh definitely," I said. "I can buy this."

"You fellows sure lead cushy lives, you investigators."

"So tell me about the Buick."

"Well, I'm all alone, see. Lived in this town all my life, and now it's just me and Fritz. Live in the back room there, free rent. I watch over the place at night. You know, kids will steal a car and joyride, and then wreck the got-damn things. We had one youngster drove a car right into the river, that's what our youth is like today."

He chewed pie.

"You can still get a got-damned good piece of pie in this town."

"Tell me about the blue Buick," I said.

"Well, it was the nicest car in the garage. Leather seats and a radio installed, a heater and an ivory steering wheel. Beautiful machine. No wonder the gangster punk wanted to steal it. Creepy, I tell you, he looked like the son of Boris Karloff.

"Well, that Buick he wanted was boxed in, see? I had to move three cars to get to it. And when I start it up, the whole got-damn garage fills with exhaust, and here comes another little fellow. This one with gold teeth. Talking like a hillbilly, you know that accent, like an ignorant got-damn hillbilly. And he's carrying a Thompson machine gun. Arrogant little bastard, this Gold Teeth. He says to

Boris Karloff: 'Come on, the whole town will be awake.' And Boris Karloff says, 'I'm not leaving without my Buick.' "

The pie was fabulous, with a crunchy crust, tart apples and tangy touch of cinnamon. A sip of weak coffee spoiled the sensation.

"And so two more gangsters come in. To the garage. And I said to myself, what is this, a got-damn gangster convention? Now these other two were bigger. And one of them slugs me with a pistol."

He bent his head, parted his thinning hair to show me the scab on his scalp.

"Well, hell, I fell to my knees. Now the two fellas who come in later, they were big guys. Did I say that? Gold Teeth and Boris Karloff were short and slender. The big guys, they talked like Rebels, too. Are we bringing gangsters up from Georgia now? We don't have enough here?"

Sophie poured Marty more coffee, and I declined a refill.

"So they drove into town in their own car," I said, "and left with a blue Buick."

"Nope. They took both cars out of town. Their own and the Buick. Loaded with stuff from our stores. Clothing mostly. The two big men, they drove a Chevy jalopy, and Gold Teeth and Boris Karloff, they drove the beautiful Buick. They put me and Randall in back of that Buick. We nearly strangulated on the got-damn clothes back there. They drove us over into a Minnesota cornfield, now it's five below zero, and four in the morning, middle of got-damn nowhere and they let us out. Gold Teeth says: "We ought to shoot you but we was raised Christian.'

"That's what he says exactly, just like that. We was raised Christian. You tell me what kind of Christian leaves two fellows out to freeze to death in a cornfield."

"When did you notify the police?"

"Notify the police? Randall is the police! What the hell is wrong with you? They took our constable hostage and held a tommygun to his got-damned head."

"You didn't freeze to death, obviously."

"We walked to a got-damn farm house and pounded on the door. Farmer answers with a got-damn shotgun. I said to Randall: We're going to get killed in this thing yet. Well, does the farmer have a phone? No. Does the farmer have a car we can borrow? Well, he's got an old truck, but it's up on blocks for the winter. Horse and got-damn buggy, that's how we got into town. Farmer bitching and cursing the whole way. Randall got frostbite ears out of it, and I got a lump on the head. Doctor says it might've knocked some of the sense clean out of me."

"So the little guys, Gold Teeth and Boris Karloff, took off in a Buick."

"I hope they're happy with that Buick. It's a thirteen hundred dollar luxury vehicle. We've been waiting two months, but insurance won't pay a dime until they send some got-damn idiot here to talk to me.

"Pilgrim Insurance," he said. "No wonder they can build a skyscraper in Chicago. They never pay money out. They keep it all for the got-damned Communist executives."

"I see," I said. "Descriptions?"

"Descriptions? I just told you."

He took a deep breath. "One of the big guys had blond curly hair, the build of a prizefighter. The other guy, snarling, dark haired, scar on his chin like from a knife fight. What insurance company are you with, anyway?"

"I'm not an insurance investigator, I'm just trying to help the police."

"I told you three times, Randall is the police."

Randall proved to be a nervous little cop with a drunk's rheumy eyes. He was about as talkative as an oyster. He chased me out of the police station after revealing nothing. So I drove my jalopy back toward Minnesota, mulling it all over. Okay, the Buick was stolen in Hudson in January. Two months later, it was torched along with the bodies of Sadie and Rose. Who were Gold Teeth, Boris Karloff, Blond Curly and Scar Chin? Where did they come from? And why would they murder a couple of sporting ladies from Duluth? And then to Janie's question, why light them on fire on the Saint Paul river docks?

Or maybe, these four Southern robbers didn't kill the girls. Maybe they were just robbers. Maybe the Buick was stolen from them. Maybe they sold it to another gangster. It did seem peculiar, to go to the trouble of stealing this car, an expensive and beautiful model, only to set it on fire. They could have stolen any jalopy to burn those women in.

I wrenched my Ford into a parking spot in downtown Saint Paul. I wanted to buy a newspaper and so searched the car for change. That's when I spied, under the passenger seat, Sadie's lipstick-tube cigarette lighter. I held it in my hand. It gleamed in the spring sunlight. "You forgot something, kid," I said to nobody. I twisted the tube and it lit. I remembered her face behind a flaming match, up in the hotel room. You were just a lost soul, Sadie, that's all. You didn't deserve to burn.

I put that lighter in my pocket, hustled across Rice Park and up the stairs of the federal building.

This building could have been in Munich, a castle right out of a German fairy tale. The ground floor was a bustling post office. I mounted the marble stairs to the offices of the Division of Justice. Hat in hand I inquired whether Agent Heater was available. All three typists looked up. One said, "I'll see. Your name?"

Roland Heater was a thin, cheroot-chomping G-man. When I entered his corner office, he was tilted back in his wooden chair, his cowboy boots propped on his desk. I'd heard it was a firing offense, in J. Edgar Hoover's outfit, to as much as loosen your cufflinks. Heater wore a dark gray suit with a red tie yanked down, shirt collar unbuttoned. By federal standards, this man was a rebel. The cheroot wagged in his mouth as he beckoned me to sit in a hardwood chair that faced his desk.

"Powers, eh? What do you got for me, Powers? What's on your plate?"

"The Burned Ladies."

He plucked the cheroot out of his discolored teeth and yawned.

"None of our federal business," he said.

I found myself staring at the gritty soles of his tooled boots.

I said: "Just another gangster murder in Saint Paul."

"Homicide? See Jim Crumley."

"It's hard to miss him," I said.

"Powers, why are we wasting your government's time this afternoon?"

"Stolen Buick. The ladies were burned in a stolen Buick."

"So?"

"The car was driven across state lines."

The cowboy boots swung off the desk.

"Now that," he pointed at me, "that's federal."

"And Crumley," I said, "mysteriously knew who these girls were just an hour after they were burned."

"You think Crumley stole the Buick, drove it across state lines and burnt up the girls?"

"You're kidding, right?"

Heater didn't answer that.

He looked over his cheroot as if surprised to find it between his fingers. "Special Agent in Charge. You know what I'm in charge of? Reports. You hear the click-clack of the typists out there? Mr. Hoover adores reports. We've got more typists than we have agents. So what I'm asking you, Powers, is to give me something I can write up. Unless it rolls through a federal typewriter, see, it doesn't exist. Give me something to write up or get the hell out of my office."

"Crumley knows who killed them," I said.

"Some day they'll erect a statue to Jim Crumley in this town. He'll have his hand out, palm upward. I can see it now, big as life, over in Rice Park. They'll need to pour a hell of a lot of bronze." He tapped his ear. "Who's paying you to bird dog the case of the burned Buick?"

"You guys care about the car, but not the dead girls?"

"We don't write the laws. See Congress. We just enforce them."

"Don't make me laugh, Heater. There hasn't been a law enforced in this town since 1919. Unless you count traffic tickets."

"J. Edgar Hoover aims to change that."

"Okay, Heater, the Buick was stolen by four guys in January over in Hudson."

"Alice!" shouted Heater, and a lanky woman shuffled in and sat behind me with a steno pad.

"Guy number one. Gold teeth. Five three. Hundred and ten. Southern drawl, carries a Tommy, claims to be a Christian. Guy number two, five-five, skinnier. Wears a straw boater, no Southern accent, greasy dark hair, noticeably creepy eyes."

"Creepy eyes." Heater snickered. "That's a good one. I'll put that on the wire. Attention all agents: Look out for a guy with creepy eyes."

I described Blond Curly and Scar Chin, and said that the robbery occurred at three in the morning, and with that, Heater ran out of patience.

"We read the newspapers up here, Powers. All of us ..." he spread his arms ... "can read."

"So now?"

"I write a report and we wait. It's not like you came in with names and addresses."

"Crumley knows."

"The next time Inspector Crumley and I speak," said Heater, "will be in a federal courtroom. We're watching, Powers. When the time is right, we will take action. Now get the hell out of my office."

CHAPTER SIX

Standing on his front porch, Papa Alt looked like a captain scouting the Atlantic for icebergs. The iceberg was his brewery, steaming and whistling, calving off trucks, a police payoff in every barrel of beer. Like the other brewers in town, the Hamms and the Bremers, Papa Alt was the corner bootlegger on a grand scale.

This morning Papa wore a double-breasted suit and a red bow tie. I sat on the porch with him at a table in front of a bay window. A pale, nervous serving girl brought coffee in delicate cups. As she melted away, Papa said: "They were burned to death?"

"No, shot first, like it said in the newspapers."

"I don't rely on the newspapers."

"I asked Doc Ingerson directly," I said. "The women were dead when the car was set afire."

Papa Alt cleared his throat. He pulled a red handkerchief out of his breast pocket and blew his nose, gently.

"And the gang?"

"Apparently you were correct," I said. "There's a new gang in town, from the South, and they do carry tommyguns."

"Ah."

I didn't want to tip all my cards to Papa Alt. I wasn't sure what game he was playing. So I said: "This gang may have something to do with certain robberies over the winter, but I'm just getting to that part of the investigation."

"Burning women? This is not the Saint Paul way," he said.

Well it is now, I said to myself.

"This is not our way here," he insisted. "These gangsters are worse than animals. Not even the most vicious animal would do this."

The coffee cups rattled when he pounded the table. He sat back. He sighed.

"Oh, what have we done here?" he said.

A truck squealed to a stop at the brewery gates. I noticed rifles and shotguns racked behind the guardhouse windows. Just this week, that arsenal had been put on prominent display.

"I have sent my grandchildren away," Papa Alt said. "I have hired bodyguards for my son and daughters. We have a wedding in the future. The Alt family does not hide."

Well, he was hiding his grandchildren. But it's a bad idea for temporary hires to point out the boss's contradictions, so I let that go. I wanted to pursue another idea. Papa Alt had the police department in his pocket. Otherwise that brewery across the street would be dark and silent.

"Mr. Alt," I said, with all the deference I could muster, "it may be obvious, but have you tried talking with the police?"

"The police?" he said. "Did the police bring Mr. Rutman back alive?"

"No," I admitted. Rutman was a bootlegger, kidnapped and tortured by gangsters who were never caught.

"Did the police prevent the kidnapping of Mr. Gleckman?
"No."

Leon Gleckman had been the king of booze merchants back in the '20s.

Papa said: "Was not Mr. Gleckman under police guard, twenty-four hours a day?"

"Yes, he was. And he was kidnapped anyway. I get your point, Mr. Alt."

"I need to know who these Southern gangsters are," he said. "They do not respect our rules."

I got it now. By the terms of The Deal, Saint Paul's gangsters committed their crimes outside city limits. In respect for The Deal, the Rutman and Gleckman kidnappers had hustled their victims out of town. But a double-execution, brazenly committed downtown, meant Papa Alt and his cronies had lost control of gangland.

He crossed his arms. "I want their names. I get results from you, or I find another man."

Asking at the Green Lantern about a guy with gold teeth and a buddy who looked like Boris Karloff, well, that kind of thing had gotten Rose and Sadie killed. My safest play was with a woman whom no gangster took seriously, Lillian. She was a Colored cook who worked two jobs, one serving cops and the other serving crooks.

She was a nice-looking woman of 40, slender and with a creamy complexion. She had stiff, no-nonsense short hair, and penetrating eyes behind cat-eye glasses. She worked lunch at the Talk and dinner at the Lantern. I had never seen her rest, seldom seen her smile. Lillian took the streetcar home, and I arranged it so I walked past her on Wabasha Street on a misty evening.

"Lilly," I said, "headed home? I'm going your way."

My Ford was parked around the corner at the police station. I let her in and ground the starter.

"Flooded, maybe," I said.

Two uniformed cops in raincoats walked down the concrete steps arguing over who owed whom a drink.

"There's a guy looking for me," I said. "I owe him money. You haven't seen him around, have you? A little guy, gold teeth, from the south somewhere."

"Um-umm, not me," said Lillian.

"Don't tell anybody I was asking, okay? The guy might be mad at me."

"Okay," she said.

The car smelled of gasoline and Lillian's perfume.

I pushed the starter button again, too soon.

"This goddamn jalopy," I said.

"Be thankful you've got a car. A lot of people would love to have a car, any car."

Chastised, I sat quiet.

"Powers, what's your game?"

"Aw, you know me."

"Well, yes, I've known you for years, and we haven't said fifteen words, and all of a sudden you make up this excuse to drive me home."

She coughed.

"Although I appreciate the ride, I really do. These bones are tired, let me tell you. Rondo trolley service? You could grow old waiting for a streetcar."

With the next grind of the starter, the car sputtered, rattled and finally behaved like it had an internal combustion engine.

I snaked around downtown and started up Rondo Avenue. The black people of Saint Paul lived along a strip, a streetcar line really. It was pretty much like Randolph or Payne or any of the white streetcar neighborhoods. The most visible difference was the shacks on the street corners, mom-and-pop operations that sold newspapers, medicines, fried chicken, bootleg booze, fresh vegetables, numbers tickets, soda pop, cigarettes, canned goods … dozens of businesses, none with a permit. Their owners paid tribute weekly to the Rondo Police Station.

"Franklin Delano Roosevelt," I said as we plodded behind a van. Tail lights out, its side panels advertised no business or trade. I guessed it was moving booze through the night. "Roosevelt's going to ruin this country."

"How do you mean?" asked Lillian.

"Wet," I said.

"We'll make it," said Lillian. "We were Wet before and we'll be Wet again. You'd better believe it. This country just keeps rolling along. I'm not afraid of Franklin Roosevelt."

I said, "Yeah, well people in my trade are."

She sputtered: "Your trade? What is your trade?"

I made a left on Dale Street and drove into an alley lit by one flickering streetlamp.

"Lillian, I would never leak a word."

"All right." She sighed. "The man you want is Little Shorty, but I don't want to end up dead over it. Leave me out of it."

"With the gold teeth?" I asked.

She stared through the misty windshield, her eyeglasses fogged. "Don't get me involved in your gangster business, that's all I ask."

"Where can I find this Little Shorty?" From inside my rain jacket, I pulled my wallet, and drew out what I hoped was a five dollar bill. Lillian palmed it.

"It's a day's pay," I said. "A day's pay I gave you."

"He goes with a little blonde named Paula," Lillian said. "They come in after midnight. She's a drinker. She was pretty once, but it looks like somebody smashed her face with a shovel."

"So Paula and Little Shorty, they come in late and stay …"

"Until Harry chases them home. Little thing like that Paula, and she can drink until dawn."

Lillian opened the car door. "Good night. Please, I have children, so keep me out of it."

"I don't even know your name," I said.

CHAPTER SEVEN

The Green Lantern parking lot was surrounded by shabby brick apartment buildings. One of those was the Wabasha Men's Hotel. It was run by a Mrs. Peterson, a thin bespeckled woman with tied-back iron-gray hair. She charged a buck fifty a night, and had four rules, posted in the parlor:

10 p.m. curfew !
NO radios !
NO drinking !
NO females in the rooms !

She lived in the parlor, from where she monitored her inmates. Mrs. Peterson offered a weekly discount, but I took the room by the day. It had a rancid smell I didn't care to identify, and a rank bathroom down the hall. I never used it. The Town Talk restrooms were clean, and just a minute away.

On my second night of surveillance I saw, walking from the lights of the Town Talk and into the shadows, Swede Fanlund and a much smaller man. I lost them in the dark, but then the Green Lantern's back door opened in a flash of smoky light and let them in. I felt a burning sensation in my right bicep. I had a tiny round scar there to remember Swede Fanlund by.

I was sorry to see he had returned to St. Paul after an absence of years. He'd been lurking on Chicago's North Side, some people said, with the O'Banionites. Others said he was running with Detroit's Purple Gang. No matter, I remembered him as the schoolyard bully of Sacred Heart Boys Academy.

I distracted myself from those memories by reading, and I had plenty of material: the three Saint Paul dailies, Dashiell Hammett's latest, *The Glass Key*, and magazines, my favorites being Startling Detective Adventures and the Saturday Evening Post.

All this reading matter had something in common: Lies. When I tired of reading Lies, I turned to the Truth, the Daily Racing Form, and worked up handicap angles. For casual betting, it's jockeys on, jockeys off, a key to reading the sneaky trainers of today. Also, it helps preserve your bankroll if you never bet Sportsman's Park, where Al Capone rides in every race. My handicapping paid off with a couple of cheap winners down at the, ahem, Royal Cigar Store, but that was the only profit I got from three nights of surveillance.

On the fourth night, at 2:30 in the morning, they motored in. Little Shorty drove a DeSoto, dark red, gleaming in the reflection of street lights. As its occupants got out, I studied them in my racetrack binoculars. Paula was wrapped in furs against the March night, and wore a dark pillbox hat. Little Shorty wore a gray suit and was hatless. His dark red hair was severely trimmed at the sides, but piled high on top. Either of them could have been children, they were that small.

"Was it you, Shorty?" I whispered to no one. "Was it you who burnt up those girls?"

Stiff and cold in my dark room, I watched until a dull dawn broke. Not long after, Paula and Little Shorty emerged from the back door of the Lantern, crossed the parking lot and pushed into the just-opened Town Talk.

I sneaked downstairs and waited chilled in my car out on

Wabasha. They dawdled over breakfast but finally emerged, Paula stumbling, Little Shorty taking her arm. Into the DeSoto they went, and as they pulled away, I prayed to Henry Ford that his jalopy would please start.

I followed them up the hill, past Cathedral and mansions, over to the corner of Dale and Grand. Just a few blocks from the Rondo neighborhood, Grand Avenue was the shopping and boozing thoroughfare for the white swells of Crocus Hill. The handsome four-story brick apartments where Little Shorty parked were as luxe as could be rented in Saint Paul. Into the alley door they went, Little Shorty patting Paula playfully on the ass. I took down the license plate number, but knew they'd come back stolen.

I had taken enough risks already. If Little Shorty was Gold Teeth the town robber, he owned a tommygun and was a wanted man. No man, especially a wanted one, can be tailed for long without catching on.

All I had to do was figure out what happened to the stolen Buick between January, when it was stolen and March, when it was set ablaze. I quit tailing Gold Teeth, and drove away with a plan in mind.

CHAPTER EIGHT

I was in bed with Myrtle when Hula Girl began her prancing premonition of a knock on the front door. I rolled out of bed and worked into my trousers just as the actual knock sounded. I opened the door on the chain because it could have been a door-to-door salesman, a bill collector, or worse, Lieutenant Bulldog.

I was happy to see Janie's freckled face but stepped into the hallway rather than let her in.

"Can we talk inside?" she whispered.

"I have company," I said.

Her face was a map of apprehension.

"Doc Ingerson's lying," she whispered.

"He's running for mayor so I assume he's a liar."

"Can we talk somewhere where nobody can hear us?"

"Well, there's the car."

We trooped down four flights of stairs. In t-shirt, trousers, and bedroom slippers, I was unprepared for the blast of cold in the parking lot. Janie at least wore a thick grandma-knit sweater.

We sat shivering in my car, windows iced by our frosty breath. According to the newspaper it was five below this morning, but I was sure the sun had warmed it to a balmy zero.

"The Burned Ladies," she said. "There was a struggle."

"You want to go for coffee?" I said, teeth chattering. "I'll run upstairs and get a jacket."

"Absolutely not. Look, the younger one …"

"Sadie," I said.

"…was clonked in the head and shot behind the ear. The other one, Rose, was shot twice in the forehead."

"So why is that a big surprise?"

"Defensive wounds. The younger one …

"Sadie," I said.

"… fought them."

"What do you mean by defensive wounds?"

"Forearms," said Janie. "I'm guessing. She was trying to hold off a pistol whipping?"

"They can tell that on a burned corpse?"

"They can, especially when there's broken bone."

A surge rose in me of pure, evil, vengeful anger.

"Which probably means," Janie said, "it was two guys, only two guys, a double date. They couldn't have put up a fight if it was more than two guys. But they did fight. They struggled like hell. Rose, she was almost strangled, with a chain she wore around her neck. She fought them too."

I pounded the steering wheel with my fists. "No! They are not going to get away with it."

"You're snorting, Powers, my Lord, take it easy."

I sucked down a breath of frigid air.

"See, it's the Nobodies," I said, "that's how the Nobodies are treated in this town. We lay down and let the Somebodies walk all over us. And if some of the Nobodies get stomped to death, well there's plenty more where they came from. That's how this town works. These girls had every strike against them. An Indian and a Jew, from out of town, two used-up prostitutes. The ultimate Nobodies. It's not okay, Janie, it's not okay to beat them, shoot them and burn them."

"I didn't say it was okay, Powers."

I realized I had a bare-handed death grip on a frozen steering wheel. When I let go, my fingers were numb.

"Are you calmer now?" Janie asked.

"Maybe," I sighed. "Chain? Did you say Rose had a chain around her neck? I'm thinking back to the night I met her at the Green Lantern. She wore a heavy gold necklace, with a crucifix on the end."

"That's what I was told."

"How did you find all this out?"

"Confidential source. But there's more."

"Spill, then."

She swallowed as if gagging on castor oil.

"Their faces," she said, "had been splashed with nitric acid."

I covered my face with my chilled hands.

"Acid?" I said through my hands. "You know Janie it says in the Bible that God made us higher than the animals and little lower than the angels. But I think He actually made us lower than the animals. A lot lower than the animals."

I dropped my hands from my face.

"What exactly is nitric acid?" I asked.

"I don't know, I didn't take chemistry. One more thing, if you can stand it, Powers. The killers took the took off the license plates and tried to file off the engine serial number."

"They sure went to a lot of trouble," I said, "when they could have just run these girls out of town. Everything the killers did points in one direction. They needed to prevent identification. Which means Sadie and Rose are linked to a Somebody. They were meant to die anonymously because a Somebody in dear old Saint Paul, Somebody well-known, was behind this crime. And that Somebody knows we're looking into it."

"We?" she asked.

"Well, it's we now, isn't it? Janie, how did you find this out?

Why didn't Doc Ingerson tell me?"

In the mornings I can be especially dim. "Oh," I said. "Doc didn't tell me because he's running for mayor and doesn't want to get mixed up in the politics."

Then I saw a flicker in Janie's eyes.

"Which one of Doc's med students are you dating?"

She looked into her lap. "Not exactly dating. Flirting, maybe. Oh, I guess you're right Powers, it's just two prostitutes, so nobody cares."

I wanted to smoke my pipe so bad that my hand went to my t-shirt, as if it could be there.

Janie said: "Thornton says whatever you do in this town, beware of Big Ryan."

"Thornton's right."

"What kind of town is it, where honest citizens can't go to the cops? Where people live in fear of the police chief?"

"How about Crumley?" I said. "He knew the names of Sadie and Rose before they were taken to the morgue."

"They're in on it, the bastards. Those rotten cops set those girls up."

"You are jumping to conclusions," I said. "But I like your conclusions."

She yanked the chrome door handle. "I'm off this case. I'm leaving it alone. This dirty town. I'm not going to be the next corpse toasted in a car."

"Janie…"

"Please, Powers, I don't want to talk about this any more."

She slammed the car door, walked down the icy concrete steps to her basement apartment.

I felt satisfied when Janie slammed her apartment door. She would be much safer letting this dirty town wash its own laundry. She didn't want to talk to me? Rejection never felt so good.

Mrs. Strutz was glaring from her cracked-open apartment door on the third floor landing. She gave me the Minnesota Silent Scolding. The poor old lady had listened, I was sure, to Myrtle's lusty lovemaking.

Yes, Myrtle was a screamer.

"Sorry about the noises," I whispered to Mrs. Strutz.

She scowled and shut the door.

When I reached my apartment, Myrtle stood in the doorway like a human barricade.

"Let me in, I'm half frozen," I said.

"Who's Little Miss Cutie Pants?"

"We're not dating," I said.

Myrtle wore a silk slip and white bra. Her hair was like a dark helmet of curls. Her face was pale, all makeup washed off except eyeliner. She had a cute, round face with a dimpled chin.

"Oh, I'm not worried," said Myrtle. "Because you'll no longer have a dick if I catch you sticking it to that teenager."

"She's not a teenager. Let me in."

"What's the password?"

"Free love."

"Now you're talking, buster." She stepped back. "Make me some coffee, will ya?"

I padded into the kitchen. Hula Girl followed me to await the treat she demanded after my every entrance. I dipped my hand into the peanut bag and threw her one. She caught it in the air and vacuumed it down whole. Snowflake, he patiently crushed the shell and extracted the nut.

"Hula Girl could play outfield for the Saints," I told Myrtle.

"Make it half strength. I don't want a cup of mud."

"You know," I told Myrtle over my shoulder, "I drive to Midway to get fresh coffee."

"Save yourself the trip," said Myrtle. "Stale's all right with me."

I scooped coffee into the percolator's aluminum basket.

"Folgers, MJB, Chase and Sanborn, it's all been sitting in a warehouse in Guatemala for years. Fresh, you need fresh ground coffee. Use plenty of coffee, and don't let it perk too long."

"I'll give you fresh," she said. "What did your freckled little girlfriend want?"

Myrtle lit a thin saggy cigarette and the kitchen began to smell of dopey perfume. Gasping like a fish, she held the smoke in her lungs and blew almost nothing out.

"She's not my girlfriend and she ... you know, the Burned Ladies."

"What about the Burned Ladies?"

"Everybody in town's talking about it."

"Who's everybody?"

"Don't you read the papers?"

"Who's got time to read?" She sucked down another cloud of smoke.

"What do you do all day?"

"Believe me, buster, I'm working all the time."

She took one last drag on that fragrant cigarette, closed her eyes against its smoke. Then she snuffed it out, delicate, in a saucer.

"Why does your little girlfriend care about the Burned Ladies?"

"She's a reporter."

"For which one?"

"Daily News."

"That rag. They can't even spell newspaper."

"I thought you didn't have time to read?"

"I thought you were making me coffee."

I set the percolator on the stove's burners, turned on the gas, struck a match, lit a blue flame. Above the stove was an inspiring three-window view of the Cathedral, poking its cross into the sky.

"I had my picture in the Dispatch once," Myrtle called in.

"Not on the society page, I take it."

"To hell with society."

"So it was a mug shot, then."

When I served Myrtle the milk-sugar confection she mistook for coffee, she was sitting on the sofa near my big console radio.

"That thing work?"

"It's a little early," I said. "The neighbors."

"Screw the neighbors," she said.

"Downstairs," I said. "Mrs. Strutz. She's cranky, she's got arthritis. Besides, there's nothing on at this time of the morning."

Myrtle grabbed last night's Dispatch from the coffee table and leafed to the radio page.

"You're right, nothing," she said. "Bing Crosby, how can anybody listen to that phony in the morning? There's no man in the world as nice as he pretends to be. Every time I hear Bing Crosby sing I need a drink to get over it. How about a movie?"

She examined the listings.

"Well," I said, "they don't start until noon."

I fiddled with my pipe, dropping tobacco in, tamping with my pinkie.

"You're not going to smoke that vile thing, are you?" Myrtle said. "You ought to try putting maryjane in there sometime. That'll take you off tobacco forever."

I lifted the glass humidor and sniffed tobacco. "Heavenly," I said. "There's a shop on Snelling, sells twenty flavors, no Prince Albert for me."

"I don't believe in princes either," said Myrtle. She slapped the newspaper down onto the coffee table. The big headline read:

LINDY IN DISGUISE HUNTS BABY

"Your teenage sweetheart," Myrtle jibed, "is she trying to solve the Lindbergh kidnapping, too?"

She sipped.

"Now that's how I like my coffee, mild and sweet." She patted her hairdo. "Like me."

"What's playing?" I asked.

Snowflake appeared, like a fluffy white ghost, at the door to the bedroom. That unwavering, brown-eyed stare was his way of asking whether we were coming back to bed.

"I see they got a trained seal act at the Orpheum," Myrtle said. "You ever seen one? A trained seal?"

"I don't need a circus, I've got Saint Paul."

"This ain't no circus, this is vaudeville. They tell jokes and the seals applaud."

"Movies, Myrtle, what movies are playing?"

"Strictly Dishonorable, with Paul Lucas." Her lips curled. "Never cared for Paul Lucas. He's kind of a drip. Ladies of the Big House, with Sylvia Sydney. Just what I need, a jailhouse picture. They want to know about jailhouses, they can ask me. Jails stink, let them try to get that piss smell into a movie."

Hula Girl rushed the front door just before a heavy knock sounded.

"It's Freckles, your girlfriend," guessed Myrtle. "She forgot her bra."

But that wasn't Janie's delicate knock. I opened the door to see Sam Tanaka. He was dressed in khaki slacks and a black jacket, bright red scarf, a driver's cap held in one hand.

He peeked in at Myrtle.

"Having a good time?" he whispered to me.

"Always," I said.

"Boss wants to see you."

"Jack Peifer?" Myrtle called from the couch. "Do they serve

breakfast over there?"

"It's a steakhouse," I said.

"So?" said Myrtle.

"So next seating is in nine hours," I said. I turned to Sam. "Give me two minutes, I'll be down."

When I closed the door, Myrtle had a hand to her hung-over head. "Oh, an audience with Pope Jack," she said. "Aren't you the big shot?"

Shot, that's what I was thinking. I rushed into the bedroom and grabbed my Army forty-five. Myrtle walked in behind me.

"Help me, will you?"

I held out a holster and turned my back.

"It clips in there."

"What do you think I am, a choir girl? I've been around, buster."

She clipped the holster to my trousers at the small of my back, and slipped the pistol in. It felt as big as a bowling ball back there. At the coatrack near the front door, I worked into shirt, sport jacket, shoes and socks, overcoat, gloves, scarf, fedora.

"Frosty the snow man," said Myrtle.

"Strange dream I had," I said. "A frozen devil."

"Oh now it's dreams, Doctor Freud."

"It's cold out there." I snatched my pipe from the coffee table.

"They'll just take that peashooter off you, if they want to kill you," said Myrtle.

"If they wanted to kill me, they wouldn't send Peifer's chauffeur."

"Then what's with the cannon?"

"It gives me that warm glow to carry it," I said. "Please don't play the radio loud. Mrs. Strutz … downstairs…"

"Okay, big boy," Myrtle said. "Go get 'em. If they give you trouble, shoot 'em in the balls. It's the only sensitive part on a man."

"Feed the dogs?" I said.

Myrtle kissed me, French style.

CHAPTER NINE

Sam insisted that I sit in back, like I was a Somebody.

The Packard's heater, unlike my Ford's, was capable of warming a car even on a zero degree day. Still, as Sam drove toward the Hollyhocks, I shivered in the rear seat. The vision of those two charred corpses, the memory of that morning's stink, sent a sick, electric feeling through me. I squirmed trying to make peace with the holstered forty-five clinging to my back. It seemed for a crazy moment that Sadie's hungry ghost rode in the seat next to me. I asked that ghost: What happened to you, skinny girl? Where'd you go wrong? Did you get into a car with the wrong man?

And who was that wrong man?

When Minnesotans want to avoid earnest conversation, they discuss the weather. I called out to Sam: "Yeah, there are only two seasons in Minnesota. Snow and mosquitoes."

He drove, grim and silent. The entire route, down Summit Avenue, was lined with the mansions of the Somebodys. They were all here: Somebody's railroad, Somebody's department store, Somebody's newspaper chain, Somebody's bank and trust. At the intersections of this fine boulevard, the city had just installed traffic lights. We were catching them all red.

"Warm front coming," I said. "Or so says the radio. Soon we'll be swatting bugs."

I doubted Sam would deliver me to an execution, and that

thought eased my mind. But maybe he was simply be following orders, with no idea what was at stake. Sam was Japan-born. He trusted authority. That worried me.

I leaned forward to talk over the seat.

"Come on, what the hell is this about?"

Sam looked at me through the rearview mirror.

"All is uncertainty," he said. "You're a horse player, Mick, you realize there are no sure things."

I dropped back into luxurious leather. "You're getting time off on the first weekend in May. Right?"

"The boss knows I would like that. Trouble is, he might go down himself. If so, I am stuck."

"Yeah," I said.

"Playing the role," said Sam.

This Japanese trust in authority wasn't what it seemed, Sam once told me. It was part of a game. Master and servant were true equals, each playing his role, fully aware that it was all theater.

"Well," I said, "if you want to play the role of detective, here's a mystery. Did Jack take a phone call from Duluth, a female? In the last week or so?"

"Not that I know of. But there's so little I know."

"Maybe he dipped into the safe to loan this girl fifty bucks?"

"Mick, I'm not his banker and I don't work the switchboard."

"But you would tell me if you knew, right Sam?"

He left that question hanging and turned onto the bucolic if frozen Mississippi Boulevard. Along the right, the great river flowed underneath its icy winter disguise. Along the left, in frosty mansions, lived the spillover from Summit, human beings disguised as lawyers, executives and doctors. The lone public building on this exclusive boulevard was the Hollyhocks, a gangster casino disguised as a steak house.

Sam drove that olive-painted Packard up the circular driveway and deposited me at the Hollyhocks' steps. Peifer's minions had cleared those steps of ice and snow, lest the sheep slip on their way up to be fleeced. In the chill dining room, behind a maze of chairs upended on tables, the lovely Violet sat at the bar, brooding over coffee. She looked at me and then back into her cup. I'd intruded into a private moment.

I hustled up the wide, carpeted stairway and through the casino room. Slot machines lined the walls. White tablecloths covered the craps and roulette tables. At the end of a dark hallway I found an open door to Jack's office. The man himself sat behind a beat-up oak desk.

A chained Doberman Pinscher, having lost all spirit, merely picked its head up as I entered. Its jaws moved silently, as if it were trying to remember how to bark. It sighed and dropped its head.

"Don't be a stranger, come on," Peifer said. "Sit down, take a load off."

The room had small, high windows that let in only a filtered soft light. Shoved back in a corner was a gray steel safe, big enough to bathe in.

I removed my topcoat, threw it over the back of an easy chair. From the bar behind him, Jack grabbed a cut-glass decanter. He poured dark liquor into a cocktail glass, held it toward me.

"Too early for you?"

"I no longer indulge," I said.

"Hair of the dog," he said. He sipped. "Should I tell you why you're here?"

"Please," I said.

"We had an understanding with that cocksucker O'Brien," he said.

I nodded. He was talking about the County Prosecutor, who in January had lost an election. I figured that Jack's casino had all along been operating under the benign and knowing gaze of county officials. But O'Brien had lost in a landslide to Michael "Irish" Kinkead, a tall, tweedy, pipe-smoking, bespeckled, brogue-spouting product of Limerick.

"I'm sure you know all about it," Jack said. "Everybody in town seems to know my business."

He swiveled the chair. "Just," he said, "when we were starting to make a buck."

He gulped whiskey, his face taking on a moody cast.

"Am I cursed? Am I doomed? Every business I've ever started blasts off like a rocket ship, then…" his hands described a falling arc, "boom, crashes to earth. I try not to take it personal, but I get the feeling I'm doomed."

"We're all doomed Jack. You're a Catholic. You know about Original Sin, don't you?"

"Sin, sure," Jack said, "But there's nothing original about it. Say, was the sheriff sitting out there when you drove up?"

"The sheriff?"

"Yeah, his deputy. In a marked car, a black Dodge."

"I didn't notice."

"He'll be around, don't worry. A deputy's been parked there ever since the Irishman went into office. Now I got nothing against the sheriff personally, but some of my clients, they see his deputy sitting out there, they go elsewhere for the evening. You know. In-dim-a-dation."

He swirled whiskey in that glass. "I liked O'Brien, I really did. He ran the county fair and square. This new Irishman, he ain't on the level."

He sipped. "He's sending me a message. You know how it works, Powers."

I shrugged.

"That's what I like about you, Powers, man of few words. Now look, I need Irish Kinkead on my side but I can't go see him myself. That would start every tongue in town wagging. So I was hoping you, you're one of them, you're Irish, you're known all over town. You could make a gesture of genuine friendship on behalf of this extablishment."

"How much?"

"For you or for him?"

"For him."

After a long pause, Jack said: "You negotiate."

"All right."

"That's why I need you. You're a high school graduate, right?"

I nodded.

"Unfortunately," Jack said, "people believe we're generating fabulous sums of cash out here when frankly, we're just breaking even. So it's not like I'm made of money here."

He looked into his glass. "They want twenty percent." He began a coughing spell that only eased when he drained his whiskey glass.

"Of everything?" I asked. "Or just the upstairs?"

"Every drink, every roll of the dice, every Caesar salad, every platter of sirloin. They want twenty percent of it all. I can tell by your reaction that even you consider that highly unreasonable. And guess what? They know how to hurt me. They will let the restaurant keep serving because they know I lose money on food. And they will shut the bar and the casino, where all the profits are. So see, they can ruin me without closing me down, the bastards, after how well I've treated them, here and my downtown place. You remember that, right? Great chop suey. Everybody in town ate there but I went broke on the food. Food is no good, that's why I hate food, you can't make a dime off of food, believe me I have tried food."

He sighed.

"You think I want to run a steakhouse? To hell with steak. Steak disgusts me. You need good teeth to eat a steak, and I've got wobbly teeth. I've got a brother who's a dentist but I can't stand to be in the chair. I squirm around and the drill nicks my tongue, see?"

He stuck out his tongue, as if to show a gaping wound.

"Why do I run a restaurant? Only to keep the wives from detouring the husbands out of my clip joint. That's the only reason."

Jack walked to his safe, worked the combination, and came back with a rubber banded wad of cash.

"Five hundred," he said. "Working cash. Don't spend it all in one place. A tip will get you in the door and then, see if you can get me a hundred a week deal. Hundred flat. Even that's going to kill me."

"A hundred a week."

"And I don't want to see the sheriff's car parked in the driveway ever again."

"And my get is?"

"Fifty flat," Jack said. "Just for the handshake. Plus if you work a good, fair deal, a hundred bonus. You know I never let my couriers … well, I'm a generous man, too generous, and it's bad to be generous in this business because I'm always giving stuff away."

"And then I get the weekly bag job?"

Jack nodded. "Sure," he said. "Think about it. Once you take the job, it's yours."

What he meant was, if you take the job, you either do it quiet or get yourself killed. But I had chosen this life, and there was no going back. A hundred fifty is more than a month's pay down at the Swift stockyards and frankly, I have no stomach to stand in lakes of blood cutting up cattle all day. You can't get those jobs anyway, they are passed down father to son. Nobody's hiring anywhere, never mind a guy with no legit references for the last ten years. So a month's pay for a morning's work?

"I'll take it," I said.

Jack poured himself a swallow of liquor. I took my pipe out of my side pocket, tamped down the tobacco that was already in it, and fired it up with a match.

He held up his glass, I lifted my pipe.

"Deal," he said. "Here's to them who wish us well, and all the rest can go to...."

He drank.

"Hell."

I felt a nasty chill all through me.

Saint Paul was full people who called themselves Irish, but were one or two generations removed from the Emerald Isle. Kinkead was not a Removed Irishman, but a genuine immigrant of the worst sort, the kind who winks at the Statue of Liberty on his way to law school. I guess people liked hearing his charming brogue on the radio, because he had no trouble winning his first election, and was now top prosecutor in Ramsey County. He'd made charming but phony promises that he intended to clean up crime.

Except for federal cases, it was now Irish Kinkead who decided who to prosecute in Saint Paul, and who to let go. He was a card-playing, whiskey-drinking buddy of Police Chief Big Joe Ryan. With the two of them running the machinery of justice, there were no rules, there was no law, and your every step in this town should be a cautious one.

Kinkead ruled from a crumbling sandstone castle in downtown Saint Paul, a block from the Mississippi. Sam let me off at the back entrance, and the elevator operator took me to the third floor. A large, jowly, dark-haired woman sat like a guard dog in the alcove.

"I'm to see Mr. Kinkead. On the River Road matter."

"Just a minute," she said, and pushed through a smoked-glass door lettered RAMSEY COUNTY ATTORNEY in gold script.

When she returned, she shut the door gently and whispered: "Mr. Kinkead will send someone to see you."

"Now or …?"

"He will send someone to see you, sir."

"But he doesn't even…"

Her voice rose in irritation. "Sir, he will send … someone … to see you."

"Okay," I said and put my hat on.

How this was going to work I could not figure. But I could figure breakfast, so in the gleaming marble lobby I dropped a nickel and called my apartment. Myrtle answered. I invited her to take the streetcar to the Town Talk.

I walked up there, freezing on Saint Peter Street. The cruelty of Minnesota's winters is not just their length and temperature, but the capricious winds that blow unhindered off icebergs at the North Pole. Huddled into my overcoat, holding my hat to my head, I passed windblown citizens scurrying to dental appointments, to get their watches fixed, to buy leather gloves, to make withdrawals from their always-shaky banks. I was grateful for the warmth, finally, of the Town Talk. I shed coat, hat and gloves, read the Pioneer Press and sipped weak coffee. The main headline shouted:

HOUSE REJECTS WET PLAN

I turned to the funnies. Prohibition was dead, maybe not in this election, but soon. And then all of us who make a living at night and in back rooms and alleys, we'll be joining those broken souls lined up at soup kitchens.

It was only a six-block streetcar ride, and Myrtle arrived while I was on the second cup of coffee. I flagged down Opal for my Adam and Eve and ordered for Myrtle, two strips of bacon and a hard boiled egg, mustard on the side.

Myrtle resented my reading the newspaper, and snatched it.

"Hey," she said. "How did it go at the fancy joint?"

"It went."

"He had something for you?" she said. "Good. Let's go to Florida."

"Long train ride," I said.

"Let's fly."

"Me? In an airplane?"

"I'd do it," said Myrtle. "A crash wouldn't bother me. It would be such a bloody, romantic way to die."

"I don't know," I said. "There'd be a fire, right? All that fuel?"

"Killjoy."

"I don't want to burn to death, all right?"

"How would you like to die, Mick"

"With you in my arms, darling."

"You got a special way of lying makes a girl feel good. But don't worry about burning up, Mick. You couldn't even start a fire in weather like this."

"Couple more days of cold," I said. "And it'll be warm again."

Myrtle sputtered. "No wonder I need my furs." She shivered. "Look at us, it's almost Easter."

I was suddenly aware of a looming presence at our table. He wasn't a big man, but he threw an awful long shadow. He stood between us and the plate-glass windows.

"Bobby," I said.

Serious Bobby Pearson wore a straw boater and a sloppy, neutral-gray suit with a tie of the same color. He was tall and fit except for a slight paunch. He was maybe forty, with the face of a wizened cherub, blue eyes magnified by rimless eyeglasses.

"You know Myrtle," I said.

"Everybody knows Myrtle," he said.

"Huh," said Myrtle.

"I'm going to sit down," said Serious Bobby.

He pushed my coffee cup to make room for his elbows.

"I can't stay for breakfast," he said. "There's a man in the car. He's the biggest man in town, and he's got every virtue but patience."

Opal delivered breakfast into a pause in the conversation. I let mine sit. Myrtle peeled her egg.

Serious Bobby said: "There's an introduction fee, I take it?"

"A three-run homer," I said.

"Not a grand slam?"

"I understood three runs was enough to win the game."

"Let me ask the scorekeeper," said Bobby. He popped up, strode for the door and, as we could see through the windows, let himself into a long dark Lincoln.

Myrtle held a bacon strip up, savored its aroma, bit it in half.

"That's Irish Kinkead's man, ain't it?" she said. "The weasel does business right in front of me."

"Keep you voice down, will you? You should be flattered. They trust you. Most girls they would have driven off."

I now had no appetite for poached eggs or cold coffee. That forty-five was jammed back there, reminding me that this was a dangerous game. When Bobby pushed back through the door, he ushered in a blast of North Pole.

He sat with us.

"A three-run homer," Bobby said. "Congratulations to the batter, and now, salary negotiations."

I said, "Fifty a week."

Bobby sputtered. "Be serious now. I'm not going to take that to the scorekeeper. He's thinking percentage."

"Well, that's why we're negotiating."

"Let me see," he said, and headed toward the door.

"They have no respect for me," Myrtle said. "I'm nobody. I'm beneath their notice."

"That's what you want," I said. "Believe me."

"Well, it makes a girl feel low."

Bobby rushed through the door, sat and said with a grin: "Ten percent of the rake." He held out his hand. "Deal? Seriously, now."

I let Bobby's hand hang in the air.

Myrtle dipped the end of her egg into mustard, and decorated it with salt and pepper.

A squad of bundled-up detectives bulled in and headed for their corner table. They held the door open long enough to suck all the heat out of the place. They pretended not to notice that their chief, Big Joe Ryan, was sitting out there in a chauffeured Lincoln.

"Can't do that," I said. "Percentage is out. A hundred RBIs. Every week."

"Let me see," said Bobby, and walked off.

Myrtle cocked her head at me.

"What?" I said.

"Little boys playing marbles. That's all this is, a game of marbles, for boys who never grew up."

She ate the egg.

"Tastes like it was made by Goodyear," she said. "I think they boiled it last Christmas."

Bobby returned. He waved cheerful at the cops' table.

"A hundred weekly," he said as he sat down, "plus five percent of the upstairs action only."

"Okay, look, Bobby, I need to talk to the scorekeeper."

"No can do," said Bobby, and shook his head for emphasis. "Seriously, now, that is a no-go."

"Because the manager of my team, he's ready to move us across the river. There's another league he can play in, with all new umpires. Some of the ballparks we're looking at are so small, a hundred bucks would take care of every umpire in the league. Tell him that. Hell, most of our fans are from Minneapolis anyway. The team moves, let's say to Inver Grove, our fans won't have to drive far. Tell him that. Bobby, we want to play in your league, but goddamn it you're killing us. Don't kill the home team, Bobby. Don't make us move across the river."

Bobby set his straw hat back on his head. Despite the temperature out there and the chill draft in here, he was sweating.

"The scorekeeper loves you guys," Bobby said. "You know that. Seriously, he loves everyone, that man. He's got everyone's best interest at heart. So I'll see. Maybe he's ready to fall in love."

Bobby again forged out into the cold.

"Do you think she's got a nice ass?" Myrtle asked.

"Who?"

"Opal."

"Sure."

"Nicer than mine?"

I laughed. "Nah."

Myrtle said. "I do. I think she's got a nicer ass than mine."

"Myrtle," I said and covered her hand with mine. I looked into her dark eyes and she withdrew her hand. She scarfed down that second piece of bacon.

"Don't make no declarations of love now," she said. "I can't stand when you're sincere."

"I know you."

"You don't know me at all, buster. You just think you do."

Bobby returned.

"A hundred RBIs every week," he whispered. "In six months, we renegotiate. Upwards."

He leaned over me, staring down.

"Deal?"

"Deal," I said.

"Let's be serious, now," Bobby said. "No handshake, just your word."

"Absolutely level," I said.

"Say the word," Bobby said.

"Serious," I said. "We have a deal."

"Serious, then," Bobby said. "I'll come right in and get it. Myrtle," he tipped his straw hat to her, and then walked over to chat up the detectives.

I slipped into the men's bathroom. In the corner underneath the copper pipes that fed the water heater was the drop space. I used my pipe tool to pry up a short piece of floorboard. From my inside sport coat pocket I took a rubber banded bundle of bills, lay it in the dusty hole, and replaced the floorboard. At the sink I washed my hands and looked in the mirror. Pale from the long winter. Chapped lips. Hairline dropping away. Beginning of the double chin. Badly in need of a shave.

"You'll be all right, champ," I told my reflection. "It's payday."

CHAPTER TEN

The next morning you could almost believe in Spring. Cathedral Hill sent streams of snowmelt through downtown and into the mighty river. The sun had warmed my Ford, which started with just a light application of choke. After stopping at Western Union to wire words of reassurance to Papa Alt, I parked on Grand Avenue, and prepared for a day of surveillance.

On the theory that nobody could go for long without stopping at the neighborhood druggist, I chose the Rexall Drugs across from Gold Teeth's apartment. I bought Startling Detective Adventures to read at the counter over a cup of coffee. The MYSTERY OF THE SLAIN HONEYMOONERS kept me entertained for one cup. Then I took a slow walk around the block. The grandees of Grand Avenue were, like the green tips of tulips, just venturing out from their long winter. Most shoppers were dressed in furs and heavy coats, as if this warmth was an illusion. I trod the alley underneath my targets' window. All her shades were drawn, windows tight against fresh air.

Back at the Rexall I caught the pharmacist in a quiet moment, and leaned over the counter. He may have been an Italian or Greek fellow, dark hair, olive skin, stubble even after a close shave, squeaky clean and dressed in crisp whites.

I said, "Excuse me, but would you have any uhm, I think it's called nitric acid?"

His head jerked as if I'd asked for arsenic.

"That is not a pharmaceutical," he said. "That is an industrial product."

"Do you know where a fella could get some if he needed it for, you know…"

"It's very dangerous," he said. "Terrible chemical burns." He wagged a finger at me. "It's for fertilizer, for explosives. A fellow should know what he's doing before he handles it. What do you want it for anyway?"

I shrugged. "What do most people want it for?"

He gripped the counter like he was anchoring himself to deliver a scolding. "I suppose it could be used to clean metals. Any big industrial lab would have it. But I would be very, very careful if I were you."

I stood looking out the window, half at my reflection, half at the busy street, when up walked Sadie's ghost. She stopped to gaze at a display of baby care products: a doll in a bassinette surrounded by packs of diapers and bottled lotions.

No it was not Sadie's ghost, but a young woman in pink, hand to her head to cut the sun's glare. She took a long look in, and then walked on. She was pregnant, unmistakable on that skinny frame.

Nitric acid. Terrible burns. Pauper's grave. Nobody from Duluth would claim Sadie's body, I'd heard.

I am going to get you, Gold Teeth, I promised Sadie's ghost. If you didn't burn those girls up, you'll tell me who did.

I returned to the counter for another cup and then another, moving into a booth after the breakfast rush, and opening the Dispatch to take a run at the crossword puzzle. I outlasted one waitress, and ordered a grilled-cheese sandwich to appease her replacement. I played the pinball machine, adding a few pennies to the fortunes of Tom Filben. It was after the lunch rush when she walked in.

I had been stalling for five hours and could hardly shake myself up for action. But it was her, no doubt, the woman with the smashed-in face. She was thin, had blond hair with streaks of red, was tiny, vulnerable looking, almost a little girl, but wrapped in an enormous mink coat. She wore a purple hat tilted sideways over pinned up hair, and walked wobbly on high heels. When she approached the prescription counter I sidled over and faked an interest in greeting cards.

She talked with the pharmacist in near-whispers and then stood back, chewing gum and examining the menu board. She approached the counter and ordered a ham sandwich, which was wrapped in wax paper to go. She sat on a stool and waited until the pharmacist handed a half-pint bottle through the window to his boy clerk. She asked the boy to fetch a bottle of Nervine Pills from under the counter. He bagged her purchases and took the money. I turned my back and walked down the aisle, toward the phone booths. I lurked a booth as she paid for the sandwich and walked out.

Since Gold Teeth's DeSoto was nowhere in sight, and since she had ordered lunch for one, I decided to work my game. At the magazine rack, I picked out Colliers, Horror Stories, Three Love Novels, Photoplay, Cosmopolitan, Hollywood, Redbook, True Confessions, and Radio Stars. It was a 90-cent investment I figured would pay dividends.

All sorts of guys, having lost their jobs, were going door to door now, selling laundry powders, candy assortments, neckties, encyclopedias, meat, milk, eggs, and even magazine subscriptions. Housewives bought out of boredom, or sympathy, or the simple inability to slam the door in a broke fella's face.

I was wearing my best gray suit with burgundy tie, and hoped I looked like a man who'd fallen from economic grace. Magazines in a briefcase, I entered by the back door and crept up to apartment

206. Listening in the hallway, I heard only the squeal of a neighbor's radio.

I knocked.

"Just a minute."

She opened the door as far as the chain would allow. Cigarette wobbling in her lips, she sized me up and said: "Now, what would you want?"

"Madam, the Publisher's Guild has authorized me to give away magazines absolutely free to deserving readers ..."

She glanced at my briefcase.

"What's the catch?"

"No catch, ma'am," I said, and waved a copy of Cosmopolitan. It featured a glamorous color head-and-shoulder shot of a young blonde, with luscious lips, a sun hat, and the suggestion that the rest of her was nude.

"We just need to fill out a short survey ..."

She plucked the lipstick-stained cigarette from her lips, blew smoke out the door.

I coughed. "In return, you receive a year's free subscription to any five of these ..."

I slipped the magazines out of the briefcase, fanned out the splashy covers.

"... or to practically any magazine you could name."

"It don't sound kosher to me."

I smelled daytime drinker on her breath.

"It's promotional, ma'am, promotional. The Publisher's Guild believes you'll love the magazines and become a lifetime subscriber. You see? Everybody wins in the end."

"Yeah, everybody wins, all right."

She closed the door.

"A guy's gotta make a living," I shouted.

I heard soft footsteps going away, then approaching again. She opened the door. In her hand was a shiny chef knife with a foot-long blade.

"You said free, right?"

"A whole year free," I said, my eyes fixed on that knife. "The five magazines of your choice."

"Come on in," she said. "But watch the monkey business."

I slipped in.

"Leave the door open," she said.

I stayed wide of her, and set magazines and briefcase on a fine, dark dining room chair. The furniture was rich but sparse, as if they'd just moved in.

The dining room table was big enough to host grandma's Thanksgiving dinner. Above it hung an elaborate crystal chandelier. A china closet, gleaming with dark tropical wood, held very little china. Brocaded white curtains were cinched back with gold-colored ropes. Set into the crook of the wall was a pink golf bag with clubs sticking out.

Paula was barefoot, swathed in a purple robe. She stood in a corner of the dining room with that knife held relaxed at her waist. She had an unmistakable face, a bad thing for a criminal. She would have been as pretty as a magazine model, but her nose was flattened so much that it acted like a trumpet, her every word nasal. Above her right eye was a jagged, ugly scar.

"My husband will be home any minute," she said.

Her hands glittered with diamond rings, but no wedding band.

"He will be delighted," I said. "We have all the mens' magazines available. Argosy. Dime Western." I winked. "Even some of the French ones."

I fanned the magazines out on the all-glass coffee table. I ran my hand over its surface.

"My, this table's quite stylish," I said. "It must have been very expensive."

"What?"

"The coffee table."

"My husband makes a good income," she said.

"Which brings me to the survey," I said. I pulled out a pad of forms I had bought at the stationers, and clicked my ballpoint pen.

"These things are the salvation of every lefty," I said.

"What?"

"Ballpoints," I said. "You're not a lefty are you? It's a special torment to write with a fountain pen if you're a lefty. Everything smears. The nuns, I went to school with the nuns, and they had it in for us lefties, let me tell you."

She sat on the couch opposite. Between us was that glass coffee table and a lush Persian rug. She set the knife on a lamp table next to a porcelain figurine of a shepherdess.

"So," I said, "If you don't mind, the questions. You're married, I take it, and your husband's occupation ..."

"Steel," she said. "He's in the steel business."

"Ah," I said. "I take it he's an executive?"

She folded her glittering hands in the lap of that purple robe.

"Oh, I don't know exactly what he does, really. You know how men are. He doesn't like to talk about his work."

I scribbled and said: "And do you work outside the home?"

"You've got to be kidding."

"A lot of modern women do," I said, brightly.

On an end table, beside the knife, lay that brown prescription pint she had bought across the street.

"Sounds like you're not from around here, but I can't quite place it," I said.

"You ever heard of Galveston?" she asked.

"Sure," I said.

"It's in Texas," she said. She retrieved a cigarette from a gold snap case.

"Ah," I said.

"So what's your racket?" she said. "I mean before you started hustling magazines. I take it you lost your job."

"Yeah well it was kind of a stinky job," I said. "I was in the fertilizer business."

"Sure," she said. "It's hard times on the farms too. So you sold farm fertilizers?"

"Right, and the chemicals along with them, you know, like nitric acid, that sort of thing."

I watched her face so intently that time almost stopped. I saw no flicker there, no guilt, no recognition.

"You kind of spook me with that stare," she said.

"Sorry. Tell me, your husband, where is he from?"

She blew smoke.

"Mama's boy," she said.

"Pardon?"

"His mother's crazy and he's always running over there. That's where he is now. I'm a little worried about what he'll do if he finds a strange man in the living room."

"So he's a local man, then."

"God no."

"Just for the company's records, I'd like to get his name."

She swallowed smoke.

"Bergstrom."

"S-T-R-O-M?"

She nodded. "Fredrick."

"And your name?"

"Paula.

"And your husband hails from?"

"They're a couple of Okies, him and the mother."

"Oklahoma, then?"

"Ain't that what I said?"

She snatched up that prescription whiskey, poured some into a rose-decorated coffee cup. She retreated to the fainting couch and watched me.

"You're a queer duck," she said.

"What do you mean?"

"I don't know. Something funny about you."

"I'm not exactly Eddie Cantor," I said.

She lifted an edge of a shade and peeked out at Grand Avenue. Then she walked over to a built-in bookcase that held not books, but a single, ceramic figurine: Valentine cherub, entwined. She leaned against that bookcase and stared at me.

"Very nice threads," she said. "You don't look like a magazine salesman to me."

I tried to bring a wounded look to my face.

"Believe me, lady, I wish I had a steady job."

"You and everybody," she said. "I guess you're all right. Hock them clothes, mister. Go around in rags and people will buy out of pity."

"I wish I lived on Grand Avenue. I'd say your husband does all right, looking at you."

"Yeah, well don't look too hard, my husband's the jealous type."

"So he's a tough guy?"

"He can take care of himself."

I handed her the stack of magazines and she sorted through them, dropping the rejects to the glass coffee table.

"I'll take these," she said when she chose her five. "I want 'em now. I took your survey, didn't I? Look, I don't want you here when my husband comes home. He can be trouble."

"Okay," I said and gathered up the rejected magazines.

"Thanks," she said. "Your name is…"

"Patrick," I said. "Patrick Powell. I've got your address, and your subscriptions will start with the next issue."

I snapped my briefcase shut.

"Yeah well good luck to you Patrick."

"A pleasure," I said, and shook her tiny glittering hand.

I drove from "Paula Bergstrom's" apartment directly downtown to see McAmbly. Since Saint Paul's cops rarely bothered to enforce the law, I parked in a spot marked SQUAD CARS ONLY. Sequestered in his attic hideaway, McAmbly was reading the Racing Form.

"You claim to make money at this game," McAmbly said, as if we'd been in the middle of a conversation.

"A little," I said. "But it's dicey. It's gambling, Billy. Ups and downs. Game of chance."

"Yeah, well, I can't figure it." He closed the Form in disgust.

"Hey, guess who's back in town?" I said.

"Jesse James?"

"No, Swede Fanlund," I said. "I think I saw him sitting in a car once. And I know I saw him the other night going into the Lantern."

"With that many enemies, I'm surprised he lived to be forty years old."

"He had to come back for a reason," I said.

"Probably on the run," Billy said.

"I still have the scar," I said.

Billy gave me a dim look. I interpreted that to mean: You're not going to bring up all that high school stuff, are you?

I slid the rejected magazines across his desk: Startling Detective Adventures, Colliers, Photoplay, Cosmopolitan, Redbook, and Radio Stars.

"Prints," I said.

"What good are fingerprints?" he said. He closed his lips over a stifled belch. "With our filing system?"

"BCA?" I said.

"Hit or miss," he said.

"Feds?"

"They don't talk to us anymore. I heard that's the order from J. Edgar himself."

"I've got a gangster girl. Lives in luxury on Crocus Hill, but no manly stuff in the apartment. Kept woman. Drinks before noon."

McAmbly belched. "Nothing wrong with that."

"Wears furs and diamonds. Plays golf. Does not work."

"I can dust 'em," he said. "But we can't do much without the Hoovers."

Beer breath leaked through well-spaced teeth. He ran a rough hand through his salt-and-pepper hair.

"I give up on this game," he said. "All crooks. I don't know how you do it."

"Horse racing?"

"It's fixed. Like the fight game. I can let you look at the cards," he said.

He led me into a dark, musty alley of file cabinets.

"Women," he said. "As criminals, they don't last long. You could go through all of Saint Paul's bad girls in ten minutes."

I took the file folder back to the dusty window, laid it on a crude workbench. There was one card for each woman, compiled by the Bureau of Criminal Apprehension. I flipped through a few and came to Myrtle's, a front and side view. Underneath someone had written SHOPLIFTER in bold handwriting. Two convictions, 1929 and 1931.

Currently on probation. Known wife of VICTOR "SLICK" MARTIN, AKA THE PROFESSOR, AKA PROFESSOR BANKS. Bank robber serving sentence in Wisconsin.

I turned the card over to the front side again. Myrtle looked cute, wearing a dress with a big bow up front, like a sullen schoolgirl brought to the principal's office.

Only when I looked closer did I see her disguised anger and muted shame.

A few cards later I found a face that was only vaguely familiar. I was seeing "Mrs. Paula Bergstrom" before her face was smashed. It was not a criminal's front-and-profile shot, but a pretty girl at a lakeside. Some cop had pressured the family to turn over this photo, which had been crudely glued to the Bertillion card. The young woman was posing lakeside hugging a big oak tree.

PAULA HARMON it said on the front.

On the back it said:

> Wife of bank robber CHARLES HARMON.
> Convicted with CHARLES HARMON, American Express
> Robbery, Davenport, Iowa, 1929. Probation.

I called McAmbly in and asked for the card on Charles Harmon. He delivered it, but the back of the card was blank.

"What the hell, Billy?"

He shrugged. "Government's cutting back."

He examined the card.

"No use filling in the card of a dead man. Back in October. Kraft State Bank, over in Menominee. Remember it?"

"Can't keep track of the bank robberies without a score card."

"Mess," he said. "Dead bodies, running gun battles …"

"So Charles Harmon, dead in October."

"Dead as they come."

"So Paula Bergstrom was Paula Harmon a few months ago and now she's a widow, the pampered girlfriend of Little Shorty."

"Who's Little Shorty?"

"Aka Gold Teeth. I don't suppose you have him cataloged under either name."

McAmbly waved. "The brass, the last thing they want is good records."

He picked up the Racing Form.

"It's a crooked game, I tell you."

CHAPTER ELEVEN

The link between Paula Harmon and the Kraft State Bank Robbery pushed me in a new direction. Gold Teeth and Boris Karloff were the leaders of the gang Papa Alt feared. But why did he fear them? So far their only known crime was a midnight raid on Hudson, Wisconsin, twenty five miles away. Their only link to the murders of Sadie and Rose was that stolen Buick.

I thought this over while smoking my pipe, staring out my apartment windows at the crazy intersection of Seven Corners. It was even more chaotic that usual, because workmen were digging up a pipeline. The traffic cop, poor sap, was trying to stay out of the way of a steam shovel and seven streams of auto and streetcar traffic. I found that traffic mess hypnotic. It was speaking to me, playing into a hunch.

Paula Harmon was living much too high to be accounted for by the haul from the midnight Hudson raid. Her dead husband was a bank robber. Perhaps Gold Teeth and Boris Karloff had robbed the Kraft State along with Charles Harmon. Now that Harmon was dead, maybe they were re-organizing, using that Hudson raid to finance their next big bank job. If so, they may have stolen the Buick to use it as a getaway car after a bank robbery.

If I was right, what Papa Alt really feared was something he would never admit to an outsider. He feared this gang was going to break The Deal, the decades-old compact between Saint Paul and its criminals. No bank within the city limits had been robbed during

Big Ryan's long tenure as chief. Saint Paul banks had become fat targets, lightly guarded. Maybe Gold Teeth and his gang were ready to defy Papa Alt and Big Ryan by pulling a Saint Paul bank job. If so, Papa Alt's only son, president of the bank, was a fat goose ready to be plucked.

If any of this was true, it might also indicate a hidden rupture in Saint Paul's underworld. Maybe Big Ryan was in cahoots with the gang, and about to double-cross Papa Alt. Maybe Irish Kinkead, and the new regime in the county building, had made demands that threw the whole system out of whack. I watched Seven Corners, busy, busy with its many crossings, its broken, buried pipelines, and felt I was on to something I was just beginning to understand.

I was still working this puzzle in my head twenty minutes later, as I pushed through the shipping doors of the Daily News and into the press room.

I snaked past rolls of paper as big as my Ford. They were stacked near a printing press the size of a whaling ship. Men, only men, wearing aprons, worked over clattering hot typesetting machines. By the time I reached the composing room, the soles of my shoes were slippery with ink.

In the composing room, men, only men, worked with Guttenberg's invention, 400 years old unsurpassed. Lead letters were being assembled in frames to make up dark mirror images of a newspaper page. The printers were too busy to notice me.

Janie sat in a cramped break-room. Behind her was a counter that held newspapers bound in leather books. An electric percolator, streaked with boiled-over coffee, was set on a grubby table. A cardboard shamrock and a gold-and-green paper leprechaun were pinned to one inky wall.

"How is it outside?" she asked.

"Oh, warming up."

She wore a white tennis visor and the straps ruffled her red locks. In the harsh light of the break-room's overhead lamps, her face looked especially pale.

"I can't get them," she said. "She's a bitch."

She cleared her throat. "Territorial," she added. "She's a mother bear, and the library is her den. Those clips are her children."

I sighed.

"But I took notes," she said. She flipped through a skinny reporter's notebook, pages covered in a hasty scrawl. "Kraft State Bank robbery, right?"

"Right, late October."

"Menominee, Wisconsin, you've been there?"

I shook my head.

"It's okay to cross the river and visit Wisconsin, you know. We're not cannibals."

"I know that very well, young lady. I shall be a Wisconsin property owner someday."

"What could that possibly mean?"

"Forty acres of pine trees and potato fields. Just outside Eagle River. My sisters and I are the heirs. What town are you from anyway?"

"Waunakee. It's the only Waunakee in the world, that's our town slogan." She pursed her lips. "It's the dullest Waunakee in the world, too. More cows than people."

"Okay, the bank robbery."

"Four men. The Kraft State Bank was owned by a fat cat named Kraft."

"No surprise."

"His two sons worked there. Nineteen and twenty two years old, the boys. One of the robbers kicks the twenty-two-year-old to the floor, demands more money, then shoots the kid in the ribs. The boy is lying there bleeding. Meanwhile, the alarm is ringing and the he-men of Menominee are gathering with deer rifles outside the bank. So the robbers take the nineteen year old boy hostage. During the getaway, some idiot townsman empties his revolver into the bandit car. Result: one dead robber, one dead banker's son."

"So four robbers, one killed."

She shook her head.

"Two killed. A posse chases them along dirt roads. The sheriff gets off a few shots at the car, bandits drop another body and keep going. That body was your man, Charles Harmon. Might have been shot by his fellow thugs, for all anybody knows." She closed her notebook. "Nobody claimed the body. Another bank robber in pauper's field. How ironic."

She sighed.

"How sad. That beautiful nineteen year old boy." She narrowed her eyes to a mean look. "Don't run away now. How does this fit in?"

Quite well, I thought. Certainly Papa Alt had read about this robbery and the killing of the banker's son.

"Any of the witnesses mention a robber with gold teeth?" I asked. "Or one that looked like Boris Karloff?"

Janie looked down at her notebook and shook her head.

"Then I'm not sure," I said.

"Are you sure of anything?"

"I'm a horse player," I said. "Longshots win all the time. Look, Charles Harmon was married to a Texas girl. He's been dead five months and she's already taken up with another gangster. She's living up on Grand Avenue like her name was Pillsbury."

"And her connection to the Burned Ladies is ..."

"Her new boyfriend was in the gang that raided Hudson. The Buick Sadie and Rose died in was stolen in that raid. I wonder if there's some connection, besides Paula, between the Hudson raid and the Kraft State Bank robbery."

A grunting pressman intruded, hefted the percolator, found it empty, cursed and stomped off.

"Everybody's grumpy waiting for spring," Janie said.

"It's already spring. Get out of the newsroom."

"Who's the new gangster boyfriend?" she asked, and leaned in to add quietly: "I want this story."

"I thought you wanted out."

"Well I want back in, if that's okay with you. I'm helping you here, right? I'm bored with the Women's Page. I'm tired of you-know-who getting all the good stories. They hand everything to him, just because he drinks with Major Hoople."

"Okay," I said.

"Don't you dare screw me, Michael Patrick Powers. I don't want Goggles to get his sweaty hands on my story."

I held up my hand like a boy scout taking the oath.

"A scout is trustworthy," I said.

She said: "You're no boy scout, Powers."

On the way back to my apartment, I walked past a tavern that was festooned with paper shamrocks. I tried to ignore Saint Patrick's Day. Even in my drinking days I stayed home on this awful holiday, an insult to the Irish. Most Irish don't drink, although you wouldn't know it by their reputation. So now that I'd joined the Irish majority, I planned to spend the evening at the movies with Myrtle. She didn't care one way or the other about Saint Patrick's Day. We planned an evening at the theater, and it would be quiet, with all the drunken louts jammed into the speakeasies. We'd attend the first showing, coming home early to avoid tipsy drivers and the drunks on the Sibley streetcar.

I walked out to Robert Street, bought a bag of popcorn at Candyland, stopped at a newsstand to read the headlines:

NO SIGN OF LINDBERGH BABY

I took the Sibley streetcar, eating popcorn as it lurched along, earning glares of disapproval from my seatmate, a proper lady. But most of the seats were occupied by drunks, dressed in green, headed for the Cathedral, chattering about the parade. I was spilling kernels, munching as I thought my case over.

So ... Little Shorty Gold Teeth doesn't live with Paula. He's always running home to mama. Paula's drinking away her loneliness. And maybe her grief over her bank robber husband. But how much grief? She's living the luxe life as her dead husband rots in a potters grave.

Paula Harmon ... she's got everything money could buy but nothing can soothe her desperate feelings. She buys more and more jewelry, drinks more and more, and finds no comfort. Takes Nervine pills with whiskey. Hmm. I hopped off the streetcar the Western Union on Seventh and sent a telegram to Papa Alt:

SUSPECTED CONNECTION
KRAFT STATE BANK ROBBERY

But I wondered: Why wasn't Papa Alt getting the dirt from his buddies, Big Ryan, chief of police, and Harry Sawyer, chief of gangsters? Yes, there was a rupture underground, somewhere, but unlike those workmen digging up Seven Corners, I couldn't find the pipeline.

I caught another streetcar up the hill, and this one was almost solid green with beery rowdies heading up to join the parade. I hopped off just before the Sibley Tunnel.

As I approached the lobby of my apartment, I saw movement behind the glass door. I expected Mrs. Strutz or maybe Little Elmer to pop out. But when the door opened with a flash of reflected sunlight, two men emerged. One was tall, pale, hatless, in blue work clothes. The other was short, dark, dressed in a gray banker's suit.

The short man, I'd had words with him in the Green Lantern, the night I met Rose and Sadie.

The tall man was Swede Fanlund. From out of his overcoat he brought some kind of weapon.

I ran zigzag for my Ford.

Footsteps thudded behind me. My pistol was upstairs and I cursed myself for not carrying it.

I ripped open the car door and plunged the starter button. I was breathing like a race horse, frightened off my wits, but feeling strangely alive. The car started and I jerked it into reverse just as Swede leveled a sawed-off shotgun at my windshield.

I stomped on the accelerator. My car careened backward into a split rail fence.

A long, long moment passed as I slumped at the steering wheel, stunned. Swede's dark partner yanked open the passenger door. He took two-handed aim with a huge revolver.

I stomped the gas again, plowed backward through the fence and down the hill until my car, thumping and screeching, came to a halt. I was tilted up looking at the sky, but only for a moment. Then I saw the Cathedral going past as if I were on a thrill ride. The car rolled on its side with a tremendous hollow thud.

I felt that my life was over, but I was at peace. I gazed at pure blue sky awaiting the appearance of God or at least the Archangel Michael. I knew two goons were gunning for me, but it no longer mattered. I was not of this Earth anymore. The nuns had been right all along. There was a Heaven.

Somewhere off in the distance I heard music, bagpipes and drums, my ancestors' welcome to Irish Heaven. It would be a realm of whiskey, tea and soda bread, but no famine, no hangovers, no gout.

Then dark figures began to surround my car. I thought I would see Dad again and maybe uncles Matt and Joe. I passed out and only came to when rough hands pulled me out of the Ford and lay me on half-frozen mud. I was screaming no no no no but they lifted me anyway, young strong men, beer on their breath, dressed in Kelly green. And when, I shaky and coughing, rose on my elbows to look in panic for my assassins, they were nowhere.

My ruined Ford, one wheel spinning, engine smoking, lay on its side, blocking the Saint Patrick's Day Parade.

"You had enough to drink Mister?" said one of my rescuers. He was a college boy built like a football lineman.

I wiped my bleeding lips. My wrists throbbed with pain, like someone had put them in a vice and squeezed. My car was leaking liquid into the street, making a puddle of green, Saint Patrick's favorite color.

CHAPTER TWELVE

I was playing Sam Tanaka on the half-frozen greens of Como Golf Course. Behind us, zoo birds cried for spring. Not three weeks ago, people were skiing on this course. The greens underneath our spiked shoes were the texture of cold butter.

Sam, a careful putter, lipped out. My second putt was a gimme, the length of a cigar, but my hands were shaky and I missed it short. Sam slipped his putter into his tan leather bag. When he hoisted the bag over his shoulder, he looked like a golf pro, wearing blue sweater, drivers cap, tweed trousers, white shoes.

"I wish I had good advice for you," said Sam, after watching me finally sink the ball. "No car insurance?"

"Are you kidding me?"

"Does McAmbly have room?"

"With six kids?"

"Myrtle?"

"Myrtle," I sputtered and shook my head.

"I'm living in a back room myself," he said. "Saving money."

"I've got no choice," I said. "It's too late for me, Sam, the packing houses aren't hiring and railroads are laying off. I'm too old to be a locomotive fireman anyway, you've got to build those muscles young."

"Bull?" he said.

"And shake down hobos for a living? I wouldn't take it even if I could get it. If there's anything worse than a cop it's a railroad bull."

Sam lay his bag against a green wooden bench. The clubs rattled against his Remington pump-action shotgun. Shading his eyes, he scouted the 9th hole.

"I understand, Powers," he said. "None of us can return to the dull plodding life. We are not oxen, we are men. None of us were meant to stand in one place all day, plucking chickens or bolting fenders."

"The thing is, Sam, a man with capital could run up to Winnipeg and drive back with a load. All it takes is money. Rent the truck. Finance the load."

I glanced over my shoulder. Was that Swede and his Italian buddy on the 6th hole? A glance at the shotgun in Sam's bag helped me feel a little calmer. Look, I told myself, they wouldn't dare gun down Sam, Jack Peifer's best man. And they weren't going to make him a witness to my murder, either. I took a deep breath, trying to stay calm.

"Too far for the chippie," Sam said. "Too short for the driver."

He selected his driver and choked down the grip. He glanced at the green, far off, dog right.

"Winnipeg?" he said. "The risk is coming back with nothing. Or coming back dead. It's not like the old days. There's a hijacker behind every bush now. People are desperate. I make it 20-to-1 you don't return with that load. And then what do you say to your Uncle? Gee, sorry, I blew your money and came back empty?"

He shook his head. "It's a level of risk I cannot accept. I like our chances in the Derby better."

"Six weeks from now, though."

"In the Derby, nobody will blast our brains out if we lose."

He squatted to tee up, stepped back for a practice swing. With a powerful stroke, he sent the ball flying into the left fringe.

"Pulled it," he said.

"Not your worst," I said.

"All I can ask." He rattled the driver into his bag, yanked off his driving gloves.

I said: "I don't even know if I could find an Uncle for a run to Canada."

"Filben," Sam said. "A reckless man."

I stood over my shot. You can't swing the golf club too slowly, I told myself. I shanked it, an ugly, errant drive into dead weeds.

"It plays," said Sam.

We walked side by side over the dormant grass. My eyes made a paranoid sweep of the bare trees, which hid, I was certain, squads of assassins.

"The hell it plays," I said.

"Powers, you can't expect a good game in your state of mind."

I found my ball, stood over it, took deep breaths, and hit a fat looper to the middle of the fairway.

"Terrible, but it's all you need," said Sam.

"I've got no choice but to go home," I said. "I can't stay at the hotel forever. How can I negotiate a truce? I don't know who's declared war on me."

"You said you knew one of them?"

"Douglas Fanlund. Known as Swede. High school bully grown up to be a thug. Went to school with me and Billy McAmbly."

"What did you ever do to him?"

"Nothing that deserves the death penalty. That's why I say he's working for somebody."

I let that word hang, an opening should Sam choose to take it. Sam's boss was a Somebody in this town. But his face gave me no clue.

"You're in a tough spot," he said. "Maybe blow town."

"Where and with what money?"

"Churchill?"

"Can I grind it out down there? The Derby's one thing. You can hedge the Derby with all that rube money in the pool. But day by day? All those crappy claiming races?"

"You never know," said Sam.

"I can see myself spending my last quarter on a Form. Scared money never wins. Sam, you know that."

"Never is a strange concept," Sam said. "Explain it to me."

"I'll never master this game, how's that?"

My ball was sitting up on half-frozen grass, and I whacked it with a five iron. It dropped dead at the edge of the green.

"Mud sunk," I grumbled. "Made a crater up there."

I carried my bag to the fringe and watched Sam poke an eight-iron damn near into the hole. He two-putted though, and I matched his bogie over a rugged bumpy green.

"Strange game," Sam said. "If you write the number four on a card, you feel all excited. If you write the number five, you feel ashamed. And yet the pleasure is in playing. It's a mistake to focus on the number."

He lifted both balls out of the cup, flipped mine to me.

"Sam, this is the only town on Earth where I can make a living. In our game, you've got to be known and trusted. I can't just move to Des Moines or Chicago. So I wonder if you could put an ear to the door. What does Jack know that could help me? I mean, he's sort of my Uncle, right? I worked the Irish Kinkead deal for him."

Sam lit a Lucky Strike, tossed the match toward a frozen pond.

"Come on, Sam," I said. "A subtle inquiry?"

"What is the difference," he said, "between maybe and perhaps?"

"Ah ..."

"Think about that," he said.

The sight of my apartment building, and the fence I'd wrecked in my backwards escape from the gunmen, filled me with an awful electric dread. Sam carried his golf bag and I carried mine into the lobby. A glimpse of that shotgun stock in Sam's golf bag calmed me as I knocked on Little Elmer's door. Elmer had entertained Snowflake and Hula Girl for two days, and spoiled them. The dogs took no particular interest in my return. I tipped Elmer, he limped back into the darkness of his apartment, and we, men and dogs, climbed the stairs. I let the dogs squirm outside the apartment door for a moment, to sniff for trouble.

I set my golf bag against the wall.

"Here goes," I said to Sam. Then I opened the door to find my place had been tossed.

A hurricane would have done less damage.

The dogs ran for their window seat while I wandered around the ruins of my domestic life. Cereal, coffee, cans of soup, a burst bag of sugar, boxes of crackers, bottles of soap and vinegar were all down in a mess on the kitchen floor, amid a scattering of pots and pans. In the dining room the China closet had been flung open, and my mom's dishes and platters, some shattered, lay on the hardwood. I knew without looking that the silverware was gone.

Sam, grim and silent, pulled out the shotgun and cautiously poked its muzzle into the bedroom.

In the living room, hats, jackets and coats were piled on the floor. The furs I'd been storing for Myrtle were missing from the hall closet. Some vicious bastard had knifed the speaker of my beautiful Philco.

In the bedroom, clothes were heaped on the bed, all the chest drawers pulled out. My forty-five and an expensive leather shoulder holster were missing. The ammo in the sock drawer had been stolen too. I sat on the bed, head in hands. Snowflake hopped up and began licking, trying to get at my face. Hula Girl watched, curious, from the doorway.

I realized I had forgotten to close the front door so I chained and locked it. I went to the phone in the living room, and picked it up, dead, cord snipped at the wall. A surge of pure rage rose in me and I opened the window and threw the phone out. Four stories down there, it sunk like a long black asteroid in a universe of melting snow.

"Look at this," I said to Sam. "No damage to the front door."

"Perhaps the janitor let them in," Sam said.

"Or somebody copied my key," I said.

"A well-known trick of coat-check girls," he said.

Sam set the shotgun against the wall, and lit a cigarette.

"If they watched me head out of the hotel with my golf bag," I said, "they knew I wouldn't be home for hours."

"Mick, I must be back at the club."

"It's okay, go, go," I said. "I'm not staying here."

We led the dogs downstairs to Little Elmer. I re-engaged his services as dog sitter and gave him a dollar. Until I changed the lock, I couldn't risk a return of the thugs, and blocked from my imagination what they might have done to my dogs. At twenty-five pounds each, they weren't fearsome enough to fend off gangsters. Driven by anger, I pushed out the door and into Sam's coupe. He dropped me, unarmed, at the Green Lantern Tavern.

Harry Sawyer's Green Lantern was legendary all over the American underworld, from sea to darkening sea. From the Green Lantern, crime spread like a spider's web all over the Midwest. But the tavern itself was an absolute sanctuary. Gunplay in here would be fatal to the fool who started it. Even the most notorious gangsters checked their guns at the door. Here in the headquarters of crime, Harry enforced a peace that eluded the rest of the city.

The Green Lantern wasn't only for criminals. The tavern needed to fill its booths. Good citizens were welcome to eat, drink and gawk for gangsters. Reporters from all three dailies were among the regular drinkers. But newspapers never dared print the name of this tavern. When absolutely necessary, they referred to it as "a Wabasha Street café." Likewise, Harry's name was never mentioned in print.

It was three in the afternoon and quiet in there. Bess was reading a Film Stars magazine behind the bar. That bar served only to support the lolling head of a lone drunken gangster. Reilly, I supposed, was over at his day job selling tickets on the ponies. I wandered down a dark hallway, through a maze formed by cardboard boxes of booze. I tapped on the office door that said KEEP OUT.

"Harry?" I said. "Powers."

"Aw fuck," Harry barked from behind the door.

I pushed in.

"My nap," he said.

It stank in there. Harry was a quart-a-day man, and although he never appeared drunk, his person and his office had taken on an end-of-the-world stink. The office had no windows and was dark until Harry pulled the chain of a single glaring bulb. He sat back in a leather easy chair and farted.

A bottle of unlabeled booze sat at his bloated, naked feet. He was nearly bursting out of his pinstriped trousers, and his white shirt was pulled open for a comfortable fit. His black hair was tousled into a pile atop his head, his dark shifty eyes were bloodshot-wet. Behind him was a locked combination safe.

"What the hell brings you in?"

"Business," I said.

"Better be," he said. "I just fell asleep."

"Sorry."

"Gonna be up all fucking night again."

"Sorry Harry."

"I heard you were running errands for Peifer."

"True," I said.

"What the hell you doing in here then?"

"Does that make us enemies?"

Harry grunted.

"I might need a favor," I said.

"Jack's your man."

"But I need protection. I understand you're the man for that."

"You understand bullshit," said Harry. He reached for the bottle at his feet. He picked it up, examined it in the light. "The shit they're bringing me now, I wouldn't feed it to a cow."

"What does it take to get some relief here?" I asked.

"From what?"

"Somebody doesn't like me."

Harry sputtered. "You bring this problem to me?"

"I'm standing here, Harry."

"Sit down, then," he said. "Sit down and drink with me."

I sat on a tufted chest that looked it came from a whorehouse rummage sale. Harry handed me, in shaky hands, a dirty glass half filled with amber liquid. I sniffed it. I sipped. I told myself one drink wouldn't bring on the gout.

Harry gulped booze and said: "I should be asleep right now. Hell, I'm not going to get any sleep. You see this?" He pushed a velvet-lined tray of diamond jewelry under the harsh light. "You got any use for this kind of crap?"

"Not my game, Harry. You looking to lay it off?"

I wondered who had tossed somebody's house to get that jewelry. Had they knifed the radio, out of spite?

"No market anymore," Harry complained. "Jewelry stores aren't moving nothing. Society dames, they're selling their fucking jewelry. Nobody's buying. Glut on the fucking market, and these guys, they bring crap in here like it was 1925. Well, the gold rush is over. They bring this crap to me and I got to take it."

"Why do you have to take it?"

"Because I got to take it."

"Even if you can't move it?"

"I got to take it."

"Well if you have to, you have to."

"And I got to, believe me."

I swallowed whiskey. It spread a relaxing warmth through me, and I realized how tense I'd been.

He said: "I hear you're working for Papa Alt too."

"Me?"

That warmth disappeared. Alarms went off in every lobe of my brain.

"People come in here with rumors," Harry said, "normally I don't listen to that shit. What does Papa Alt want, anyway?"

I took a deep breath. "I thought you and Papa were friends."

"We're like this," Harry said, and crossed his fingers. "You know what that is? That's a German fucking a Jew."

"Beer's disappearing from the Alt Brewery," I lied.

"Oh yeah?"

"Papa wants me to find out who's stealing it."

"Whole trucks or barrels or what?"

"He doesn't know."

Harry tossed down the rest of his whiskey.

"Thanks for lying to me," he said. "Get out of here so I can sleep. I'm up until four in the morning around here."

"Fifty a week, maybe?" I said. "I can make that."

Harry whistled. "Who do you need to keep off you?"

"I figure you know that, Harry."

He squirmed in his chair.

"Two guys," I said. "One of them might be The Swede. I don't know the other guy, Rico. I've seen him in here."

"You got fifty I'll give it a try. You can't trust nobody in this town anymore, the whole thing's going to shit. We used to have a deal in this town where a guy knew where he stood. No more. Gimme the fifty. It's a half-ass offer but let it be a lesson to you. Peifer can't help you, but Uncle Harry can. See, that's why guys shouldn't work for that asshole. Jack only cares about Jack. That's the fucking lesson here. Now give me the fifty, and don't go parading around like you're John Fucking Barrymore. Stay low, and pay up. Jack Peifer, you see what a pussy he is now?"

"Can I call you Uncle Harry?"

"You fucking Irishmen, I have a soft spot for every one of you."

CHAPTER THIRTEEN

If there's anything worse than a Ford, it's a Plymouth. At least my Ford did not quit in traffic, and didn't smoke so bad you had to drive with the windows open. Lucky for me, spring was here for good.

In that rattling Plymouth, I tailed Gold Teeth in stages from Paula's house, first to the Robert Street Bridge, then two nights later across the bridge into Little Mexico. A day later, I trailed him up the hill to where his DeSoto turned off in a suburban alley. Having little to do during these nights of surveillance, I worried to pass the time.

My living expenses were usually $100 a month, but with the payoff to Harry, they had suddenly tripled. On top of that I owed Filben $250 for this stinking Plymouth. I was making $10 a week, reliable, for the Peifer bag job, and $50 a week, temporarily, from Papa Alt. My other bag jobs were hit or miss. It was like getting a big bonus one week, and nothing for weeks in a row. You didn't have to be Einstein to calculate there was no road from here to Easy Street.

Five weeks to the Derby, that was my tranquilizer. If Sam and I got lucky in Louisville, I might be able to skip town for a while. Sure, Harry had issued a protection order on me, but that was an expensive deal. And it didn't change the fact that a Saint Paul Somebody wanted me dead. Swede Fanlund and his partner Rico were just hired guns.

The night I tracked Gold Teeth home, I stopped at Western Union and sent Papa Alt a three word message:

TARGETS DOMICILE DETECTED

That had a sophisticated ring, I hoped. Western Union doesn't charge extra for big words.

Next day, I returned to Robert Street's suburban end on the pretext of getting the Plymouth a lube job. Across from the Gold Teeth house was a gas station run by a wide, short woman. It was the cleanest gas station in town. The woman was maybe thirty years old. She wore white overalls with the name SHELLY stitched across the breast pocket. She climbed up from the lube pit when I drove in, wiping her hands with a blue rag.

"Lube and oil?" I asked.

She glared at the Plymouth. It might have been a dead, stinking whale beached at her gas pump.

"Not right away," she said.

"Well, eventually?" I asked.

"This afternoon," she said.

"One o'clock?"

"Um, probably."

"Two?"

"More likely," she said. "I'm by myself here. Can you leave it? Work piles up."

"Well, I've got free time this afternoon," I said. "I'm patient. And I really need that lube job."

"You from the neighborhood? "

That threw me for a moment. "Thinking of renting around here."

"Expensive," she said, and tossed the rag into a barrel. "I drive in myself."

I parked that Plymouth in front of a barber shop and walked around the block twice, just to get the feel of the neighborhood. There wasn't much to distinguish it. Suburbs had sprung up in cornfields during the Roaring years. The houses were modern boxes, the trees young and scrawny. Unlike downtown, there was room out here, and each house had a small backyard and alley. When they extended the trolley system out here, Robert Street had begun filling up with drugstores, grocers, auto parts shops, speakeasies, hardware stores, butchers and so on.

In the alley behind Gold Teeth's house stood a one-car garage, the last trace of winter's snow in its shadows. Parked in front of the garage door was a rusty 1928 Essex. Gold Teeth, I surmised, kept his precious DeSoto in the garage.

I drove over the bridge to downtown and stopped at Downtown Dutch's Pawn to look over pistols. A dusty display case beneath the cash register contained watches and cigarette lighters. One of those lighters was gold, and shaped like a lipstick tube.

"Dutch," I said and pointed, "let me see that lighter."

Dutch had lost a forearm in the trenches. Which side he'd been fighting for, I was never sure. Every day, his wife pinned back one arm of a clean white shirt. She used a big gold safety pin, as if to call extra attention to his wounds.

Dutch, his every move unbalanced, lunged for that lighter, dropped it into my palm.

"Pelieve me," he said, "your princess will love it."

It had a squiggle of filigree, and a nick on the lip. It was Sadie's, and had been stolen from my apartment.

"Who brought this in?" I asked Dutch.

"Punk kid, never seen him pefore."

"That's the answer you give the cops. How about a real answer?"

"It's a pusiness answer," he said, spittle flying from his lips. "People do pusiness in private here."

"What else did this punk bring in?"

Dutch shrugged. "Poke around."

"You sure are informative," I said. "How much for the lighter?"

"Puck twenty five," he said.

I laid change on the counter.

"You want to peek at pistols, Powers?"

"How about silverware? Get any new sets in lately?"

"Funny you should ask," he said, and stooped to lift something from under the counter.

It was a beautiful, polished mahogany box. It was inlaid with stones in a pattern that formed the script-letter Y.

That Y was for Young, my mother's maiden name.

"Go ahead," Dutch said. "You'll see. Absolutely peautiful. In perfect condition."

I lifted the lid back on its brass hinges. There in red velvet lining lay the gleaming silverware my grandmother Young had bequeathed to my mom. This box of dinnerware was grandma's hope that my mother would live a prosperous, respectable life. It was a hope crushed by my father's illness, and his long absences from work. This was the precious silverware my mother had hung on to, even when she had to borrow the grocery money. This was the gleaming treasure that only appeared on special occasions, and had otherwise been hidden in a back closet of whatever hovel we were renting. My hands shook, my eyes welled with tears, something lumpy caught in my throat. Here in front of me was the dream of an honest, beautiful, loving woman taken from this world far too soon. This was all that was left of her. Not gold, not diamonds, just silver utensils.

"I'm practically giving it away," said Dutch.

"I can't afford it," I said.

"Porgive me Powers, you stared at it for quite some time."

"I don't give dinner parties," I said.

"Think investment," Dutch said. He picked up a gleaming fork, turned it in front of my eyes. "You can't go wrong with precious metals."

"Shoot me a good price."

"Porty," he said.

"Outrageous," I said.

"Por you, Powers, special," he said. "Porty for anybody else, special price for a pellow veteran. Let's say twenty-five, plus I throw in a pottle of silver polish."

The knives all stood up in the lid, like shiny sentries. The forks and spoons lay nested, all with their kind. Order and beauty, that's what I was thinking. I had caught my mother, once in a while, opening this box just to behold order and beauty.

"I'm kind of stretched right now, Dutch," I said. "I'll give you a five on her, put it on layaway."

Dutch smiled and I knew I had agreed to pay too much.

"Lock and key now," I said. "I don't want to come in and find this gone. I want the paperwork. Twenty five and its mine."

He dropped the lid and the little bronze latches snapped into place.

I found parking behind the police station and climbed the back stairs to see McAmbly. Billy, red-faced, was eating a baloney sandwich and drinking from a bottle of Hamm's beer. He dropped the half-eaten sandwich on the wax paper it had come in, wiped his fingers on his tunic, and said something.

"What?"

He swallowed.

"Radio cars," he said. "Each car with a radio now."

"So the cops can listen to Burns and Allen?"

"Who?"

"Burns and Allen."

"Who's that?"

"What century you living in, Billy?"

"I'd prefer the eighteenth."

"So radio cars?"

"Yep. Get this. KSTP? They're going to pause the programming and broadcast the calls."

"So?"

"So you're listening to a nice orchestra, and then you hear McGraw's scratchy voice say, Car 29, Seventh and Wabasha, Robbery. Do you want to hear that? You're listening to music, for Christ's sake. Stupid idea. The commercials are bad enough, now police calls? Broadcasting, all that's gonna do is fill the scene with gawkers."

He tossed the beer bottle, clank, into the trashcan with its many brethren.

I said: "What do you hear about Swede Fanlund?"

"I'd love to read his obit," Billy said. "Other than that?" He shrugged. "Why?"

"Just wondering," I said.

"The hell you are." He belched. "Another thing. Beer in cans. It don't taste the same. I tried it, okay, I don't want to be a cave man, I don't take a horse and buggy to work, but Jesus H. Christ, beer in cans?"

"Here it is," I said and ripped a page out of my spiral notebook. That page bore a description of Gold Teeth's DeSoto and the five digit license plate number.

Billy looked at me with bleary eyes. "It'll take a phone call."

"So make the call."

"If you hit the Derby I want to see something."

"Case of beer," I said.

"In bottles," he said.

He, and sandwich, disappeared behind a black curtain that separated the file room from the photo room.

I spread the Dispatch on the counter. There was still hope for the Lindbergh Baby, its headlines said. I skipped that story after the first paragraph.

UNPAID CHICAGO TEACHERS
LIVING LIVES OF MISERY

That story told everything in the headline. I skipped it to read about Minneapolis bootlegger Bruce Campbell, shot dead by a cop. I read that entire story, following it off the front page. I didn't know either deceased or cop. Minneapolis, in some ways, was as far away as San Francisco. A different gang ran things over there. Even Harry couldn't help you on the West Bank of the Mississippi.

I figured this dirty Minneapolis cop had been trying to hijack a bootlegger's load. Because normally, running rum is not a capital offense. Normally, you just made your payoff to Copper Joe and drove on.

Maybe Sam Tanaka had given good advice. Rum running had gotten too treacherous.

McAmbly pushed through that black curtain sporting a grin.

"Got us again," he said, smiling gap-toothed. He slapped my notebook page on the counter.

"Your DeSoto is registered to Robin D. Banks," he said.

"Oh no."

"I'll give Filben credit for creativity," he said.

"And balls," I said.

"When you're the Big Prick's fishing buddy, the fish practically jump into the pan."

"Address? I don't know why I ask."

"Robin D. Banks lives at the Palace Theater."

"Filben, he should have been in vaudeville."

"You see this?" McAmbly said, and tapped the newspaper. "They're cutting our pay."

"No," I said. "They won't dare. It's just politics."

"I got six mouths to feed, for Christ's sake."

"I'll buy you lunch next time, Billy."

"Okay, but ham, not baloney," he said.

I stopped at the Saint Peter Rod and Gun Shop, named after the street, and not the First Bishop. There I priced a nice Smith & Wesson six-shooter, $12.50. But maybe, I reasoned, I didn't need it, as long as I kept up my payment to Harry. So I walked out unarmed and kept my appointment with Shelly the Mechanic.

I arrived at 1:30 and this woman, despite her previous claim, had absolutely nothing to do. She was sitting at her desk, smoking a cigar, and reading Modern Detective Magazine. At second glance I saw she wasn't reading, but doodling in the margins. Her pen-and-ink creatures were tommygun gangsters and their molls. She reluctantly folded the magazine.

"That lube job," I said.

"I'm on break right now," she said.

"You're the owner, right?"

"That's why I need my breaks," she said. "Nerves."

She tapped ashes off her cigar.

"I'm all alone here," she said. "I've got no help."

"Well I'm in no rush," I said. "Like I told you, I'm thinking about moving out here. Clean air and all. The coal smoke downtown. You know."

She kicked back in her chair. Behind her was a sparkling clean window that displayed a set of Goodyear Tires.

"Mexicans," she said. "That's the main problem. Mostly they

stay down the hill, but…"

She puffed her cigar.

"Ah," she said, "people complain about them, but honestly, they're no worse than the Irish. You're not Irish, are you?"

"What about your neighbors?"

"Dutchers, mostly. Right across the street, they own a speakeasy, down near the stockyards."

"And them, over there?"

"Okies," she said. "Renters."

"Next door?"

"Are you a burglar? An encyclopedia salesman? What are you?"

Before I could answer she said, "Micks. She works at the Emporium. He's a typical Irishman, stays home and drinks all day."

"You see much of the Okies?"

"They're like bats. They fly out at night. Except for the old lady. The sons, that's an all-night party. I see them sneak home after I open up some mornings."

"What time do you open up?"

"Six. It's a twelve-hour day here."

"How many sons?"

Shelly held up two fingers.

I asked: "The old lady, she's an Okie too?"

"Oh yeah. Don't get her going, you'll never shut her up."

"You don't know their names?"

She pursed her lips, shook her head, then perked up: "Anderson?"

In order to camouflage my interest in the Okies, I interrogated Shelly about the other neighbors until she climbed down into the pit and began to change the oil in my Plymouth.

As she worked, I leafed through Modern Detective Magazine, and admired Shelly's gangster doodlings.

"You like gangsters, I see," I called down to her.

"My next life," she called up, "I'm going to trade in my wrenches for a tommygun. It's cleaner work and the money's better. Female bank robber, wouldn't that be a hoot?"

"Yeah," I said, but I was staring at the Gold Teeth house. Okies. I began wracking my brain to dig up some desperado or private eye I knew in Oklahoma.

I called down to Shelly in the pit. "They drove a Buick, didn't they?"

"Who we talking about?"

"The Okies."

"One of them brought a Buick in here, for an oil change, yeah."

"One of the sons, right?"

"Yeah, nice guy."

"Gold front teeth?"

"No," she said. "I know who you're talking about, little guy with gold teeth, he drives a DeSoto. This was the other one. Taller guy, with dark, slicked-back hair. He took good care of that Buick, shame when it was stolen."

"Stolen?"

"Yeah, stolen, that's what he told me. Stolen in a blizzard. Who steals a car in a blizzard?"

Red kerchief over her head, she began to climb out of the pit.

"I don't push my nose in, mister," she said. "They're gangsters, obviously."

"Huh?"

"Bootleggers! Come on, man. They're out all night. They always have new cars."

She snapped her fingers at me.

"When is a crime not a crime?" she said. "When it's a federal offense. You know what I mean?"

I nodded.

"You drink," she said, "don't you?"

"On occasion."

"Well, does that make you a criminal?"

"No," I said.

"The kid who owned that Buick, he may be a gangster, but he's all manners. He's driving a fancy Hudson now. Takes good care of his cars."

She shrugged. She wiped a stainless steel wrench clean and hung it on a pegboard.

"Dollar fifty," she said.

She insisted on writing out a receipt. As I waited for that, a black Dodge pulled up in front of the Okies' house. Lieutenant Bulldog McMullen popped out of the car, ran around the house and into the side door.

"Cops," she said. "You see them over there once in a while." She shrugged and handed me the receipt. "I guess it's about that Buick. Stolen cars? With all that goes on in this town, you'd think the detectives had something better to investigate."

A few seconds later, Bulldog McMullen reappeared. He hurried back to his Dodge, and with a glance over his shoulder, pulled out reckless into traffic, made a screeching U-turn, and headed downtown.

CHAPTER FOURTEEN

Bulldog McMullen was a homicide cop, and he was in on The Deal. Investigating an auto theft was far beneath him. I could think of two reasons for his visit to Gold Teeth's house: to collect overdue protection money or to deliver a message from headquarters. His visit confirmed that the Gold Teeth gang was working with the knowledge and consent of Police Chief Big Joe Ryan, enforcer of The Deal.

Out-of-town criminals were slow to realize it, but they were the cows and Saint Paul was the slaughterhouse. The criminals paid the cops ten percent of their haul as protection money. But that was just the beginning. Money laundering cost twenty percent. Stolen items such as furs and jewelry lost ninety percent of their value when fenced. Criminals purchased their autos from Filben at inflated values, and paid extra for false license plates and bogus registrations. Local rogues like me ran errands for hefty fees. Madams, card sharps and barkeeps all put their hands in the gangsters' pocket. So The Deal caused criminals to go from flush to broke in record time. Depleted of cash by the system, gangster simply had to commit more crimes.

I lit my pipe with Sadie's lipstick tube lighter and pondered the mystery of the purloined Buick. It was the greasy-haired Boris Karloff guy who had stolen it in January during the raid on the town of Hudson. In March, he told his mechanic, it was stolen from him during a blizzard. That was the last storm of the season, on the night Sadie and Rose were murdered.

Boris Karloff took good care of that Buick, and you don't change the oil in a car you're going to burn. So maybe it really was stolen from him. But it was also possible he loaned that Buick to the killers of Sadie and Rose, without knowing what was to happen to it and them.

All I had to go on was that Buick, and the certainty that it had been stolen by the Gold Teeth gang. The gang was on good terms with the Saint Paul police, so why was Papa Alt so afraid of them?

Some kind of betrayal was in the works. That was all I could figure.

There is no camouflage as convincing as walking your dog. Hula Girl served as apprentice detective while I pulled surveillance on the Anderson house.

An old lady in rundown stockings came out of that house ass-first. She yanked a chain, choking a stubborn black-and-white bulldog. It was one of those miniatures, bred as house pets. The woman wore a mink stole over a tattered dress. Her pinky sparkled with a diamond ring.

Her dress met her knees, where thick stockings had her varicose veins surrounded. She pulled that bulldog down the stairs in a fit of temper, tugged it across a muddy yard and into the gravel alley.

The dog trotted behind her, panting, toward the downtown skyline. When they were a block away, I leashed Hula Girl and eased her out of the car.

It was a cheerful spring day, but snowy reminders of winter clung to every shadow. Bare trees were afraid to send tender feelers into a dangerous world. Hula Girl watched our targets, whickering, hoping to further her life goal, which was to meet every dog in the universe.

Hula Girl pulled me down the alley faster than I wanted to go. I turned her around. Mrs. Anderson was a slow dog walker, so I had to zig and zag to meet her. Hula Girl stopped to pee at the sandstone walls of a funeral home. Toward us walked Mrs. Anderson and her bulldog.

"Can my dog meet your dog?" I called.

She frowned, this short, square-built woman. But as Hula Girl and the bulldog circled each other, Mrs. Anderson allowed a tired smile. She was a craggy woman, perhaps 60. The bleached hair was supposed to make her look young, but nothing could hide her wrinkled skin and a wary, wounded look in her eyes.

"Whew," I said, "Lucky you're dressed in fur. Will the warm weather ever get here?"

She stepped back to allow a young mom to push a baby carriage past. She tightened the bulldog's leash.

"People hereabouts believe this to be spring?" she asked in a croaking voice.

"Really isn't much spring up here," I said. "Sort of rolls right into summer."

"Well, I haven't been here for summer yet."

"You haven't? Well, it's delightful. Summers are easy to take around here. Just warm enough, and breezy."

Hula Girl won a staring contest with the bulldog. It climbed the stairs to escape her challenging gaze.

"We're going to the lakes this summer," Mrs. Anderson volunteered.

"Oh?"

"My boys promised we would take up a cabin."

"Ah. Which lake?"

"Oh, I don't know the lakes in these parts."

"Well, we have plenty of them."

I avoided asking direct questions. If she was a gangster mother,

her suspicions might be easily aroused.

"I was born in New York City myself," I said.

"Oh were you?"

"Railroad family. We moved here when I was a little boy. My dad. A mathematician. Railroad timetables, that was his job."

"They're great fishermen, my boys," she said.

"Walleye. That's the fish around here."

"Oh." She held her nose, "I don't eat fish."

"Walleye is a very mild tasting fish."

I put out my hand for a shake.

"Patrick Powell," I said.

"Mrs. Anderson."

"And this is Hula Girl," I said.

Mrs. Anderson had scant interest in Hula Girl.

"Your dog's name is...?"

"Rascal," she said. "He hates the outdoors."

"Oh really?"

"He's afraid of everything," she said. "He can't stand loud noises. The squeal of the trolley car drives him flat-out crazy. I time his walks by the streetcar schedule."

"Ah."

She fixed me with a stare. "I believe you're a gentleman, Mr. Powell."

"Oh really?"

"I have a feeling for things. In the hills where I come from, I'm known as a seer. I have a sixth sense. People come to me for life readings."

"Wow," I said.

"I surely can read cards and tell fortunes. The cards speak to me, Mister Powell."

"Perhaps you should set up a little business. People would pay a quarter to hear their fortunes."

Mrs. Anderson, in a blush of modesty, waved that off.

She glanced over her shoulder. I followed that look to see a scowling face in the tiny front door window. The face was mostly white hair, beard and mustache.

"Rascal needs to go in," Mrs. Anderson said. "I hope to see you around, Mr. Powell."

She walked up the stairs. I allowed Hula Girl to tug me down Robert Street.

We circled the block. The houses were fancier one street back. It was renters who lived on noisy Robert and the steadier folks back here. I put Hula Girl in the Plymouth, and sat behind the wheel, rescued my pipe from the glove compartment, lit up with Sadie's lighter, and sat for a contemplative smoke.

What had I learned? In this house lived a mother, father, two thieving sons and a cowardly bulldog. They had police connections, but hadn't lived in Saint Paul for long, so they were in on The Deal. One son had stolen the Buick during a raid on Hudson. The other, Gold Teeth aka Little Shorty, kept a golfing girlfriend in high style on Crocus Hill. He drove a DeSoto acquired through Tommy Filben. Certainly these Anderson people had their roots far south of here, to judge by their accent. They had money enough, when so many people were broke, to summer at a lake cabin. And the boys loved to fish.

Whatever they were in the Ozarks, up here they were land pirates, raiding small towns and retreating to Saint Paul, where they enjoyed police protection. Maybe they were involved in the Kraft State Bank robbery, maybe not. They didn't seem to be kidnappers, so I really hadn't any earthshaking news for Papa Alt. But I needed to tell him something.

I blew up clouds of tobacco smoke. I drove around the neighborhood. Hula Girl panted, happy for any adventure, an enthusiasm that puts our species to shame. She didn't care where we went, as long as she could put her little black face out the window and sniff the breeze.

I spied from a block away. I glimpsed Ma Anderson in their yard with a gentleman of 60-some years. They were walking toward the rusty Essex. I hung the Plymouth back as "Pa Anderson" drove downtown, five minutes tops. Pa parked that Essex in a garage. I parked illegal at a fire hydrant. Out of the garage walked Ma and Pa. They entered the Paramount to see "Murders in the Rue Morgue" starring Bella Lugosi.

Pa Anderson was tall, very well dressed in a three-piece brown striped suit, a watch chain stretched across his skinny belly. Hmm. Movies in the afternoon. They certainly didn't have jobs, either one of them. I berated myself. I should have pushed Mother Anderson to reveal her exact hometown. Then I would have something to take to the beer baron. If I found their exact town of origin, Papa Alt could hire a local detective and take it from there.

A gold ring tapped on the Plymouth door. That ring belonged to Pat Reilly, owner of the worst set of teeth in town.

"Patrick!

I let him into the Plymouth. "You know Hula Girl," I said.

Without being asked, the socially skilled Hula Girl leaped into the back seat.

"They're laying off," said Pat, and lit a Lucky. He rolled down the window and blew smoke at the traffic.

"Who?"

"The Royal."

"How come?"

"Not enough players," he said. "Where you been?"

"Busy."

"See? What? The economy's picking up. So they say on the radio, but you can't see it from my cage."

"What do we have, five weeks to the Derby?"

"Yeah, but nobody's playing now," Pat said. "Hell, it's all tips, that's my whole income. You win, you tip a dime, you cash the double it's a quarter. That used to be the law, right, unwritten? No more. People…"

"Go back to the Saints," I said.

"Jeesh," he said. "Best job I ever had."

He blew smoke. "Brutal bus rides, though."

He looked at me, sorrow in his face. "Should have been a ballplayer. Just for the babes alone. You can't imagine how easy those guys get laid. I can't hit the fastball, though. All field, no hit, that's me."

No field, no hit, more like it. But a man must claim to be better than he is. That's just how we are.

"So you're free daytimes now?" I asked.

"Starting today," Pat said. "They might call me back on Derby Week. Harry's good to me, though. Harry won't let me down."

"Yeah."

"So what are you doing downtown?" Pat asked.

"Out for a drive."

"Bullshit. You know it's funny I seen you. Harry wants you."

"Harry?"

"Yeah. He said I see you around, I should tell you."

"He can't pick up the phone?"

"Harry don't talk on the phone. He sees little G-men hiding in every telephone. You know they can wiretap nowadays."

"He should pay his taxes," I said, "so he don't end up like Capone. Taxes is all the G-men care about."

"Still, Harry wants to see you."

"You know what it's about?"

"He's got something for you."

"I'll bet."

"No really, Mick, he's got work."

"I know I'm a couple of days late with his money. I've got to get paid myself."

"Go see the man," Pat said, and threw the burning Lucky out the window.

So I dropped Hula Girl at home, fed her and Snowflake, walked them on the Governor's lawn, and headed for the Green Lantern.

It was a dead afternoon. Bess said she hadn't seen Harry all day. "Try his house," she said.

I drove to Mac Groveland. Here in modest but substantial houses, lived Saint Paul's professional class. In the middle of the neighborhood is Macalester College, a school for rich Protestant kids. Mac Groveland is home to managers, brokers, merchants, doctors and lawyers, and one criminal mastermind.

The three-car garage was the tipoff to his occupation, although one of his neighbors didn't seem to get it. Across the alley from Harry lived Tom Dahill, captain of detectives. Dahill, who looked more like a bank clerk than a detective, was chatting with Harry at the fence when I drove up. Dahill wore his full dress brass-button uniform, maybe on his way to some police ceremony. He saw me approach, waved at Harry, and walked off.

Harry wore a white shirt, cuffs rolled up, and a leather vest. He grasped in one hand a glass of beer, probably a boiler maker.

"You wanted to see me?" I asked.

"Gladys," Harry barked over his shoulder. "Bring Mick out a ginger ale." He set a bloated hand on my shoulder. "I like a man that don't drink. Reliable."

"Sorry I'm a little late on that thing," I said.

Harry waved that off.

"No, Harry, I need an Uncle. I've got that Swede on my bad side. Don't back off on me."

"Ah," said Harry. "You'll be all right."

"Why? What's changed?"

Gladys wore a beautiful black crinkled dress with a diamond pin at the neckline. She was a stout woman with frizzy hair and deep soulful brown eyes. She handed me a bottle of Hamm's ginger ale and retreated.

"Guys can be mad at you one day and forgive the next," Harry said, "because nobody wants to hurt a friend."

"I still don't know what I did wrong."

Harry drank beer. "They're mad but they forgive," he said. "On account of they would like a favor."

"Shoot."

"Week after Easter, stay loose," he said.

"Okay."

"It's like a ten-minute job, and you're off the fucking hook. All square. Forgive and forget."

"No more payments?"

Harry shrugged. "A favor now and then. Nothing strenuous, you know. Guy is with us dependable, what the fuck."

"Okay, so week after Easter."

"Keep your calendar open, and your mouth shut."

"Harry, when the mugs tossed my place, they nabbed my .45."

"You won't need no cannons for this job. You got a jalopy, right?"

CHAPTER FIFTEEN

Myrtle rented a swell place on Crocus Hill. She owned a lamp made of gold once, but that was in better times, when she was married to Professor Banks. Before he'd been slammed into Waupun, Professor Banks was the greatest jug marker in the Midwest. When The Professor marked the hometown First National, the robbers got a flawless floor plan, an estimate of the take, an impeccable time schedule, a couple of paid-off cops, and a getaway map complete with mileage markers and alternate routes.

Professor Banks' pencil was as mighty as any tommygun. But when the state of Wisconsin locked up the Professor, Myrtle began selling her fancy stuff. Her last good mink coat had been stolen by the thugs who tossed my apartment. I wasn't eager to inform her of the loss.

I lay in her bed, which was deep with feathers, so much that you could get lost in it. I reached for her. In the mornings, she felt warm, pleasantly chubby. I drew her to me underneath a corn-yellow blanket that had been quilted by her Iowa grandmother.

"Let me sleep, will ya?" said Myrtle.

I was in the mood for lovemaking and teased her breast.

"Not before coffee," she said. "I have bad breath."

"So do I. We'll cancel each other out."

She had her back to me, her curls in my face. Her hair smelled of chemicals, her body of woman divine.

"I'm hungry for toast," she said.

I groaned. Myrtle never cooked. The closest thing to food in her apartment was a bowl full of teabags. Toast meant rising, getting dressed, walking to the drugstore.

"Fifteen more minutes in bed," I said.

"You like to cuddle more than any man I ever met. Your mother must have whelped you too soon."

I rolled over to look out the window, but the shades were drawn. The guy across the alley was a peeper. There were hints of sunlight at the margins of the shade.

I clamped Myrtle to me. "Spring baby, spring."

"Yeah," she said, gloomy. "End of fur season. I've gotta look for cold storage."

"You could find something to do besides lift furs."

"Nah," she said.

"With all the people you know?"

"Furs is more dependable than people."

"You'd make a swell hostess."

"And be on my feet all night? I used to dance, you know, and now I have bum ankles. Dancing's for the birds."

She rolled away from me.

"Speaking of birds," she said. "Flyboy's peeping for breakfast."

She arose naked, and I admired her, from dark curly hair down to blaze-red toenails. She was not one of these slender reedy models, but had a compact body and a gorgeous, almost Italian, complexion. She was the most enthusiastic sex partner I'd ever known, but when she wasn't in the mood, forget it.

She worked into a fluffy white bathrobe that had gone missing from The Emporium. She loved to loot that department store, especially after they'd turned her down for a job at the jewelry counter.

Flyboy was a blue-green parakeet in a dull rusty cage. It was equipped for bird amusement, with cuttlebone, tiny mirrors and bells. Myrtle slipped a dollhouse teacup filled with seeds into his cage.

"He eats like a pig if I leave seed in there," Myrtle said over her shoulder. "You've heard the expression when pigs fly? That's my bird. That's Flyboy the flying pig."

Flyboy chirped.

"Wish I had wings," she said. "I wouldn't be afraid to come out of my cage. Come on, Flyboy, spread 'em."

Flyboy furiously scattered seed.

"I'll leave it open for you," Myrtle said, then turned to me. "He's like some men I know. Happier in jail. Say, you gotta go let your dogs out?"

"Nice try at getting rid of me," I said. "Little Elmer."

"How is that kid? He still walking funny?"

"Myrtle," I said, "it's polio. Usually they don't get better."

"There's a miracle cure coming," she said. "I read it in the Daily News."

With that, she bumbled into the bathroom.

I sat up on the edge of the bed. I was staring at a blank, cream-colored shade, set off by sheer white curtains. It was like staring at a movie screen, waiting for the pictures to start. I was convinced it would be a gangster film with a bloody end.

I had felt good under the quilt next to Myrtle's warm body but now I began to go sick with worry. I couldn't get out of my mind the hate-filled faces of the thugs who had jumped out of my apartment lobby gunning for me. I was overcome by the skin-crawling memory of finding that goons had invaded my home and wrecked it.

"Myrtle, I need advice."

Myrtle held a mannish outfit in front of her for my inspection.

"What do you think?" she said.

"Kind of dark for spring," I said.

"It's Good Friday."

"Oh, right."

"I'm saving the flowery stuff for Easter." She turned her back on me, showing her naked side. "The Professor always hated it when I dressed like a man."

"Oh, the Professor again."

"Do you mind a woman in trousers?"

"Depends."

"Depends on what?"

"I guess I do prefer a skirt."

"Yeah, me too," Myrtle said. "I hate to admit it."

She dropped the pants-suit on the bed and looked at herself, naked in the big round, cracked mirror. She cupped her breasts before fitting a bra.

"Help me, will ya?"

I hooked up the back strap of her bra.

"You know all these guys," I said.

"All what guys?" she said, looking at me through the mirror.

"Harry's guys," I said.

"I know some. Nobody knows them all. Some of the guys in Harry's gang never met Harry."

She chose a yellow blouse.

"That's kind of loud for Good Friday," I said.

"So? We ain't going to church, are we?"

She reached into her dresser drawer for underpants and a corset. She slipped on the pants and wriggled into the rubber torture device.

"I could lose five pounds, I'd be delirious," she said.

"The two guys who came after me, they're still hunting me in my dreams," I said.

"Well you're paying Harry, ain't you? That beats any life

insurance policy ever written."

"I was paying Harry. Now he's got a job for me."

"Better yet," said Myrtle. She grunted as her corset crushed her abdomen. "Now you're one of his boys, untouchable."

"Well, I don't know what the job is."

"So?"

"I wake up in the middle of the night, worrying. I'm supposed to drive. But what? Is this a getaway car? Am I taking somebody for a ride? I don't know and Harry won't say."

She looked at me direct, not through the mirror.

"You used to be a tough guy," she said.

"Yeah, well, when you're twenty years old, you're too dumb to know what can happen to you. But I'm twice twenty now. I can't shake this feeling. There's a double-cross coming. See, I go out on this job for Harry, and then they bump me off. That's how I figure. They got an extra reason now. I'm a witness to whatever job they're going to pull, and they love to get rid of a witness."

Myrtle sat on the bed to slip her feet into stockings, then stood to roll them up her legs.

"Look, Mick," she said, "I don't know what to tell you, honey, you gotta show up at the job."

She stared at me. "You're not thinking of lamming it, are you? No, not you Mick. You ain't a coward. Harry needs reliable men. You know how many sour grapes he's got in his vine?"

"You gals talk," I said.

"Oh do we?"

"I was hoping maybe, you know, maybe you could have lunch with Gladys."

"You wouldn't wish that on me, would you?"

"Do some spying, that's all. She might let something slip. Then at least I'll know what I'm into."

Myrtle selected a dark wool skirt and stepped into it, then

buttoned up that yellow blouse. She stood with gleaming patent-leather pumps in hand.

"Remember Rutman?" I said. "They set him on fire."

"That wasn't Harry, that was a Minneapolis gang."

"Remember Le Pre? Shot like a dog and kicked to the side of the road."

"That wasn't Harry either. That was the cops done that. Cheer up, will ya? This is your chance with Harry. Things could be good from here on. He sees something he likes, or he wouldn't use you at all. Guys are begging to be in Harry's gang."

She was right. I was becoming a wreck, like my car and my apartment.

"Trouble comes with the territory," Myrtle said. "Last winter, you remember, Crumley arrests me, and the Bulldog cleans out my fur closet. Nice cops, eh? The Professor, he was double-crossed by his number one guy, and for nothing, like Judas, thirty lousy pieces of silver."

She sighed.

"He's dead, Judas the traitor. Or I'd kill him myself. Look, I like you, slugger. I'd like to keep you around as a plaything. You're not half bad. Play for Harry's team. You're a gambler, right? Well, Harry's your best bet."

CHAPTER SIXTEEN

On Saturday, I put Hula Girl in the Plymouth and took her for a ride to the Anderson's neighborhood. The day was cheerful and I had recovered some of my courage. Acceptance. That's what had calmed me down. It seemed I had two choices: go guns blazing after Swede and Rico, or take up with Harry. The shootout option was by far the worst. The risk was death if I lost and prison if I won. There was the further danger of antagonizing whatever underworld power had hired Swede and Rico in the first place. So really, there was no choice. With Harry's job on schedule for next week, I was safe until then, or so I tried to convince myself.

In the meantime I had to do something to keep Papa Alt's $50 a week coming in. But I had another, stranger reason to keep tabs on the Gold Teeth gang. I had dreamed of Sadie. She was walking like a Pilgrim, a fat candle in hand, with a flickering flame. She was dressed in a gown, off-white, dingy. Her skin, rough and porous in life, had gone smooth in the afterlife. Her eyes were closed. Her dark hair had grown well past her shoulders, and was streaked with gray. She didn't have a thing to say, but her lips trembled. And then her face dissolved to bone.

I awoke from that dream with a scream that sent both dogs scrambling out of bed. Hula Girl low-crawled under the bed and whined. Snowflake scampered into the closet, his neon eyes glowing in the dark.

The bedroom had smelled vile, of burning rubber. I was awake two, maybe three minutes before I realized that stench was only part of the dream.

That dream came to me on Good Friday night. Now, on this sunny Easter Saturday, I walked Hula Girl on a chain leash along Robert Street.

What is it about dogs? How do they know what a doorway is? Hula Girl tries to enter every door she passes. The butcher I could understand. But the hardware store? The dry cleaners? When she sniffed the barber shop entrance, I saw, among the waiting customers, Pop Anderson. He was slumped in a chair, reading the Sporting News.

I walked on, but once out of sight, hustled Hula Girl to the Plymouth. I bribed her with a peanut, and trooped back to the barber shop.

There were two barbers, father and son. Father was occupied with a portly near-bald gentleman, the son with a squirming youngster. Most of the waiting chairs were filled, shaggy men and boys wanting to look sharp at Easter services. I stood next to a coatrack that was draped in hats and jackets, nodded to Father Barber, and took a seat amid scattered magazines in the window box.

I set my hat back, picked up a True Detective Mysteries and paged through. Pop Anderson dozed in the chair next to me. He had dropped the Sporting News into his lap. I heard the hint of a snore, sniffed a whiff of gin.

I accidentally on purpose nudged him shoe to shoe.

"Oh, sorry," I said.

His eyes flew open. "What?"

He was a distinguished-looking man in his sixties, wearing an expensive dark three-piece suit. His shoes were polished oxfords. He had a full head of white hair. If he'd claimed to be a retired small-town banker, I'd have believed him.

"Sorry, my man, if I woke you up," I said.

"Well, who are you?"

"Me? I guess I'm in line after you," I said.

His jaws chomped as if he were swallowing something bitter.

"You a Cardinal fan, by chance?" I asked.

"Yes I am."

I pointed to the Sporting News in his lap. "There's no time as exciting as spring training. What do you think about this Dean kid. You think he'll make the club?"

"Who?"

"Dizzy they call him."

"Who's he?"

"A hurler. Big prospect."

"I don't know nothing about him."

"I see you read the Sporting News."

"What about it?"

"Best baseball paper in the country."

"You're damn right it is," he said, as if he'd prevailed in an argument.

He sat back. "You want to read it?"

"Sure."

He handed me the paper. I paged through it while the clippers buzzed and the odor of witch hazel filled the air.

"Going to be a while, I guess," I said to Pop Anderson.

"You're damn right," he said.

"Well, what can you expect the day before Easter?"

"Nothing," he said.

"Long lines everywhere," I said. "I see you've got a handsome suit all ready for church."

"Me?" he said. "I don't attend nobody's church. I don't believe in God or the Devil."

"Well," I said. "You don't need to wait on a haircut today then."

"Oh, I ain't waiting on a haircut," he said. "Shave," he said. "I don't shave myself no more. Look."

He held out a trembling hand.

"Got the shakes," he said. "Don't know why. Started up over the winter and I thought it was just the cold."

"What's the doctor say?"

"Doctor? I don't believe in the doctor, son. The Doctor, the Devil and God, you can put 'em all on a slow boat to China."

"Yeah," I said. "You're damn right. Still, it's going to be all morning until you get your shave."

"That's all right with me. I'm retired."

"Ah. Lucky you. Say, why don't we go around the corner and have us a drink while we wait. The barber will keep our places."

"I don't give a damn if he does or not. I got all day."

We walked around the corner to a shabby, window-deprived speakeasy called The Last Roundup. Pop Anderson rapped the secret knock. We were admitted to a dark room, where I stumbled toward a bar lit by a single bulb. A cigarette-smoking bleach-blond girl of about seventeen demanded our drink orders in a tough, cynical voice. Pop Anderson ordered that special gin she kept under the bar. I put out two dimes for real Canadian whiskey.

"Here's to Canada," I said when we got our drinks.

Pop Anderson toasted me.

"A sensible nation," I said.

"Damn right," said Pop Anderson. "I've never been there."

"It's not far away."

"You've been there I suppose."

"Once or twice. Say, you don't sound like you're from this part of the country."

"Oh no." He shuddered as if wrestling a horrible thought. He raised the gin glass to his lips in two shaky hands.

"Tulsa, Oklahoma," he said. "God's country."

"Never had the pleasure," I said.

"Oil rich now," he said. "Dirt poor in the old days. Farmer was lucky to feed cornstalks to a mule. Now? They're all driving cars and the women are wearing furs."

"That's oil money for you," I said.

"Damn right. So what's your business, Mister?"

"Mine? Well, I supply people what they want."

That seemed to set the old fellow thinking. I looked down the bar. Two guys in grimy overalls shot pool in the corner. One thick-built man slumped alone against the bar, in a bloody butcher's apron, drinking a schooner of Hamm's. I couldn't figure whether he was a Robert Street butcher, or had sneaked out of the slaughter houses for a beer break.

"Is that so?" said Pop Anderson. "I thought about getting into that business myself, at one time. No need now. I'm sitting pretty. Retired a year now."

"Retired from what, pops?"

"Speculation," he said.

"Wheat?"

"Oil, son."

"So you hit it big in oil."

"Damn right. Oil's practically flowing down the streets of Tulsa now."

"Well good for you. You can retire on it? You hit it that big?"

He drank off the gin, slammed his glass on the bar to demand another and said: "Big enough."

Was this shaky old man the gang's planning genius? I doubted it. But I didn't believe he'd made a dime in oil. I figured he owed his prosperity to whole-town robberies. Over the last week, two Minnesota towns, Cambridge and Pine City, had been looted. Since those towns were miles away, the robberies barely made the Saint Paul papers. But the pattern of those raids was identical to the January heist in Hudson. Whether Pop had any hand in the planning or not, his boys led the raids, I was pretty sure.

"So what brought you all the way up here?"

He sighed. "The woman. And the boys. They got wandering feet. The boys play in the nightclubs. They wore out their audience down in Oklahoma."

"Musicians, the boys?"

"I got no use for 'em."

"They're not your sons, then?"

"Those two? Not by a longshot."

"Ready made family," I said.

I began to worry about Hula Girl, but remembered that I'd cracked the windows. She was a confident dog who would calmly wait hours for your return. Snowflake, he would stand paws at the windows scanning anxious for you, while she curled up in a black circle, quietly dreaming.

"Let me buy you that drink, sir. What is your name? Mine is Patrick."

"Arthur," he said.

I shook his trembling hand.

"I'm thinking of moving to this neighborhood," I said. "Fresh air. And now that they've put the streetcar out here, why, there's no need to live in the city. You can be in the Loop in ten minutes."

Arthur Anderson swirled gin in his fat glass.

"Plus," I said, "I heard the cops in this town are all right. So I'm thinking of moving out, I really am."

"We're not far from the countryside either," Anderson noted. "Nice drive, now that the weather's fine."

"See, I'm in the game, and well, I don't tell just anybody this, but I've got a little something coming in from our friends to the

North."

Anderson looked at me, hard.

"A few cases, that's all, but first rate. Very, very good stuff from the real Canadians. No adulteration. Nothing fake about it. Sealed, bonded bottles. The thing is, the goods are in hock right now. If I had a partner with a little cash, we could spring it loose."

He only stared into his glass.

"Two hundred fifty bucks, we need," I said.

He whistled.

"Well, if that's too much," I said. "A case at a time. Twenty five the case, we sell it for fifty. I'll do the driving. I'll take the risk. The thing is, I need the cash, an investment, like speculation, is what it is."

Anderson reached into an inner pocket for a packet of Gauloises cigarettes.

"Ah, you smoke the expensive stuff from France," I noted.

He offered me a cigarette, and I declined. I was going easy on the whiskey too, and hoped he wouldn't notice.

"Double our money," I said.

"Oh, I can do my sums. Young man, you don't look like you need a haircut."

I ran a hand over my crew-cut.

"Well, Easter," I said.

"You wouldn't be trying to trick an old man out of his money would you?"

I put my hand up like a boy scout. "I'm looking for a partner."

"You grew up around here?"

"Well, since high school."

"And you ain't got any friends to finance you?"

"My friends are either broke or scared," I said. "The federals have gotten nasty lately. And the Minneapolis cops, they just shot a bootlegger. You can read it in the papers."

I wanted to tease out of Pop Anderson some revelation about "his boys." I figured with enough drink in him, he might boast of his gang connections.

"Well, I'll tell you what," Pop said, "you come for dinner tonight. Let the old woman take a gander at you. She's got special powers, this woman. She's Bible-believing, with the gift of second sight. I call it Ozarks voodoo. If she believes you're okay, you're okay by me. And she's famous for her cooking. She makes chicken and biscuits like you Yankees never did taste."

"Will I get to meet the boys?"

"Saturday dinner? You never know. They barely live here anymore. All those boys do is run around at night."

I was on edge when I arrived for dinner at the Andersons. But Ma, swathed in a greasy apron, hugged me when I crossed the threshold. "Welcome to our humble home, Mister Powell," she said. "Oh, you should have brought that cute black dog of yours. You know, it's a shame, all winter we don't see hide nor hair of our neighbors."

She herded me into the kitchen where Pop sat, alone and useless, before a half-empty bottle of no-name bourbon. He looked at me and grunted, as if he barely remembered inviting me, and now was sorry. He muttered and I asked him to please speak up.

"Kate does all the preaching in this house," he said and cleared his throat. "But she don't go to church no more."

Kate glared at him. "Now don't you go telling tales."

She said this over her shoulder. She was frying chicken in a huge cast iron skillet. So Kate! The bulldog-walking grandma. She had been introduced to me only as Mrs. Anderson.

Pop Anderson, slobbering drunk, stumbled into the living room and returned with a Bible. As Ma poked at the frying chicken, Pop read passages, sometimes just his lips moving in silence, sometimes muttering stray words. Drink had calmed his hand tremors. He paged through, paged through, stopped to quote a passage, then gulped raw whiskey.

We were at the kitchen table for dinner because the dining room table was occupied by a gigantic jigsaw puzzle. It would, assembled, show the swallows returning to San Juan Capistrano. The dining room had been turned into sort of a hillbilly concert hall, with The Carter Family blaring buzzy from a radio.

Pop fumbled in his vest pocket for a crumpled blue pack of Gauloises. He pinched out a cigarette, twirled it in his fingers as he read the Bible.

"Now keep yourself upright, Arthur," said Ma. "My boys might come home for dinner." She shook steel tongs at Pop.

"Bah," he said.

"They don't like to see you in your cups."

"I ain't in my cups," grumbled Pop. He jammed the cigarette into his lips and lit it. "I'm reading on Jesus."

I decided not to remind him that he'd declared himself an atheist just an hour ago.

"Don't you go blast-feemin on Jesus," warned Kate.

"Ah," he waved her off with a smoking cigarette.

"Where'd your boys go off to, Mrs. Anderson?" I asked.

"Oh, they's got an engagement," she said. "Those boys are never home on Saturday night no more."

As Kate turned back to her frying chicken, I felt a surge of relief, although I half-hoped to meet her gangster sons. If her son Little Shorty Gold Teeth came home alone, that would be one thing. But if he brought home Smash-Face Paula, I would have a lot of explaining to do. I was hiding behind my alias, Patrick Powell, and had told the elder Andersons that I had fallen on hard luck. I'd told them I'd tried to make a living as a magazine salesman. That story might buy me enough to time to exit gracefully if Paula walked in the door. But it wouldn't be long before the Andersons figured out I was spying on them.

"Jesus was a bootlegger," declared Pop Anderson.

Kate threw her tongs. They landed on a trestle table that had been covered with cut-flat grocery bags.

"I've had enough blast-feemin," Kate shouted.

"Turned water into wine, didn't he?" Pop asked. "He didn't have no license, did he? Did he have a license from the state?"

"There wasn't no state back then," Kate said. "Was there a state back then, Mister Powell?"

I shrugged.

Kate's tone softened. "Are you a high school graduate, Mister Powell?"

"Yes I am."

"And you don't know if Jesus lived in a state? Like Oklahoma, that kind of state."

"I believe it was Rome," I said. "I believe Pontius Pilate was a Roman governor."

"Hell no, Jesus lived in Jer-ooze-za-lam," Pop said.

"You ignorant goat," Kate argued, "our guest is right, it was Rome. Was wine against the law in Rome?"

"I surely don't think so," I said.

She removed her greasy apron and threw it on the radiator.

"I've had enough of this man," she said. "I don't court bad luck by darkening the name of Jesus."

With that she stomped out of the kitchen, leaving the chicken frying.

Pop closed the Bible. "This is the most trouble making book ever written," he declared.

Kate turned up the hillbilly music to a dish-rattling level. In a moment, a door closed. Embarrassing body noises sounded through thin walls as she used the bathroom.

Pop held the bourbon bottle up to the weak light filtering in from the kitchen windows. The whiskey shone like gold.

"Your average bootlegger," he said, "never made nothing like this."

It was a round, unlabeled bottle. He jiggled it.

"Drink, Powell, drink."

"I have to go easy, Arthur. With the gout."

"Gout you say?"

"Yes sir. Very painful."

"Bah," he waved that off. "Whiskey's good for the gout. You say your whiskey is better than this?"

"It's Canadian."

He slurred: "Now don't you go telling the old woman nothing. She don't use liquor and don't approve of it. She was raised up to think it was evil."

The toilet flushed, making a titanic whoosh. Airplanes have lifted off runways with less racket.

"I'll get the money from her boy," Pop said and winked at me. "He's got a pile, that kid. And he ain't afraid to spend it neither."

"Which one is that?"

"Her real son. Freddy."

"Is he the younger or older?"

"He's the baby. He's the mama's boy. He's a young man who knows the value of a dollar, I'll tell you that."

He put a finger to his chapped lips. "Shh, don't say nothing to the old lady."

Kate bustled into the kitchen, washed her hands at the big porcelain sink and re-tied her apron. Using tongs, she picked crispy chicken pieces out of the hot fat. I began to salivate with the aroma of it. She laid the chicken out greasy on the paper bags. She opened the oven and, using heart-shaped hot mitts, removed a muffin pan that held high-top biscuits.

"Careful, now," said Pop, without moving to help.

When she set down the biscuits she returned to the oven for a covered steel pot that held boiled potatoes.

"I can mash those," I volunteered.

Kate looked at me as if I were mad.

"I'm a single man. I cook for myself."

She set the pot on the trestle table.

"I like a man who ain't ashamed of cooking," Kate said. "I'll get the milk from the icebox. Arthur, would you fetch this gentleman the milk and butter, please."

Pop sat back, stupefied, his eyes swimming in alcohol.

I fetched the milk, butter, salt and pepper and began crushing the potatoes with a steel masher.

"We like the skins on," Kate advised me. "That's the Ozarks way."

From the oven she drew a bread pan loaded with green-beans and pork fat. She grabbed the milk bottle and a flour bag and stood in front of the cast iron pan stirring gravy. All the while she hummed along with the fiddlers on the radio. Pop was tilted back dangerously in his chair, eyes closed, lips twitching.

"No man in my family can even fry an egg," Ma said. "So I admire you, Mister Powell."

"Oh, mashed potatoes is nothing," I said. "All the flavor's in that gravy you're making."

Kate's feet tapped in time to the music. She stirred gravy. I cut more butter into the mashed potatoes. Kate hummed.

"What kind of scheme does he got up?" she asked me.

"Pardon?"

"Arthur. Is he trying to drag you into one of his drunk ideas?"

"Me? Uh…" I looked at Pop, who rocked forward and rested his head in his arms on the table.

"He wants to buy a speakeasy so he can drink all day," Kate

said. "Is that right, Arthur? Are you trying to lure our neighbor into your speakeasy scheme?"

She stirred.

"I reckon he is. It just ain't come out yet. You're a grown man, Mister Powell and you seem right sensible to me. Arthur has got his virtues I guess, but common sense ain't one of 'em."

She poured the gravy into a huge bowl that was painted with tiny roses.

"He'll drink all the profits," she warned me. "Ain't that right? You'll drink all the profits, Arthur, you old goat you."

She set the gravy bowl on the counter and kicked his chair.

"Wake up and eat. Wake up and eat now. Soak that liquor up, you mist-cree-ant."

Arthur looked up, rose unsteady, and stumbled toward the bathroom.

"It's my boys keeping him in liquor," Kate said, and set bowls of green beans and mashed potatoes beside the gravy. "I have half a mind to cut this old man loose."

"Oh," I said. "I thought he had sold some oil land."

"Oil land?" She laughed. "Arthur? Why he was a billboard painter before his hands got the whiskey shakes."

In a basket lined with napkins, Kate lovingly, piece by piece, set an entire golden-fried chicken. That aroma made me want to eat hearty, curl up with the funny pages, light up the fireplace and watch out the window satisfied as the evening drifted by.

A platter of beautiful puffy biscuits were set beside the gravy and Kate whipped off her apron. She hung it on the hot water boiler and said, "Now that is country cooking."

"Looks good enough to eat," I said.

"Yeah," she sighed. "My boys. They're never home no more."

A sad look replaced the cook's joy on her face. "My one boy's in his grave. Herman."

A single tear appeared at the corner of one eye, and she wiped it. "He is in Heaven, I know for sure. I dream of him, up there with Our Lord. Do you reckon they have biscuits and gravy in Heaven, Mister Powell?"

"I'm sure they do, Missus Anderson."

The music abruptly stopped.

Pop appeared in the doorway, buttoning his belt buckle.

"Don't you come to the table undressed," Kate warned him.

He retreated into the dining room for his jacket.

"And don't you go dragging our neighbors into your schemes," Kate scolded when he reappeared.

She turned to me. "Are you married, Mister Powell?"

"Recently divorced," I said.

"Have you children to support?"

"No ma'am," I said.

"Whereabouts do you live? I don't recall."

"Oh, aways down the road. I like to walk my dog up here on Robert Street, where it's lively."

This seemed to satisfy her. Pop sat, buttoning his jacket.

"Lord," said Kate and we all held hands across the table, "please look over our friends and family. We thank you Jesus for your providin' nature, and your sweet forgiveness of all our sins, and your promise of life everlasting, and…"

Pop harrumphed.

"… most of all grant your tender mercies to my boys, wherever they may be tonight. Keep them safe from evil and harm. Amen."

" 'Bout time," grumbled Pop. "She cooks it hot and prays it cold."

He grabbed a drumstick. "A man gets hungry," Pop explained.

"How you were brought up!" said Kate.

"What?"

"Company first!" said Kate. "Use a fork. Are you a cannibal sir, or a gentleman?"

Rascal the bulldog, who had been keeping to himself in the living room, went into a frenzy of barking. Kate practically flew to the back windows, grabbing the sink ledge for balance. Down the gritty, darkening alley drove a big black car.

"My Freddy," she cried. "He's come home."

I stifled the impulse to run for the front door. I could only imagine Fred was bringing Paula home for dinner.

The bulldog yapped, but the car kept rolling, past the garage, and down the sloping alley. Kate's hand went over her heart. She turned around ashen.

"She's having one of her fits," Pop declared, and bit into a chicken leg. "It's her heart. Don't pay her no mind," he told me, chewing.

Kate staggered toward the table.

"Old woman damn you," said Pop, "you're not having one of your heart attacks, are you?" He looked at me. "She's got a bad ticker."

I helped Kate into a chair, and she sat, breathing heavy. She slumped. She shuddered. I fetched her a glass of water from the sink. She drank with a sputtering gulp.

"My boys," she said, "they'll be the death of me."

CHAPTER SEVENTEEN

The noon Mass on Easter Sunday was a combination fashion show and Lapsed Catholic reunion. Inspector Crumley was in attendance, in seersucker suit, along with his fur-bearing wife and daughter. Pat Reilly entered just after the Introit, in the company of his bleach blonde wife and her dark-Irish sisters. In the second pew sat Jack Peifer and Violet, whose wide white hat was wild with flowers. In the first pew sat the Alts: Papa in the aisle seat, then Richard, the only son, his wife and toddler. Emily, the younger daughter, accompanied her sporty boyfriend, who was dressed for a golf match. Belinda, the older daughter, prayed head down, ignoring husband and three squirming children. It was the Alt pew bought and paid for, marked by a brass plaque inscribed with their name.

Harry Sawyer was Jewish, so I wasn't surprised that his wife Gladys left him at home. Dressed in purple like it was still Lent, Gladys excused her way into a pew of parents and schoolchildren.

I lacked female company, since my substitute wife Myrtle had gone atheist, and my substitute daughter Janie was back in Wisconsin. I stood in the vestibule with Sam Tanaka, waiting out the Mass, shifting from foot to foot on the stone floor.

When I'd first met Sam, he was head waiter at the Hollyhocks. We became friends one night at closing time when I saw him making notes in the Racing Form. I was surprised by his dead-on

American accent, then learned that he'd been raised in Seattle since kindergarten. I didn't expect he'd be Catholic, but his parents were from Nagasaki, a city influenced by Portuguese traders.

After Mass, as the crowd pushed out into the spring sunshine, I saw Papa Alt talking with Father Mack at the chancery gate. I was almost certain that it was Father Mack who, knowing I was hard up for rent, had recommended me to Papa Alt in the first place. The way this town works, it's not just good to have friends, it's essential.

Myrtle did not believe in God, but she hadn't lost faith in dinner. We celebrated with a ham-and-gravy feast at the Lowry Hotel. After dinner we took a drive in the country, Snowflake and Hula Girl jostling for position at the back windows. The ride was complicated by a dog walk, a punctured tire and a stop at a roadhouse along the Minnesota River. Myrtle, even though lit up by roadhouse booze, was in no mood for romance. As darkness approached she got gloomier and finally clammed up altogether. I figured she was mooning over The Professor, locked up in Wisconsin for a crime he certainly did commit.

After dark, we dropped the dogs off at my place, then sat in the car in Myrtle's alley and argued. We were disappointed in each other. I was not The Professor and she was nothing like my Peggy.

"If you didn't want to go out," I said, "you should have just said so, instead of ruining the whole afternoon."

"Oh, you would have had a swell time, you and the dogs."

I shut the Plymouth down.

"I'm not going to invite you up," she said.

I said: "Okay. I just thought we could sit here and be unpleasant without wasting gas."

She settled into the corner of door and seat. "You can't expect nothing soft-hearted from me. Love don't count no more. It's too demanding on a girl."

"What am I demanding?"

"Well, right now you're demanding that I be in a good mood and I want to be in a rotten mood. Okay? I hate these holidays. They're miserable."

"Okay, be in a bad mood."

"I am, and I don't need your permission."

I sighed.

She muttered: "Give, handsome."

"How could two people who are so locked-in as lovers be so locked-out as friends?"

Myrtle opened the window to a chill breeze. She stuck a cigarette in her lips. She lit it with a match and tossed its tiny flame into the dark.

"Aw," she said, "you're soft hearted. You're still busted up, I can tell. You can't make up for it, Mickey. It's a dead chance. There's only one person for each of us in this world. One person that was meant to be. If you miss your chance it's gone forever. My soul mate is locked up in Waupun. Yours ran off to Honolulu."

"Pearl City," I said.

"What's that?"

"A Navy town."

"What was he, some kind of admiral?"

"Not so high up."

She blew a stream of smoke through bitter lips.

"Face it," she said. "We're a couple of losers."

"Could you blow the smoke the other way?"

"What's with you and this hatred of cigarettes? You're a smoker." She flicked ashes into the dashboard ashtray. "Old Myrtle's just waiting around," she said. "And for what? The fun's over. What's an old girl got?"

"A nice apartment, good clothes, lots of friends."

"I don't want friends."

"You want The Professor."

"That's right." She blew smoke out the window.

"What did he ever do for you?"

"Something."

"And I can't do it for you?"

"No man can. The Professor turned my switches, that's all. He lit me up. Don't take it personal, Mick. I'm probably just a teensy bit in love with you but I'm lousy at love. Deep down, I'm no good at all. I'm rotten. I'm just awful."

"Myrtle, when you're not blue, you can be a lot of fun. People really like you, don't you know that?"

She sighed. She threw the cigarette out the window.

"If people do like me, it's because I'm faking it. Don't knock anymore, Mick, Myrtle ain't home. Go feed your dogs. Go call your little virgin reporter. Bring your aunt flowers in the old folks home. Leave a big tip for an ugly waitress. But don't waste your love on me."

"The Professor got you all twisted up, Myrtle."

"Oh yeah?"

"You gave up your apartment, sold your furniture and followed him to Milwaukee and what? He turned you out."

"We had a personal misunderstanding."

"He borrowed money from you how many times, and lost it playing cards?"

"That's none of your lousy business."

"But you're the one who told me that. The Professor is the guy who got you into the fur racket, which led to, guess what, a cell in the county jail and your picture in the wrong part of the newspaper. You stole furs to make money so The Professor could run his game. In the end, the one he was gaming was you."

"I ought to slap you," she said.

"Go ahead."

"I can't be bothered."

"So this con-man, who did you nothing but dirt, you're going to moon over him the rest of your life, and shut everybody else out."

"He's crazy about me. He can't live without me. You can live without me easy. See, that's the difference."

"But he's locked up," I said.

"I've got a lawyer working on that."

"Looking for someone to bribe, I suppose."

"The Professor needs me. I'm the engine that makes his car run. He treats me bad because he needs me bad, see. You never had that in your life, did you? Somebody who needs you to survive. See The Professor's got a holt on me and I got a holt on him. That's the way it is. I don't believe in God but I do believe in Fate, Mick. It's no point to struggle."

Her voice trailed off. "No point at all."

She patted my knee. "Don't feel bad, Mick. You ain't over the hill yet. There's plenty of horny women in this town."

She retrieved her fur stole, then stepped out of the car. At the lobby, she turned under the light and blew me a kiss.

"Call me," she said. "But not too soon."

Myrtle's rejection hurt. I was tempted to drink the pain away, but then, the pain of gout is even worse than heartache. I killed the evening with a long dog walk up and around the Cathedral, and then by reading detective magazines. An overdose of milk and cookies made me sleepy, and I was dozing when the phone rang.

I stumbled into the hallway and picked up the earpiece.

"I know you're home," Pat Reilly said, "I seen the lights. Somebody wants to meet you downstairs."

"Somebody who?" I asked.

"He barks like a Sea Lion," Pat said.

I leashed the dogs. Hula Girl bites her leashes so she gets the steel chain. Snowflake, the gentleman, can be held on cheap leather. I walked down four flights and waited. I talked myself out of fear. It was Harry, code name Sea Lion, who wanted to see me. While Harry's goons might kill you, Harry himself was all business.

A cream-colored Packard drove into the parking lot, its headlights knifing into the gloom. It stopped in front of me. I put my hands on the windowsill, passenger side, and stuck my head in.

"Smells new, all right," I said. "Harry, you must be doing okay."

"So are you," he said. "Get in. No dogs."

I tied Hula Girl and Snowflake to the steel burglar bars that guarded Janie's basement window. I got into Harry's car in the soft glow of the dome light. That Packard smelled of clean leather, booze, pricey cigars and cologne.

"Powers, what are you doing Tuesday?"

"Nothing special," I said.

"That's where you're wrong," he said. "You're doing that job for me and it's gotta be done right."

"What kind of job?"

"Shut up and listen."

It seemed like a long silence before the Sea Lion barked.

"Open the glove compartment."

When I did that, I saw in its miniscule light a folded piece of paper, a crude map.

"Tomorrow," Harry said, "you follow that map." He flicked on a flashlight. His fat finger pointed to an X on the map.

"You drive to that street corner," he said. "You see a telephone pole with a police callbox attached. Get it fixed in your mind, exactly. Then burn the map. If I ever see this map after tonight, I'm going to be pissed, understand?"

"Sure, Harry, burn the map."

"You memorize, then you burn."

"Got it."

If the Dead Could Speak / 171

"Practice run, that's the key."

"All right."

"You got a watch?"

"Yeah, a pocket watch my father..."

He handed me a gold wristwatch.

"Use this one," he said. "It keeps Harry time. Tomorrow at noon, you make a practice run, burn the fucking map and then you bring me the watch."

"Okay."

"I'll set the watch. Then Tuesday at 10 o'clock exactly, you crash your car into that telephone pole. The one with the police callbox. Right there." He tapped the map. "Corner of Plymouth and Washington."

"I crash my car?"

"Make it good. Make it loud. Ten o'clock exactly by this watch, ten o'clock on the nose. You bring this watch to me tomorrow night, and I will wind it and set it exactly."

"So," I said. "Let me get this straight. On Monday I drive to Minneapolis to look this job over. On Monday night I bring you the watch so you can wind it and set it. On Tuesday morning at ten exactly I crash my car into a pole at Plymouth and Washington. It's a phone pole with a police callbox."

"You're a smart fucking guy," said Harry.

"That's all I need to know?"

"There are one or maybe two cops at that corner, directing traffic. You will make a bang so loud, and beat up your car so bad, that those cops will come over to help you."

"And maybe they won't be able to call the station, if a wrecked car is blocking that callbox."

"That's the idea. You keep the coppers as busy as you can, then when the tow truck comes, you take the streetcar home."

"Harry, you're asking me to wreck my car."

"They said you was smart, they didn't say you was Einstein."

"What if I hurt myself?"

"Don't hurt yourself. Hurt the car. Make big noise."

"But I need the car, Harry. I just got it."

"Cars, we got plenty of cars. I'll send you to Tommy. We'll take care of you."

He flicked off the flashlight. Only the faint glow of the Cathedral's perpetual light eased the darkness.

"You work for me now," Harry said. "It's a job comes with life insurance. You need insurance right now, believe me. What more can a guy ask?"

"You'll take care of me with the car?"

"Do it loud, do it on time, and we celebrate with a bonus."

He punched me in the shoulder, friendly.

"Don't worry about the fucking car," he said. "You can do better than a lousy Plymouth."

CHAPTER EIGHTEEN

On Monday I bought three pillows at the Golden Rule. I drove to Minneapolis and located the phone pole I was to crash. Two cops were stationed at the intersection. It was a busy corner, but the city, broke, was slow putting in traffic lights. The cops' lifeline to the police station was a green-painted callbox fixed to the telephone pole. I pulled into a shadowy alley, and burned the map in the ashtray.

That night, I took the watch to Harry at the Lantern, and he wound and set it. It was an expensive Bulova, inscribed on the back: *To Mel, with Love.*

On Tuesday morning I left Snowflake and Hula Girl in the care of Little Elmer and drove to Minneapolis. Elmer was instructed to call Janie if I did not return, to arrange for long-term care of the dogs.

I arrived early, with coffee and crullers. I circled the block until I found parking, then tried to read the morning papers. I couldn't concentrate.

These were busy streets, lined with shops and apartment buildings. One block away was the obvious target: The North American Bank. People pushed in and out of the bank's revolving doors, and that scared me. An armored car nosed out of an alley, and that scared me. I was in a mood that everything unnerved me, even the passing traffic.

Harry operated on the principle of maximum ignorance, so I figured I would never meet the robbers.

I was wrong.

At 9:55 a LaSalle pulled up beside my car. It was a huge, long sedan, jammed with men. The passenger window rolled down to reveal the face of a red-headed fellow. I didn't hear what he said because I was dumbstruck by a flash of gold teeth. I nodded, he rolled up the window, and the LaSalle was driven off by a shadowy driver.

Five minutes. I realized that's what he'd said only when I was gagging on the LaSalle's exhaust fumes. Four minutes and thirty seconds later, I pulled away from the curb and headed for Plymouth and Washington.

I was only vaguely aware of one cop, walking off, his back turned to me. There was no time for thought. With the pillows between my chest and the steering wheel, I drove the Plymouth into the phone pole.

A shock and shudder passed through me and my head hit the passenger window. After what seemed like a long silence, I heard a hollow crunch. Then something started hissing. Then something metallic fell, bing, to the pavement. Some driver, speeding past, honked his horn.

I was knocked dizzy, but had the wits to throw the pillows to the floor before I staggered out. I stood in the street, a stunned idiot. It seemed some sap named Powers had been in a crash. His lips were bleeding. He was seeing double. He wasn't acting when, ten yards from the crumpled Plymouth, he sat down from fear of falling.

Down on the curb, I almost became myself again. I looked up to see the white-gloved hands of a policeman waving off traffic. Then his thin hard face was level with mine. Underneath a peaked cap: pale blue eyes and moving lips.

"You okay, pal?"

"Don't know," I said.

"He don't know," the cop said.

"Can you wiggle your hands and toes?" asked a rough voice behind me.

"Sort of. I think so."

"Come on, up and walk it off," said the rough voice, and hands helped me to my feet. With a uniformed cop on either side of me, I limped toward from the Plymouth. It had knocked the phone pole slantwise.

The bigger cop, with the rough voice, inspected the car, laughed and shook his head. "One more for the wrecking yard," he said. He stretched to reach around the smashed hood and opened the callbox.

The thin cop let go of my arm. He asked me to follow his index finger with my eyes.

"All right," he said. "You been drinking this morning, pal?"

"No sir."

"What the hell did you drive into a pole for, if you're sober?"

"I ... I guess I was fiddling with the radio."

He eyed me, suspicious.

Even though I knew the "accident" was going to happen, the sight of the wounded Plymouth, surrounded by broken glass and bits of sheared-off steel, I found shocking. My ears were ringing loud and my elbow began to throb in pain.

"I hope you got insurance for this wreck," the thin cop said.

The hefty cop crossed the street to join us.

"Tow truck's coming," he announced.

My crash had failed to disable the callbox, but I couldn't worry about that now.

The big cop said: "How much you had to drink this morning?

You an Irishman? He's an Irishman, Kurt."

"I wish I had a drink right now," I said.

The hefty cop backed up. "Walk to me," he said, and then to his partner, "You check his license, Kurt?"

I walked toward them, a little dizzy. They passed my license one to the other. Officer Kurt pulled out his ticket book but the hefty guy, whose nametag said KAZMAREK, wrinkled his face.

"He's in enough trouble," said Kazmarek.

As we stood in dumb silence, awaiting the tow truck, an alarm bell rang down the block. Kazmarek and Kurt looked at each other, not sure what they were hearing. Kurt shrugged. Kazmarek hefted his pistol-belt. They trudged toward the North American Bank.

I melted away into an alley. Three blocks later I was on a streetcar. By 11:30 I was home with the dogs. I popped open the windows on a fine spring day. I made lunch, a peanut-butter-and-jelly on English Muffin, and at noon turned on WCCO. The news announcer was very excited, but the wounded speaker of my radio spoiled understanding.

I turned off the radio and rolled the complications around in my head. Freddy Anderson aka Little Shorty aka Gold Teeth, was now revealed as a bank robber working under Harry Sawyer's protection. Harry Sawyer was Papa Alt's beer distributor. Yet Papa Alt was paying me to find out who Freddy Anderson was, and what he was up to. Somebody was double crossing somebody, but who and why?

I put those questions to Snowflake, who in his wisdom declined to answer. Hula Girl, licking her chops, retreated into the bedroom, to digest peanut butter in peace.

All evening I expected the Bulldog would knock on the door, and hustle me to the "baseball room" at Minneapolis P.D. No knock came. I spent the day putting my apartment back in order, reading detective magazines, smoking my pipe, and drinking good coffee. After a midnight dog walk to the Chancery lawn, I turned in for a restless night of so-called sleep.

In the morning I walked the dogs down to Blind Benny's newsstand and there, read all about it. It was a windy morning and the zephyr nearly blew the newspapers out of my hands. Yesterday's bank robbery had been the most lucrative in Minneapolis history. The haul was $55,000 cash plus maybe $200,000 in negotiable bonds. Witnesses said there'd been between six and eight robbers. The operation was slick and professional. They were in and out in less than ten minutes, making a clean getaway to the gangster haven of St. Paul. Descriptions of the robbers were given, but nobody mentioned gold teeth, so I figured Freddy had kept his mouth shut while in the bank.

Deep in the story the writer mentioned a traffic accident up the block. But police did not suspect it was linked to the robbery, since the driver had not fled the scene. That puzzled and delighted me. Apparently, in the confusion, I had gotten away clean.

I needed to talk with someone. Not Sam, given his connection to Jack Peifer. I thought of McAmbly, but this robbery was a bigger deal than I expected. I couldn't put him in the position of knowing who was involved. Myrtle and I were on the outs. All my other friends were tied up with one rival gang or another. So I rode the streetcar to the Daily News.

On the ride down there, I glimpsed the half-hidden storefront that housed Tom Filben's Emerald Radio. Something about Filben's phony business made me realize why Harry had been so cavalier about me crashing my Plymouth. The Minneapolis cops told reporters that the crash had nothing to do with the robbery, but they knew better. Those cops knew all about The Deal. They knew the bank robbers were already back in Saint Paul, and untouchable. They knew the crashed Plymouth was a deliberate distraction. When they saw that it was registered in Saint Paul, they decided not to waste their time on it. Any inquiry would be ignored by Big Ryan's detectives. The Minneapolis cops probably even guessed this bank job was rigged by Harry Sawyer. The cops over there were too smart, too lazy, too cynical to launch a real investigation.

At the Daily News, Janie seemed happy for an excuse to leave her newsprint prison. I suggested we take the St. Clair streetcar to a hamburger joint near Macalester College, far from the gangster district.

"No streetcars," she said.

"I notice you avoid them."

She flushed. "They're full of feelers. Grabby. I've been groped."

"I see."

"I just find it so creepy. Taxis," she said. "I don't mind paying."

So we took a cab out there. Surrounded by professors and students, we ate burgers, pickles and cole slaw. We gulped root beer from frosty mugs.

"I need a break on Wednesdays," she said. "Most of all on Wednesdays."

"Why Wednesdays?"

She cleared her throat and affected a high-toned voice. "Mr. and Mrs. Worthington Sommers announce the betrothal of their daughter Alice to Philip R. French. She is of Abbot Academy, Andover, and he is of Dartmouth."

She reverted to her own voice.

"Dartmouth, don't you know. That's the kind of crap I write all day Wednesdays. In the meantime, women are being burned like they were witches, and our so-called police reporter shrugs it off and goes drinking with the cops. And our so-called editors are having lunch with gangsters."

"Major Hoople lunching with gangsters? Which gangsters?"
She chewed through a bite of hamburger.

"Tommy Filben. Yes. Filben and our editor, lunch buddies at the Saint Francis. You tell me what that was about. Jeez!"

I shut my mouth. I was going to need Filben soon, if I wanted another car. Certainly no bank would finance me.

I said, "I have something juicy for you. Juicier than this hamburger. But you can't write it."

"Then why tell me?"

"I need your advice."

"You need *my* advice?"

"I need somebody who can think clearly."

"Okay." She shrugged, sipped root beer, sat back. "Spill."

"A guy named Freddy Anderson from Oklahoma."

"Okay."

"Raised on the Bible, carries a tommygun."

"I like it already."

"Lives over in West St. Paul with his mother and stepdad. Has a brother or maybe a best friend who looks like Boris Karloff. Those guys are the Hudson robbers. They stole the Buick that Sadie and Rose were burned in."

"So they burned Sadie and Rose."

"Not clear whether they did. Now, yesterday's bank robbery?"

"Go on," she said.

"Pretty spectacular, wasn't it?"

I hemmed. I hawed. Knowledge is danger.

Janie said: "I know you were going to tell me something."

"Here's the thing. Papa Alt hired me to find snoop on this new gang that hit town. I assumed he was afraid they were kidnappers. But they turned out to be bank robbers, led by this Freddy Anderson. Strangely enough, Freddy takes his marching orders from an underworld business associate of Papa Alt. So somebody's holding out on somebody."

"Like you're holding out on me."

"Janie," I said and pushed my lunch aside. "I've gotten kind of involved."

"In what?"

"I don't know exactly."

"You mean with gangsters."

"I mean with …" I whispered … "bank robbers."

She shook her head.

"Powers, Powers, Powers," she said.

"If I tell Papa Alt what I know, it could get back to the wrong guys. How deep are Papa's connections to gangland, I don't know. The whole thing, Papa Alt hiring me I mean, it could be some loyalty test. A setup. They might be grooming me for some kind of courier role. Papa Alt knows more than he lets on and I'm not sure how to play it. If I tell him a gangland secret, he might be grateful, but then again he might double-cross me. And I have a meeting with him in two hours."

"So you're telling me …"

"There's nobody else I can tell."

"So you're telling me that …"

"A Wisconsin cowgirl is the only person I can trust in this town."

"So you're telling me that …" she leaned forward and whispered. "You are a gangster. Not just a bootlegger, a real honest-to-God gangster?"

I gave the slightest nod.

She slapped the table and bit her lips.

"Oh that is so crazy," she said. She broke into a smile. She leaned toward me and whispered: "So now I live downstairs from a big-time Saint Paul gangster. Well! That's just nuts."

"It's more like, I do favors for money."

"What kind of favors? Oh, wait. I don't want to know, do I?"
I shook my head.

"Look," I said, "making a few bucks is one thing, murder is another. Whoever torched Sadie and Rose, there's bad and there's evil, Janie, and that was evil. I would like to see their killers rot in Stillwater. I'm giving you something to work on, Janie. Maybe you'd be smarter to stay away from it. If I were you I'd give it to Thornton. Get him and Major Hoople in a room. Tell them you have a story for them, but in return, you want a real beat, off the women's pages. That's how to play it smart."

"Okay," she said and settled into the red leather seat. "Go."

"Fred Anderson, originally from Oklahoma, now of Robert Street, West Saint Paul. Hudson robbery, January 5. Double murder and burned corpses, March 7. Big bank job yesterday. And remember the Kraft State Bank robbery, over in Wisconsin? All connected somehow, but how? There's a new gang in town and they know what they're doing, and this guy Freddy Anderson is the leader."

I held up my index finger as a warning. "There aren't many cops you can trust, although I know a few. Talk to my friend Billy McAmbly up in Bertillion. But be very, very careful. Don't go asking questions of people you don't know. Assume everybody's crooked unless you know better, and know it for sure. Hell, your boss is probably a crook."

"Major Hoople? He just gets a cheap thrill out of lunching with gangsters."

"Don't be so sure. So what are you going to do with this story?"

"You mean the Burned Ladies? Well, I don't want to give it to Goggles. Can I trust the G-men?"

"Maybe."

"I can drop it in their lap and have them feed it back to me as an exclusive. Thornton does that all the time. That's why he's survived so long. He makes it look like the authorities have broken the stories he's dug up. Hands it to them on a silver platter. It's a love fest, I'm telling you."

Her eyes were shining.

"But the G-men have no authority in murder cases," I said. "I already tried that. Janie, you don't know who to trust, who's in bed with whom. I can't tell you how careful you should be."

"If Thornton can do it, I can do it. The Burned Ladies," she said. "I can see it in True Detective. They pay fantastic. You're my source, Powers. Finally I have a gangster source."

"Janie…"

"Don't talk me off it because I'm a girl. Don't you dare tell me to become a feature writer. I am not going to write about charities and matrons. And if you don't help me, Powers, I'll find somebody who will. I want to get them, whoever burned those girls."

"You can't assume it was Fred Anderson. A: He didn't steal the Buick himself, and B: That car could have changed hands after it was stolen. And C: The girls were in contact with Filben and Peifer. This Anderson gang is working for someone else."

"Oh tell me who."

"That would be against the code. But there's nothing to prevent you from guessing."

"Harry Sawyer."

"I can't say yes even if I mean yes."

She pushed her lunch plate away.

"I paid for the cab. You're buying lunch, right Powers?"

CHAPTER NINETEEN

Friday was April Fools, the day of my appointment with Papa Alt. It was raining hard when the taxi delivered me to the Beer Mansion. Rivers of mud ran from Papa's tulip garden, washed down the sandstone cliffs, and into the Mississippi below. His butler led me around the side of the mansion, under dripping eaves.

Papa stood, consulting with women, underneath a striped tent. As I had read in Janie's society column, Emily Alt intended to marry the son of a Minneapolis banker.

The tent was set up with bare tables and wooden folding chairs. I recognized two Saint Paul beat cops, in plainclothes, hired as bodyguards. Papa broke away from the wedding planners and crooked an imperial finger at me. He stood in a wet corner of the tent, where a hedge separated the Alt estate from its merely prosperous neighbors.

Papa wore suspenders, damp white shirt, red bow tie askew. He appeared worn down by worry. Last time I saw him he looked like a vigorous captain of industry. Now he seemed like an old man, creased and pale and dull-eyed. Maybe the wedding preparations had sapped his energy. Maybe his bank, like so many others, was failing. But more likely, the alliances that made up The Deal were shifting under his feet, throwing him off balance. No question, Papa Alt was a partner in The Deal. Papa and Harry and Chief Big

Ryan, with Jack Peifer knocking on the door and Serious Bobby as go-between, that was the nucleus of The Deal. The question I had never resolved: Why had Papa Alt hired me when he already had the ultimate in underworld connections? Who was it he didn't trust?

Hot and damp underneath my raincoat, I shed it and draped it over my arm.

"Mr. Alt," I said, "I have an answer for you, although I don't know if you'll be happy with the answer."

He grunted.

"The women you first inquired about..."

"I inquired about no women," he barked.

My head jerked and I looked squarely into his bloodshot eyes. Reflected there was a man of ferocious will who had built an empire against the odds, and against the law. I backed down.

"Sir..."

"I inquired about a machine-gun gang," he said.

"They go by the name of Anderson," I said. "Although I'm fairly sure that's an alias. They moved here in early winter, from Tulsa. They now live on Robert Street, just across the city line, in West Saint Paul. The two leaders of the gang are living with a mother and possibly step-father. These gangsters likely participated in midnight raids on several small towns, and in bank robberies in Minneapolis and Wisconsin. They were visited at least once during my observations by Saint Paul detective Bulldog McMullen, for what purpose I cannot say. There is no strong evidence of their involvement in any murders, sir. And I don't think you have to worry about kidnapping. They are not kidnappers."

He put his thumbs behind his suspenders.

"Splendid," he said. "I have assurances from a man who is in no position to offer assurances."

"They came here for a specific purpose sir, and it was not to kidnap anyone. They had a target in mind, and their mission has lately been accomplished."

Papa harrumphed. He turned to look at the wedding planners, who waved him over. He left me standing like a dripping statue in that corner of the tent.

His butler touched me on the elbow.

"May I escort you out?" he said.

Whatever signal Papa had given him, I missed it. I followed the butler under the mansion's dripping eaves. A yellow taxi I hadn't called idled in the street. Alt's butler handed me a folded white envelope.

"In return," he said. "All matters remain confidential."

I took the envelope. I nodded. I put out my hand for a shake but the butler returned a hostile stare. I dashed for the taxi.

This was the beginning of the most profitable day of my life. Inside that envelope was $50, the exact amount of my rent, which was due that afternoon. Just before lunch, I borrowed my sister Kelly's car, and shuttled the weekly payoff from the Hollyhocks to Serious Bobby. That put $10 in my wallet. I rewarded myself with a Coney Dog at the Gopher Tavern.

The rainstorm flew north to replenish Lake Superior, and then Mexico sent us a pulse of sunshine. I stopped at the Royal and played the second race at the Fairgrounds. I won on a horse named George Gee, at 7-1. That was $16 minus a $1 tip for the clerk. Pat Reilly was not in his cage, but Horace, the head cashier of the Royal, had a job for me too, $20 in advance. The job was to talk to Serious Bobby about who had the rights to run a Sunday night card game at the Saint Francis hotel.

I thought I was really raking in, but then I drove home to find Pat Reilly waiting in the cab of a bootlegger's truck. He beckoned me over, asked me to sit in the cab, and handed me a cheap leather wallet. Lucky Strike bobbing in his lips, he said: "Harry's your uncle now."

I looked into the wallet, which was stuffed with cash.

"It's good to be the man's nephew," Pat said. "You'll see."

He pressed the starter button and put the truck in reverse.

On my way up the stairs, I counted what was in the wallet, and toted up my one-day score at $595. That was six months' pay at the stockyard.

I walked Hula Girl and Snowflake up to the Cathedral and back. After that hard morning rain, it was turning into a glorious afternoon, and it seemed like there was only good weather to come, the long winter behind us. Every trace of March snowstorms had been swept away by the driving rain. Snow? Ice? In the warm sun, who could remember?

I took the streetcar down to Essenmeyers and bought the dogs an excessive amount of German sausage. I treated myself to a red-striped summer shirt at Rothschild. Back in the apartment, I fed the dogs, and put four $50 bills in separate envelopes, the rent taken care of all summer. I slipped $5 into my top pocket, a spring bonus for Little Elmer. I mentally reserved my spending money for the summer, and calculated that I had $200 to invest in the Derby. That was in five weeks, and after the Derby, if I got lucky, well it seemed anything was possible.

On top of all that, Harry owed me a car.

So crime does pay. That night I took Myrtle via taxi to the Lowry for dinner, and then to the Boulevards of Paris to dance to the music of Ben Pollack. Myrtle was thrilled to think that this national orchestra was playing Saint Paul. The prospect of a night's dancing brought her out of her funk, and it seemed like our last argument had never happened. Myrtle and I were dressed up fine, like we were an executive couple.

When Ben Pollack's boys took a break, Myrtle huddled with

Loretta, honcho of her Free Love Group. They were planning an all-girl trip to the Chicago World's Fair. It was to open next spring, and Myrtle and Loretta were already looking over railroad timetables and hotel rate cards. I stood in one corner of the bar and sipped a ginger ale. Billy McAmbly, his suit-coat open for ventilation, joined me.

"Get me out of here," said Billy. He lit a cigarette with a silver lighter.

He waved that cigarette and I stepped back with a shudder, a bad memory: Billy and me and Swede in a fenced schoolyard.

Billy asked me: "Who did you come with?"

"I'm treating Myrtle tonight," I said.

"Myrtle." He laughed. "She ain't a cheap date. I thought you were broke?"

The band was coming off break, the trumpeter tooting his horn, the drummer tapping the snare. Billy and I walked down the dark hallway between bathrooms and stepped out the side entrance. Shiny cars, some chauffer-driven, pulled up, headlights bouncing in the night. Out burst the city's swells, wrapped in furs, glittering with diamonds.

"How did I miss out?" McAmbly said. He lit yet another cigarette. He held a cocktail glass, rattled its ice cubes.

"Judge," Billy said, nodding to a man dressed in a tuxedo.

"Municipal court," Billy said when the judge passed. "No need to pay a traffic fine if Judge Quick is on the bench. Mickey, where did I go wrong?"

"Not too late to get in, Billy."

"Oh, it's after midnight for me. Once you get on Big Ryan's shit list, you never get off. Remember the nuns saying, this is going on your permanent record? Well, my permanent record says: Too Smart For His Own Good."

He crushed the cigarette under his scuffed, police-issued shoes.

"I backed the wrong horse, see. I joined the Elks, it shoulda been the Moose. So I'm raising six kids on $110 a month. Good luck finding them a mother now. Sure, I drink free and cadge the odd lunch, but all the real money is flowing in the sewers underneath my feet. A nightclub like this operating in the open, advertising in the newspapers even, sending a river of cash downtown, and I can't even dip my toe in it."

He drank whatever liquor clung to the ice cubes. He adjusted his tie as if it were strangling him. I was alarmed by the redness of his face. He looked in that half-light like a hanged man.

"Big score over in Minneapolis," he said.

I nodded. A lean woman in a white dress sewn with pearls swept past us.

Billy said: "You don't know nothing about that Minneapolis job, do you?"

I shrugged.

"You got your ear to the rail," he said. "I heard it was a ten percent job. Hail to the Chief."

McAmbly smoked as if he were angry at the cigarette.

"Pretty slick," I said. "Whoever pulled it off."

"Kansas City gang, I heard."

"Oh really? Not the marker, though. That was way too slick, Billy. The marker had to be local."

"You know and I know," he said.

"Yeah," I said. "Probably Eddie Green."

"The kid is good."

A familiar young woman in a green turban and low cut busty dress paused to tip the doorman. She led a group dressed much like her, and then I realized it was Emily Alt, out with the bridesmaids on her last single fling.

"Whoever took that bank in Minneapolis," I said. "Nobody hurt, that's the way to do it. They got the cash, not a drop of blood on it. The Bloodless Bank Robbers. I'd go along with that. The bankers, they're a bunch of thieves anyway. Okay, some of the bank clerks got the crap scared out of 'em, but now they got a story to tell their grandchildren."

"I'm out of luck," said Billy. He gave me a searching look. "How you doing?"

"I've got Aunt Doris," I said. "Someday, I'll own a farm over in Wisconsin."

"Now you're a goddamned rich farmer?" His eyes flashed Celtic anger.

He threw the ice cubes at me and walked inside.

CHAPTER TWENTY

"I don't understand you horse gamblers," Janie said.

We sat on opposite sides of a picnic bench outside our apartment building. Mild sunshine beamed from a friendly sky. Using a schoolboy's ruler, I tore charts from the Racing Form.

"Isn't it fixed?" she said. "Isn't it corrupt?"

"Janie, look around. I know men who've been railroaded to Stillwater Prison for crimes they did not commit. Last fall, the police executed the owner of a bordello, and left him on the road to die like a dog."

I looked at Hula Girl and Snowflake.

"My apologies to the dogs," I said. "Street executions! The cops are worse than the gangsters in this town. The county prosecutor stiffs cases left and right. Federal liquor agents drink with the bootleggers. Half the judges have their hands out. The mayor is on payoff to look the other way. The governor stinks of Minneapolis gangster money, and appoints crooks to the State Police. College boys have been paid to throw basketball games. And you're worried about a jockey taking it easy in the stretch?"

"You don't have to be so hostile."

"Am I being hostile?"

"A little bit."

If so, neither Snowflake nor Hula Girl sensed it. Snowflake lay snout down in the grass, content. Hula Girl crouched under the table, watching a squirrel that scolded us from the oak tree. An electric smell preceded a streetcar grinding out of the tunnel. I sipped coffee and ate the delicious last of a buttered roll, then set the plate down for the dogs to lick.

Janie read a headline from the Daily News:

MINNEAPOLIS BANK BANDITS
CALLED CAPONE MEN

I shook my head.

"What do you mean?" she asked.

"I mean what people usually mean when they shake their heads."

She said: "Thornton's source was Captain William H. Shoemaker, Chicago Police."

"Liar is just another name for a cop."

She dropped the Daily News and picked up the Minneapolis Journal.

" … the robbers were affiliated with the gang of Al Capone, dethroned hoodlum lord," she read.

"Wrong."

"Now how do you know?"

I was writing fractional race times in my notebook.

"I said how do you know?" Janie demanded.

"I know what I know."

"That's a circular answer."

"Janie, follow the logic. Cops are liars. Thornton has to write whatever the cops tell him. Therefore, Thornton writes lies and the Daily News prints them. The cops are using Thornton like a trained seal."

She sat with that, thoughtful and quiet.

I said: "I see Crumley brought one of the bank robbery suspects back to Saint Paul. So the Minneapolis cops let the prince of corruption take away a suspect in the biggest bank robbery in city history? Well, that tells me these Minneapolis arrests were just for show. Reporters need to file stories. Cops need to make arrests. That's how it is."

She had a look on her face like she'd broken a tooth.

"Crumley and Big Ryan are masters of misdirection. Wherever they point, look the other way."

"You know who the robbers are, exactly?"

"I have a pretty good idea."

She put her head in her hands. "Well, we have a State Police now."

"The Commander drinks with Harry Sawyer."

"The G-men, then."

"Bank robbery is not a federal crime. Janie, there's nobody to go to. The crooks are in charge." I folded the Racing Form.

"Compared to Saint Paul," I said, "horse racing is a bastion of integrity. Sure, the races are full of crooked people, but the horses are honest."

I opened the Daily News to an inside section. There, in a splash of studio photos, a story anticipated the wedding of Emily Alt.

"Is that your work?" I asked.

"That's me," she said. "Late-breaking weddings." She sighed. "You wouldn't give a girl a hint, would you?"

I sipped cold coffee. Snowflake rose from the grass and stretched.

"Bet to win, never to place or show," I said.

"Come on, Powers, one little thing I can work with."

"Remember the fate of Rose and Sadie?"

"They're not going to murder a reporter, Powers."

"Don't bet on that."

Hula Girl put her sweet black face into Janie's hands, and Janie rubbed her behind the ears.

Janie said: "The female witnesses at the bank picked out one bandit as particularly handsome. I wonder who that was?"

I shrugged.

"Don't you think that's odd?"

"Maybe all the rest were particularly ugly. Janie, look, if you have some cockeyed notion that a lowly reporter is going to switch on the light of truth in this town, forget it. I know you're jealous of Thornton, but he's just another sucker in the audience. He gets free admission, but that doesn't make him an insider. All the real action takes place off stage. The bankers are in on it, the hotels, the pool halls, dice rooms, the pawn shops, the card rooms, the nightclubs, the race wires, the whore houses, all the fences dealing in money, jewelry, hot bonds, furs… There's millions of crooked dollars flowing through this town and I can't imagine anything short of war that would stop it."

I handed her the Daily News.

"This newspaper's not even worth two cents," I said. "Hell, I'm a gambler myself. If the Royal ever stops bribing the cops, Crumley would raid it, and I would be in handcuffs, along with all the other horse players."

"Well, I'm not going back to Wisconsin and milk cows."

"And I won't get you involved with the gangsters of this town. If you're going to do something crazy, do it on your own."

"Oh, bug off Powers," she said, and walked off toward the basement door. Hula Girl followed her, then turned around as if looking for instructions.

I shrugged.

Hula Girl turned tail, as if she understood.

Sometimes I think Hula Girl understands everything.

The Noon Mass attracts the reluctant, the stragglers, the hungover. They can't hope to recover their Faith, but might find an after-Mass drinking companion. They won't let go of their Catholic upbringing, but can't live by it either. I was one of them.

The Cathedral is the size of a stadium, with side altars to a dozen saints. Toward the end of Mass I got restless, sneaked out of the pew, and into the alcove of Saint Patrick. I dropped a quarter into the tin slot at the bank of candles, which gave me the right to light five of them. Mom, thanks for keeping us all together when Dad was sick, I don't know how you did it. Dad, I wish you'd had an easier life. Myrtle, it's okay to let go of the Professor. I held the taper in shaky hands, above the votive candles. Two more to go, Sadie and Rose.

As I lit the candle for Rose I realized in shame that I had taken money from a gang that may have killed her. Maybe it wasn't the Gold Teeth gang that did it personally, but still, it was all part of The Deal. And now I was a part of The Deal. Rose's candle sparkled as I fired it. As I lit Sadie's candle, all five candles threw shadows on the marble snake under Saint Patrick's feet. I said the first prayer I had uttered since high school. *Saint Patrick, you drove the snakes out of Ireland, you can drive these Ozarks thugs out of Saint Paul. In the name of the Father, the Son and the Holy...*

I had a horrible vision of Sadie, in her grave in the black, black earth, half covered in dirt, trying to rise on her elbows.

I was shocked by a slap on the back and a whisper: "I thought that was you."

I turned around to see Reilly.

"You need to buy me a drink," he said.

I looked over his shoulder, expecting to see his usual following of dark Irish women. The sisters, his wife included, must have gone to an earlier Mass.

Ite missa est, the priest said from the altar.

Deo gratias, responded the crowd.

Kneelers were slammed, pews were bumped, boots sounded on flagstone as the crowd moved for the many exits.

"Tell me something," Pat said. "They threw me out of altar boys, I couldn't get the Latin. The priest says, what does he say at the end?"

"Go the Mass is ended," I said.

"Right, and the crowd says *Deo Gratias,* which even I know means Thank God. So why are they thanking God? Because the Mass is finally over?"

"Pat," I said, "the Church is about mystery, not answers. Mystery."

"No wonder I never got it," he said.

As I started toward the side exit, Pat put a hand on my arm, steered me back into Saint Patrick's altar, lit only by candles. They threw wavering shadows across Pat Reilly's unshaven face.

"Look, Mick, speaking of answers, I got one. See, the question is, can you be loyal to two armies, and the answer is no, negative, never. You gotta choose. Caesar or Hannibal."

"Says who?"

"Says Caesar. Believe me you want to be with us Romans. Not them barbarians."

"Carthage," I said. "They weren't barbarians."

"What?"

"Hannibal. Carthage, they were just as civilized as the Romans."

"Hannibal's no good," he said. "You need to go to Hannibal and turn in your sword. You're fighting for Rome now."

"Caesar says this?"

"Caesar was what-do-you-call, adamant."

"Do I have a little time?"

"None. No time exactly on the clock. Believe me, Caesar would know if this doesn't get done."

"Okay," I said. "Tell Caesar I salute Rome."

"And only Rome."

"I get it, Pat."

"Just making sure," he said.

I crossed the street to my apartment building, climbed the four stories, and that's all the time it took to realize I had to do as Pat asked. Harry, aka Caesar, was my uncle now. If I told all I knew about him, he'd go to prison for a long time. So we had our own deal, unspoken. Harry would protect me, in return for the occasional favor and absolute loyalty. The penalty for treason was to join Sadie and Rose in Saint Paul's Book of the Gruesome Dead.

Having no car of my own, I dialed Sam and asked if he could fetch me for a cozy with his boss. He showed up in Jack's Packard. I admired this machine every time I got into it: the deep shiny olive-green paint job, light green pinstripes, immaculate canvas top, leather seats the color of sand, and chrome on just about every surface. It was such a beautiful car that Harry Sawyer was inspired to dump his brand-new Hudson and buy a Packard. Whatever Jack had, Harry wanted too.

Unlike most of Sam's passengers, I sat in the front seat.

Sam, usually an impeccable dresser, wore greasy overalls. I set down a manila envelope filled with clipped racing charts. I sat back and enjoyed an open-window drive, the first of the season. I admired the Mississippi, which was just waking up to its free-flowing nature.

"Up to date as of yesterday," I told Sam. "The charts."

"Do we risk a thousand apiece?"

"Ahhh," I said. "More like a fiver."

Sam's face set into disappointment.

"Still time, though," I said.

"Probably, yes, probably we have time."

We speculated about Phar Lap, the wonder horse, and whether anybody would ever challenge him again after his awesome win in Tijuana. Sam figured Phar Lap would end up back in Australia. We discussed Economic, Stepenfetchit, Burgoo King, and Gallant Sir, our horses in the derby. Gallant Sir's recent win at Hawthorne, Sam thought, was a stellar showing against a strong field. This was Sam's specialty: the class angle, or as the rubes would put it, who beat who.

We turned into a driveway that was blooming with tulips and daffodils, although the path itself was a frosting of mud. Sam slipped the Packard into the garage. He opened the hood and snatched a sparkplug wrench off a paint-spattered workbench.

"He had to buy a V-12," Sam grumbled.

"You could eat off that engine," I said.

"This may be my last Derby," said Sam, and began wrenching out sparkplugs. "They have excellent racing, you know, in Japan."

I wandered to what Sam called his "corner office" at the back of the garage. It was illuminated by a harsh mechanic's lamp. There atop a beat-up desk lay a dark green rice bowl, wooden chopsticks laying across it, like an exhibit in a museum. On a shelf were a few dusty, loosely bound books in Japanese. Keeping them from falling over was a bronze sitting Buddha. Nailed to the wall above was a dark wood crucifix with a silver Jesus. Propped up in a frame at the back of the desk was a photo of a Japanese woman. She was dressed in an overcoat, and standing on the deck of a ferry on a foggy day. She rested each arm on the shoulder of a tiny child, boy and girl. I knew better than to ask about them. Ever. You don't touch a man where he's sore.

I could always sense a controlled anger in Sam. We have this in common: our women left us. But Sam's sorrow was worse, because his son and daughter had been taken back to Nagasaki by his homesick wife. There was going to be a full-on war between Japan and China, Sam was certain. Although he rarely spoke of it, his life goal was to return to Japan with enough money to rescue his family.

I left Sam to his mechanical chores and walked up the concrete path toward Violet. She wore a white pants-suit, and it billowed around her skinny frame. She looked like an Arabian virgin in white, but with the palest, most Scandinavian shade of skin. She directed the gardening efforts of an elderly Japanese couple. For some reason, Jack hired just about every Japanese who applied here. Most had been dining car waiters, laid off or retired from the Empire Builder.

Violet ignored me, as she did most of Jack's seedy friends. I climbed the stairs, hustled across the empty dining room, up the sweeping staircase, through the cigarette-stinking casino.

Jack's office door was open. Father McCarthy O'Sullivan occupied the visitor's chair.

Father Mack wore an open green polo shirt over black trousers and mirror-shiny shoes. He held up a big meaty hand to me, snorted, and said, "Well, I'll be going, then."

Even five words out of Father Mack's mouth betrayed him as immigrant Irish. *Will, Ayellbe goin den.*

"Michael," he said, rising. "Good to see you in church this morning."

"Father." I watched him edge out the door. The man was six-foot-six and his footsteps sounded heavy in the creaky hallway.

"Jack, you're getting religion," I said.

He waved that off.

"I'm offering God a bribe," he said. "Violet's dreaming of a Cathedral wedding. Nothing but the most glamorous affair will suffice."

"She has to dream?"

"She's Lutheran."

"Oh," I said.

"The hated enemy. A married couple can't be Lutheran and Catholic. It's one or the other. No tolerance."

"Jack, that's what I came to talk to you about."

"Bah," he said. "Business. Say, are you going to Opening Day? Everybody's excited. I've got two tickets for you somewhere."

He began opening desk drawers.

"I can't wait to see the new ballpark," he said. "I hope to hell this one has decent restrooms. Don't you hate to piss in a trough? Here they are, Saints versus Mudhens. You'd think the opener would be against the Millers, wouldn't you?"

I took the two tickets he handed across the desk.

"Bring your girl. Hey, who are you seeing? Not Myrtle, I hope."

"Jack, I need to beg off the bag job."

"Beg?"

"Yeah, I sort of need to drop it."

Jack leaped up from his desk, threw open a window, and bellowed: "Sam!"

Then he sat back at the desk.

"What's behind this?" he asked.

"I'm getting busy," I said.

"No," Jack said, and shook his head. "You're not busy. I'm busy. You are at my beck and call."

He picked up a pencil and tapped it on his felt blotter.

"You're shafting me," he said.

"Look, I want to play the horses full time."

"Don't bullshit me," Jack said.

He leveled such a penetrating look at me that I got the willies. My testicles sought shelter. Goosebumps rose, hairs stood on end.

"Who you working for?"

"Harry," I said.

"Son of a bitch," Jack pounded the desk. He reached into a side drawer and pulled out a gleaming stainless steel revolver with a pearl handle. He pushed it across the desk at me.

"Take this," he said.

"I'm not a trigger kind of guy," I said.

"You'll need it," Jack said. "Because when Harry's done with you, he'll bump you off. Take it. Take that pistol, I'm telling you."

I grabbed it, I looked it over, it was so shiny I could see my own reflection. Footsteps sounded in the corridor and Sam appeared in the doorway.

"Tanaka," Jack said, "take this traitor son-of-a-bitch out of my office and never let him set foot on my property again."

Sam wiped his hands on his greasy overalls, then stood blocking the door. He was short, but all muscle, and no question could give me a good fight.

He put a hand on my shoulder.

"Let's go," he said.

I looked at his stone-set face, then into Peifer's angry eyes.

"Boss?" Sam said.

"He's not out of my sight yet?" Jack said.

"You wait outside," Sam told me.

"Go!" Jack shouted.

I backed into the hallway and Sam whispered, "Wait downstairs. Take a breath of fresh air."

I retraced my steps to the porch. Violet and Father Mack were chatting in the sunshine. She was leaning, flirtatious, against the porch railing, as if daring the priest to seize her for a kiss. I stayed in the shadows and fumbled for my pipe. I just had time to light it when Sam, calling from the grand stairway, beckoned me back to Jack's office.

"Go on in," Sam whispered, and gave me a pat on the shoulder.

Again I was seated in Jack's lone visitor's chair, and again Sam blocked the doorway.

Jack stood near the window and pointed at me.

"You're lucky," he said. "Sam spoke for you."

I nodded.

"Sam revealed to me that you are friends."

I nodded.

"You can keep the wheel gun. Compliments of the Hollyhocks, where smart players always win."

He allowed himself an ironic smile.

"Sam," he said, "what do we do with assholes like Powers, when they're dear, dear friends and we can't kill 'em?"

"We put them to work," Sam said.

"That's right Sam. We put them to work. Now scram, both of you."

We descended the stairs into the dark barroom. Sam walked behind the bar and made us each a whiskey-and-water.

"What the hell was that about?" I said.

"He's almost certainly blustering," said Sam. "He wasn't going to bump you off. Not over a $10-a-week job."

"You're sure?"

"People exaggerate," said Sam. "They say Jack is a killer. No, but he uses that reputation to his advantage."

Sam was kidding himself about that, but we're all lying to ourselves about something.

"Drink," he said.

"Gout," I said.

"A sip," Sam said, and we clinked glasses.

"All the Master wants from you," Sam said, "is to have a spy in the enemy camp."

"That..." I said, but Sam shushed me, finger to his lips.

"Just say yes. Bring him a tidbit once in a while."

"... could be dangerous."

"Come on, you're a horseplayer. Life's a gamble. You're

hedging, that's all."

"I don't know, Sam."

"You have little choice," Sam said. "You've taken the man's money, as I have. We belong to him now."

"What's he after?"

"Harry's got the cops by the balls, we all know that. Jack doesn't want to interfere in the protection rackets. But you know, people used to come to us with dirty money. Now it all goes to Harry. Jack is very distressed about that."

"Hot money."

"Yes."

"That's what this is about?"

"Yes. For sure. You know that bank job last week, very, very nice haul. But not one dollar, and not a single bond, has been exchanged over here. Used to be, we would get a split. Some to Harry, some over here. Now we don't see a thing, and I remind you, that's the biggest bank job since the Denver Mint."

Sam tossed down his drink.

"It's the easiest game, pure money. You take in ten thousand dirty, you give back eight clean, you keep the two. It could not be safer and Jack is very, very upset that Harry's got all this action now. Why? What has changed? This is what the boss wants to know. Why are we cold all of a sudden?"

He sighed.

"I would like to know as well. It affects me, Mick. It affects my income. When the Master does well, so do I."

His head turned and he stared out the windows. Over his shoulder, he said in a voice I could barely hear:

"We live in a time of great danger. Read the newspapers, Mick. Demons are being unleashed all around the world. If war comes to Japan, a woman and small children, without a man to stand up for them ..."

He finished his drink.

"This is child's play, Mick. This is child's play compared to what is coming."

CHAPTER TWENTY ONE

When I arrived at Myrtle's apartment building, I found her on her knees, crying, in the alley. I caught her arm as she lunged for the back door.

"Don't run away." I said. What's got into you?"

"Leave me alone, will you?" She wiped her tears with a dirty hand.

"I'm your boyfriend, remember?"

"Boyfriends call before they come nosing around."

Her eyes glistened with anger. I followed her upstairs and when we pushed into her apartment, I noticed the bird cage, empty, on the dining room table.

"No Flyboy?" I said.

"I buried him."

"He's dead?"

"Why else would I bury him?"

"Sorry."

"You Catholics believe in God. What kind of God kills an innocent bird on Easter?"

"He died on Easter?"

"Overnight. You got any use for a bird cage?"

"Myrtle, get another parakeet."

"He was my one and only." She pulled off her tufted green-and-blue sweater and sat with it around her forearms. The sweater was like a fluffy pair of handcuffs.

"I'll never get another bird," she said. "They just die on you. I feel sick to my stomach. You know how I get?"

I put my hands on her shoulders. "I know how you get."

"Nothing's going to work out. Everything I see. Threatening."

"What looks threatening?"

"Omnibus, is that a word? It looks omnibus out there."

"Ominous?" I said. "What looks ominous?"

"That building across the street. The cars. Everything. They just have a creepy look."

"Let's get out of town," I said.

"Nah," she said.

"I have a place."

"You told me. It sounds lousy."

"You can't sit here and cry over a dead bird."

"He was special. He was Flyboy."

I dropped to one knee.

"Aw, Jeez," she said, "you're not going to propose are you?"

"Neuske's bacon," I said. "We'll have bacon three meals a day."

"Don't try so hard to cheer me. I find it depressing."

"Pack for long weekend," I said.

I went home, packed a suitcase, and fed both dogs, who pranced in anticipation of a road trip. By canine voodoo, they knew they were going along. I let them leap into the car and drove to Myrtle's. She was sitting in the lobby like an obedient schoolgirl, suitcase packed, apartment door locked. In the alleyway, she had dumped the birdcage near the garbage cans. A popsicle-stick cross marked Flyboy's grave.

"Hello boys," she said to the dogs in the back seat.

"Hula's a girl."

"It's a manner of speaking," said Myrtle. "Where'd you get this machine?"

"Filben loaner."

"Pontiac, huh," she said. "I never rode in one of these. What's the gimmick?"

I started the car.

"Ah," she said. "It's just another lousy car."

It was a five hour drive, over bumpy roads, with no radio. Myrtle might have been one of the dogs, for all she offered in conversation. We stopped at a crossroads cafe in Ladysmith, and bought three hamburgers, one to be split by the dogs. The burgers were greasy, Myrtle complained, and the root beer warm.

Unlike humans, dogs are creatures of gratitude, and give all restaurants an enthusiastic review. Hula Girl and Snowflake settled down with satisfied snorts after their burger. I drove along Federal Eight bound for Eagle River, amusing myself with some simple math. I calculated that the split from the North American job would come to about $7,000 per robber, after all the payoffs were made. I imagined how I would spend $7,000 if I had been entitled to a level share. These gangsters lived like kings. I'd be satisfied as an emancipated serf. I was in Harry's grasp now, one way or the other. If I could get level for just one job, I could escape Saint Paul. Harry would forget about me sooner or later. The Gold Teeth gang would run back to the Ozarks. Just one job, and all could be well.

Gradually as we drove along, the landscape changed from forest-and-farm to just pine forest. In places it seemed dark and forbidding, with April's low sun casting long shadows. In other places, it had been logged off, to a rough sea of ugly stumps. Myrtle and the dogs dozed until we got to Minoqua. There I bought groceries while Myrtle walked the dogs.

"Half an hour now," I said and dropped the grocery bags in the back seat.

"You didn't tell me the drive was going to take all day," she complained.

When we finally reached the farmhouse, a white-tail deer looked up in panic and bounded once, twice into the woods.

"Here we are," I announced.

Myrtle hobbled out of the car and stretched. Snowflake and Hula Girl scampered after the deer.

"It's where my mother spent her summers," I said.

"I thought you were Irish."

"American on the other side."

"You must be so happy on the Fourth of July."

"My mother's people were Midwesterners. She met my father in New York City. Before she had kids, my mother wanted to be a newspaper lady."

I put both our suitcases on the front porch and unlocked the door. The farmhouse was a ramshackle thing. Every few years, my mother's Aunt Doris and her paranoid husband Joe had added a room or an outbuilding. I passed the suitcases into the kitchen, then circumnavigated the house with a crowbar, taking down storm shutters and setting them against the chipped white walls.

"Just letting the joint air out," I told Myrtle, and ducked inside to fling open windows. I stuck my head out and told her: "Musty in here."

I turned on the water pump and opened kitchen and bathroom faucets to a steady, rusty bleed.

"What are you waiting for?" I called out to Myrtle.

"Are there spiders in there?" she asked, leaning against the Pontiac.

I had to give her time to adjust to country living. "Okay, let's eat out," I said. "We've got to go downtown anyway and buy ice."

"Swell," said Myrtle.

I locked the dogs in the house. Snowflake barked angry. Hula Girl sulked. Myrtle and I drove to downtown Eagle River. Its main street had a movie theater and two supper clubs and bright shops selling fudge and moccasins and fake Indian trinkets. We ate a roast-beef-and-mashed potatoes dinner, Myrtle sucked down two cocktails, then we stopped at the icehouse.

When we pulled into the farmyard again, the big red barn looked like a rustic painting framed by the windshield.

"I thought country living would cheer you up," I said. We pushed into the kitchen amid a canine celebration. The dogs enjoyed the spoils of a roast beef dinner. As I wrestled the block of ice into the leaky old icebox, I tried again with Myrtle.

"It's peaceful here, no?"

"I find peaceful depressing," Myrtle said.

In the living room, she slumped into an easy chair near the piano. The sun had disappeared over the pine trees.

"You play the piano?"

"My Aunt Doris did. Never took lessons. Taught herself."

"What happened to Aunt Doris?"

"Nursing home," I said.

"I'll take a whiskey sour," she said.

"I happen to have the ingredients."

At Bonson's Cash and Carry I had bought two beat-up lemons in a produce aisle that was mostly carrots, iceberg lettuce and radishes. I squeezed both those lemons into a stainless steel shaker, added sugar and Canadian Club, and tossed it all around. I decorated each cocktail with two maraschino cherries, and carried the drinks to Myrtle.

She was in the living room, leaning into the big window, staring out at the night. The Rhinelander radio station played music so scratchy that it was hard to tell who the orchestra was. I put the cocktail in her hand.

"So you're drinking," she observed.

"Once in a while."

"Like a real man. I've never known a real man who didn't drink."

I toasted her. I ate the cherries, one at a time. "Two are twice as good as one," I said.

Myrtle grunted.

I set the drink down on the piano bench, and squatted to start a cheerful fire in the barrel stove.

"What's bothering you, Myrtle?" I said. "Don't tell me it's about a dead parakeet."

"Look at my life, sport. Where am I going? What have I done?"

She drained her whiskey sour. "You know the Professor took it all out of me. He's a thief in more ways than one." She looked out the window, into the blackness of a deep forest night. "There's nothing out there."

"That's the beauty. Our own forest primeval."

"It's evil all right."

"Primeval," I said. "Natural, you know. Adam and Eve. Unspoiled."

"Ah, baloney, everything's spoiled."

"We should step out and look at the stars," I said. "You can't see the Milky Way from Saint Paul."

She rattled her ice cubes to request another drink.

Eventually she drank enough that she stumbled off to bed. I let the dogs out. As they snooped in the dark, I looked up into the moonless night at a billion stars. Cassiopeia, the Queen, I traced her royal outline in the northern sky. I heard the strange elongated call of a barred owl, and the flap of its wings as it swooped out of the trees.

In the morning, Myrtle got off to a chipper start. Perhaps it was the smell of bacon frying in a cast iron pan, or the cup of cowboy coffee. An April breeze flew in, smelling of sweet morning forest. I scrambled eggs on the grill of the wood-fired stove.

She picked up my half-read copy of *The Glass Key* from the kitchen table. "What's this about?"

"A gangster."

"What's the glass key?"

"It was in a dream. It shattered."

"No wonder I don't read books," Myrtle said. "There's enough shattered dreams, without reading about them."

I served us bacon and scrambled eggs and toast.

'What's this place worth?" Myrtle asked.

"I'd have to buy out both my sisters."

"For how much?"

"Oh, $2,500 each. One good bank job, see, that's all it would take."

"You couldn't live out here, Mick, I know you, you got city blood in them veins.

After breakfast we walked down the woodsy pine-smelling path to Snipe Lake. It was a quiet, calm lake, shaped like a giant moccasin. We had no neighbors, really. The lone cottage at this end of the lake belonged to my cousin Cindy, who hadn't been up here for years. Across the lake stood summer cabins, owned by Milwaukee and Chicago people who never showed up until July. In the sunshine, Myrtle sat on a log and removed her blouse, wool skirt, underpants, shoes and socks. She stood on the sandy shore naked, her back turned to me.

"I hope I drown," she said, then shuddered and plunged.

She bobbed up immediately.

"No such luck," she shouted.

Snowflake tested the water and retreated. Hula Girl paddled toward Myrtle, then turned for shore, trying to lead her back to safety.

Myrtle stood shoulder deep, hands crossed over her breasts. Shivering, she waded to shore. Her lips were trembling blue when I tossed her a towel. I dried off her back and butt with another towel. She sat on those wet towels, laid along a fallen pine log.

I sat beside her and said: "I wouldn't let you drown."

"I didn't mean it Mick, it's just … I feel so dark inside sometimes."

She patted my hand. "You make it better, you really do."

"Myrtle, we could live out here, away from everything. I'd need a stash though. Maybe I wouldn't make it as a farmer, but if I had a pile … You know those boys, the North American."

"What about 'em?"

"I was going to ask you."

"I don't know nothing about them."

"The split was seven gees."

"That ain't so much. The Professor got twelve once, out of a single job."

"Yeah, well, seven. Its years of free living, the way I figure it."

She shrugged, swathed in damp towels. Goose-bumps covered her flesh. She toweled off her hair.

"You ain't got 'em, Mick. I've seen the killer eyes, and I know who got 'em and who don't. The Professor didn't have 'em. There was a man stole for a living, but was as gentle as your family doctor."

Tears formed in her eyes. She swiped at them with a knuckle. "The gang you're talking about, they got killer eyes."

"So you've met them? At the Lantern?"

"A woman hears things they would never tell a man."

"Who would never tell a man?"

"The tough guys. You know my friend Loretta, she's had her head on every pillow in town. She knows more than J. Edgar Hoover."

"These bank robbers, what do they look like?"

"Short and skinny, not my type. I like a little meat on the bones."

"Okie accents?"

"One of them does."

"Little Shorty? With the gold teeth?"

"That's the one. The other one's like you. Doesn't drink too much. Time I seen him he had a glass of milk and a boiled egg. What kind of gangster is that?"

"But killer eyes."

"Gives me the creeps. Makes me shudder," she said. "Do yourself a favor. Stay away from them Mick."

"They came from the Ozarks, they'll go back there," I said. "Harry's got other guys, and there's plenty of banks."

I called the dogs, who had wandered sniffing along the lakeshore. Myrtle, wrapped in towels, carrying her clothes, followed the dogs toward the farm house. Just as we left the forest and tromped into the meadow, Myrtle stopped and looked up into the trees.

There, on a thick branch, sat two huge gray barred owls, side by side, like they were married.

"Why are they known for wisdom?" Myrtle whispered, "what's so wise about an owl?"

"They hunt in pairs," I said. "Two swiveling heads are better than one."

"Sweethearts," said Myrtle.

"And ruthless predators," I said.

"Yeah," said Myrtle, "I knew I liked something about 'em."

That night, our last in the farm house, I dreamed about those owls. The dream woke me up just past midnight, and I lay there among Myrtle and the dogs, trying to sort it out, some crazy thing, the papa owl holding a glass key in his beak and the mama owl whispering in my ears. Mama owl spoke some kind of language, it wasn't English but it wasn't a sound that ever came out of any owl.

I rolled out of bed and walked out into the deep silence of a woodsy night. The wind blew the kitchen door closed behind me. I put my pipe in my mouth and lit it with Sadie's lighter. In that flame, the only light except for the stars, I saw Sadie's homely face. *I've got five dollars worth of happy for you, Mister.*

I smelled Sadie: stale perfume and wine and cigarettes and underneath that, something damp, warm, lovely, a whiff of wildflower and forest.

The door opened behind me and the dogs scampered out. Myrtle sat beside me on the wooden porch steps.

"Got a light champ?"

I flicked Sadie's lighter.

The owls hooted. Who-who ... who who.

I lit Myrtle's cigarette and it bobbed, a red-orange dot, in her lips.

"So now it's you got the blues," Myrtle said. "I got woman sense. I can tell."

I blew smoke into the dark sky. Hula Girl sat beside me, panting into the hot night. Snowflake stared at us with green-glowing eyes.

"I can't figure out the who," I said. "I can't even figure out the why."

"You gotta give me more than that, sport, I ain't a detective."

"Back in March, the Burned Ladies, remember."

"Oh yeah," said Myrtle. "I remember. A warning to all us dames."

"A warning?"

"To shut the hell up."

"Is that what it meant?"

She tapped the side of her head. "Woman sense. It meant: Hey women, this gangster stuff is men's business and it's gonna go bad if you stick you nose in."

"I'd never thought of it as a warning to all women."

"Ask a woman, see. We're used to these things."

"Well, the dead are speaking to me right now. The dead women."

"And what are they saying?"

"They're saying *who*, like the owls. They're saying whose side are you on? Myrtle, I can't take money from these guys. But I'm too broke to turn it down."

"What guys?"

"Harry's boys. The ones that did the North American. Freddy Gold Teeth and that gang. It might have been them, beat Sadie and Rose, shot them, threw acid on their faces, lit them on fire. I don't know. It's driving me a little nuts, I can't sleep. I thought it was the heat and the mosquitoes but I can't live without money from Harry's jobs and I can't take it either. My mother would be ashamed of me. I can't have nothing to do with the murders of those girls."

Myrtle, tender, put her arm around me.

"There's times I adore you, slugger," she said. She threw her cigarette out into the weeds.

I didn't believe she loved me, but it felt good, her arm around my shoulders.

"But it ain't just the money," I said. "I can't tell Harry no. You tell Harry no, and he assumes you're either a police snitch or you're working for Jack. Harry seems like a jolly guy, but don't be fooled. You tell Harry no, you get a visit from the undertaker."

"You'll work it out, Mick. I know you. You been playing this game since Volstead went crazy. I thought you was clever, how you sneaked that booze out of the rail yards, remember, years ago, the horse-drawn sleigh?"

"Days of innocence," I said. "We were just kids, having fun, fooling the cops."

I heard a flutter. The owls flapped off on strong wings. They may have been figures of wisdom, but they were swift and silent on the attack, and they tore their prey to pieces. Somewhere in that dark forest, a little mouse was in danger.

CHAPTER TWENTY TWO

"Where have you been?" demanded Sam as I sat in the olive-green Packard.

"Out in the country," I said.

"Too bad about Phar Lap," he said.

"What about Phar Lap?"

"Poisoned," he said.

"Dead?"

Sam nodded. "Don't you read the papers?"

"The Wonder Horse? Poisoned? Who killed him?"

Sam shrugged.

"Holy mackerel," I said. "Sam, it's getting bad. Kidnapping babies. Poisoning race horses."

"Caution in all things," said Sam. "It's a dangerous world."

"What's the boss want me for?"

"He may have an excursion in mind."

When we rounded the corner of the great white nightclub, Jack Peifer was trying to learn golf on the lawn. His lazy Doberman and beautiful wife were his audience. He was swinging a nine-iron and mostly missing the ball altogether. He wore safari-shorts, his winter-pale legs looking sickly. His safari shirt was sweaty at the armpits, his liver trying to save him from last night's booze.

Violet was hiding a laugh when I walked up.

Jack swung, and hit a weak line drive, clonk, into an oak tree. The ball bounced back at him.

"Are you sure Walter Hagen started this way?" I joked.

Jack gave me the hostile once-over. Apparently men of my status were not to joke about his athletic shortcomings. He shoved the nine iron into his golf bag. With his black-and-white spiked shoes, he kicked at a scattering of balls.

"I'll leave you gentlemen," Violet said. The Doberman watched her walk away, feinted at following her, then decided to lie in the sun.

With a checkered handkerchief, Jack mopped his forehead clear of sweat and hair grease.

"Tonight I need you," he said.

"Okay."

"Normally this would be a $100 job, but I deduct $50 for Mayor Bundlie."

"Is he broke?"

"It's a campaign contribution. Mahoney the prick is gaining. Roosevelt's coming to St. Paul, have you heard? Roosevelt backs Mahoney, the Communist. I need you tonight."

"What's my role?"

"You drive. That's it."

"Jack, I can't be seen working for you."

"It will be night and it has nothing to do with me. It's dark at night, remember, nobody sees. You're driving, that's all."

"I don't own a car."

"A car is provided. You play golf?"

"Yeah."

"What's your handicap?"

"I don't keep one."

Jack's head jerked. "Then what's the point?"

"It's more fun when you don't keep score," I said. I kept to myself that I'd learned that from Sam.

Golf tee protruding from his fingers, he pointed at me. "You, you're a dangerous thinker."

I shoved my hands in my pockets, hoping to look relaxed.

"I thought we had an agreement," I said.

"We do. But irregardless. There's this one night job. It will be over in ten minutes."

I knew better than to ask why me, because I wouldn't get a straight answer. "What time?" I asked.

"After dark. Stay home. You will be called for."

"They're hitting everybody up," I told Janie.

She blew her nose into a white handkerchief. We were in her basement apartment, where it was dark enough to grow mushrooms. The April sun was enlightening the earth, but it was hard to tell by looking out these tiny, steel-barred windows.

I had brought Hula Girl and Snowflake down to cheer her up. They were in bed with her, curled up at her feet. Janie lived in one room, and slept in a daybed. Overhead ran a complex of steam pipes. The "kitchen" was a stove and sink along one wall, and on that stove I was boiling water for tea. I'd made her a peanut butter sandwich, but she had no appetite.

"Who's everybody?" she asked.

"The underworld. Mahoney's got them scared."

William Mahoney was the white-haired, fancy-talking editor of the Union Advocate. All year he'd been stirring up the Red radicals and now he was running for mayor.

"I kind of like him," said Janie.

"Well, you would, you're union. But if Mahoney wins, he fires

Big Ryan, reforms the police department, and breaks The Deal."

"Okay, Mister Insider, you're saying that Mayor Bundlie's a gangster?"

I sputtered. "Mayor Knucklehead? He's no gangster. He's the bootlegger's best friend. There's a difference between gangster and bootlegger, you know. Bundlie doesn't have to commit a single misdemeanor. He makes out nicely by spouting civic pieties and looking the other way. His city hardly resembles the one portrayed in your newspaper."

I set a pot of hot tea on the night table, and from my inside coat pocket produced a shiny flask.

"Tea and whiskey," I said. "The Irish remedy for all ills."

She sniffled and sat up.

"Thank you."

She wore a wrinkled, sweaty flannel nightgown and her hair was a tousled mess. To make room for the tea cups, I pushed aside copies of Modern Detective, and *The Glass Key,* which I had finished reading in Eagle River.

Snowflake, displaced by Janie's movements, burrowed again into the sheets. Hula Girl sniffed at the peanut butter sandwich, awaiting her tribute.

"What's your angle?" Janie said and sipped whiskey tea.

"Well, Mahoney is a Union commie."

"Oh really?"

"Gets his money from Red Russia. Bundlie, on the other hand, relies on underworld money."

"So my story is…?"

"Do you want a Commie or a bootlegger running this city? That's the choice."

"I see. And your choice?"

"Most people will choose the bootlegger."

"Well, I choose the unions."

"Do you want me to write the story for you, Janie? Gangland sources say Saint Paul bootleggers have been pressured for contributions to Bundlie's faltering campaign."

She blew her nose.

"Pad that out. That will scoop Thornton, big time."

"Okay."

"Janie, I was a legman back before the War."

"Oh really, covering what?"

"Cops and fires, nothing special. Well, okay, one time, this is my first year with the Globe, there's this guy driving a horse and wagon. This is on Fort Road. A steamroller comes along and spooks the horse, who runs in front a streetcar. The wagon's busted up, the horse runs away, but the guy goes under the wheels of the streetcar."

"Ugh, don't tell me any more."

"It was the ugliest thing I'd ever seen. I went into the back of a saloon and threw up three times, called rewrite, and then ordered a double whiskey. But the editors, see, they played up that story for a week. They had half the newsroom working on it. And I finally figured out why they played it so big. It illustrated the dangers of depending on a horse, suggesting we'd all be better off in automobiles. And guess who were the Globe's biggest advertisers?"

"Oh come on."

"It's a game, Janie. Look, this is how you build a story. You take one kernel and blow it up into a bag of fluffy popcorn. You take what I told you, get comments from both sides, what have you got? Nothing really, but it's news. BUNDLIE DENIES GANGLAND LINKS."

She lay back in her pillows.

"I'll think about it."

"Three weeks until the election," I said. "You'll be back at work soon."

"It doesn't feel like it," said Janie in the dark shadows of her daybed. "Right now, I can't keep anything down."

I felt ashamed, using Janie that way. But I told myself: She was looking to break out of the Women's Pages, wasn't she? A story linking Bundlie with bootleggers would do our side a lot of good. People like booze and nightclubs. People hate Communists. The commie Mahoney was a threat to the booze and gambling party that had run wild in this city ever since Volstead got sober.

I left the dogs with Janie for the evening and prepared for my night with a nap in the fading sunshine. I made a fried egg sandwich and brought it downstairs to Janie, but she was lights out, so I ate it myself.

I waited for hours, watching out my fourth-floor windows. Twilight became evening and I paced, I read magazines, I played game after game of solitaire. I fell asleep twice. At just after one in the morning, headlights cut the fog and parked in my empty spot in the lot.

The lights flashed three times. I slipped into my work jacket, patted a pocket, yes, the pistol was in there.

Even as I approached his car I had the awful feeling I knew the driver. His dark form moved over to the passenger side. I opened the driver's side door and he said:

"Ready, Shaky?"

A wave of sick horror rose from gut to brain.

"Swede," I choked out.

"What are you waiting for?" he said.

I slapped the car into gear and backed out. It reeked of gasoline. That smell was mixed with the stench of dead meat, like a month-old steak was lying on the back seat.

"Down Seventh until I tell you," he said.

I drove, a puckery feeling taking over me, accompanied by an attack of goose bumps. My brain held a furious debate. Was this my appointment with the Angel of Death? No you fool, nobody dared bump you off without an okay from Harry.

Most gangsters dressed swell for a job but Swede wore the dark blue uniform of a car mechanic. He was known for that. He stood out among gangsters. Most of them couldn't spend enough on their suits, ties, cufflinks, shirts and hats.

But Swede's message was: nothing fancy, I just get the job done.

Smirk on his face, Swede hummed as we drove into the night. I hated that humming. It told me he was confident and I was nothing to worry about.

Swede had been the senior bully of Sacred Heart the year I was a freshman. He was six feet tall, his hair color hard to tell, because he always wore a severe crew cut. He was a Lutheran bruiser recruited by sports-mad priests for the Sacred Heart football team. He wasn't the biggest guy on the team, but by far the meanest. In those days the forward pass was a radical experiment that hadn't been adopted by high schools. Football as played by Swede was a dirty, bruising, ball-busting game of attrition.

On initiation day at Sacred Heart, Swede and his buddies had forced freshmen to kneel in the school's asphalt playground. Using a lit cigarette as a threat, Swede demanded that the boys kiss one another. Billy McAmbly fought them off, and got bloodied for it, but I was a little guy as a freshman. I stared straight ahead, as if the bullies weren't there. I refused to kiss Jimmy Lavin and Swede burned that cigarette into my upper arm. I still have the scar, the exact diameter of a cigarette.

That's where I picked up the nickname I hate: Shaky. Swede said I was trembling like a scared rabbit, and that's why he burned me, for cowardice. That was more than twenty five years ago but the nausea, the heaving, the burning, the tears, and the laughter of the senior bullies has never faded. I avoided Swede that semester, and he mostly left me be, except for the occasional shove in the hallway. He dropped out after senior football season, to the relief of even his friends.

Now, humming in the passenger seat, Swede opened the window to spit out. He glared with contempt at a cluster of young men milling about in the night lights of the Seven Corners speakeasies.

"College boy pansies. Herman's has turned into a pansy bar. How do you like that?"

I grunted and drove along Fort Road.

"They should have their dicks cut off, that's what they deserve."

I kept my mouth clamped shut.

He said: "Every man gets what he deserves, Powers. That's the beauty of life."

I stared through the windshield at the night road.

Swede said: "What do you think the penalty ought to be for being a pansy?"

My hands were strangling that steering wheel. "Maybe they ought to be burned with a cigarette," I said.

I could feel the weight of that revolver in my jacket. Could I whip it out and plug this son of a bitch? Not unless I wanted to run from Jack's thugs for the rest of my life.

All I could hear for ten long seconds was the clatter of the engine and the whine of tires over pavement.

"Oh, a wise guy I see," said Fanlund. "With a long memory. Let me tell you Powers, somebody's got to do the right thing. Somebody's got to keep things in line. Worse was done to me. Believe me, a lot worse was done to me before I got big enough to defend myself."

He lit a cigarette. In that flame I saw, in the windshield's reflection, his hard stubbly face.

"But you went into the Army, Powers. I was surprised by that. I didn't think you had the guts for that."

"I'm not fourteen anymore, Swede. I don't weigh a hundred twenty pounds, like I did in the schoolyard. Me too. I'm big enough to defend myself."

He laughed. "Oh, are you?"

He shifted in his seat, stared intently out the side window. "Turn the corner," he snapped out. "Then stop."

We were around the corner from a barber shop. It was a two-story building with an apartment above. A long slanted wooden stairway led to that dark apartment.

"Go up there and get 'em out," said Swede.

"What?"

"The people, get 'em out. Chase 'em off."

I put my hand on the door handle and looked into his cold hazel eyes.

"We don't want them to burn up, Shaky. Just chase them off and shoo them away."

I climbed the wooden stairs. With the butt of the shiny pistol Jack had given me, I pounded on the door. Nobody answered. I looked around. Most of the neighboring buildings held shops only, but there were apartments down the road and I feared I would wake their occupants.

I pounded again. A light went on.

"Police!" I shouted.

The door opened. A young fat woman in a bathrobe answered, a half-naked boy behind her in the hazy light of the kitchen.

"Get out of here," I said. "Evacuation order. Now."

I showed my pistol without aiming it at her.

"Message from the gas company," I said. "This place is about to blow. Wake up, lady. Get your kids and run."

I stood aside as the lady gathered three children in nightclothes, a boy, a girl and a toddler. Her eyes big with fright, she pushed the children out the door and they half stumbled, half ran down the steps. I herded them down the foggy lamp-lit side-street.

"Go and keep going," I shouted.

A half-block away, I turned around to see a shadowy figure between car and barber shop. In a flash, the shop exploded in flames. I ran for the car but Swede peeled off, leaving me staring stupid at a flaming storefront. The tires of his car squealed rounding the corner. Dogs barked, glass popped, and the fire began to roar.

I made my way home through back streets, always looking for where I could ditch the gun in case the cops rolled by. They did not. Block by block I got farther from the fire until it was only a distant glow. The sirens of fire trucks had gone silent. By the time I wormed my way through steep alleys to Cathedral Hill, there wasn't any fire to be seen at all.

I had something new to think about when I sat on my couch and gathered myself for a smoke. Something besides the scary lighting up of a barber shop and the chasing off of an innocent family. I knew now, for dead certain, that Swede was a soldier in Jack Peifer's army. So it was Jack who had sent Swede and Rico after me on Saint Patrick's Day.

Why exactly I still didn't know. Was it Jack's idea or was he following orders from higher up? Why he'd changed his mind about having me executed, I didn't know. I wondered if Sam had put in a saving word for me.

The Saint Paul underworld was sort of like the fight game. There was a champion, like Max Schmeling. But there was always a challenger, like Primo Carnera, coming up fast. Harry was the champ and Jack the up-and-comer. Sooner or later there would be a heavyweight battle for the big prize.

I figured I'd live only as long as I was useful to Jack. His main interest in me was having a spy in Harry's camp. If a war broke out between Harry and Jack, I might be the first casualty. Jack was the one man in town who would dare violate Harry's protection order.

The morning papers, including Janie's Daily News, missed the arson story but the afternoon Dispatch picked it up. This was another in a series of fire-bombings at barber shops in the Twin Cities. The whole episode began to make sense when I got to the third paragraph, where Police Chief Ryan commented.

I had visited Janie early that morning but now I carried the newspaper down there, along with a flask. Hula Girl and Snowflake didn't seem to know it was me knocking, and set off barking. I had her spare key. I let myself in.

She was sitting on her daybed, swathed in the same rank nightgown, feet in fluffy slippers.

"I think I can get up," she said, and stood wobbly.

She hobbled to the bathroom and I picked up *The Glass Key* and saw she had dog eared it in the middle. I carried teacups and crumby plates to the kitchen sink. I belly-rubbed Snowflake and Hula Girl, one with each hand. When Janie emerged she had brushed her hair straight, maybe the beginning of a rebound.

"Another shot in the war," I said, and nodded at the Dispatch lying on her bed.

She picked it up.

"Paragraph three," I said. "It's quite germane."

"Germane?"

"Yeah. What's the matter with germane?"

"It's not a word you often hear in conversation."

"Well this is a conversation, isn't it?"

She read. "Okay."

"It's right there in your paper. Chief Ryan blames the unions for these fires," I said. "Mahoney is the union candidate. Mahoney is the guy who would dump Ryan if elected."

"So…?"

"So it's really the gangsters who set the fires. Motive: blame the unions."

Janie frowned.

"Thereby," I said, "smearing candidate Mahoney."

"I get it," she said, testy.

She dropped the paper. "I don't buy it. There've been, what, eight barber shop arsons. Not all of them in Saint Paul. So how does this tie in to the mayor's race?"

"Well," I said, "I didn't say the gangsters set *all* those fires. If they were really clever, they'd torch a Saint Paul barber shop, suggesting that the Commies had set all the previous fires."

"But gangsters aren't that clever, are they?"

"Your gangland source says maybe they are. It's tricky out there."

"Oh," she said, and rose to wash her dishes. Above us, the steam pipes, shutting down for the season, emitted a groan.

"How about that family?" she called, her hands in dishwater.

"What family?" I said.

"Below the fold."

I had missed it, but now saw a tiny headline:

Mother of three,
pajama clad children,
rousted by gangsters
in middle of night

The father was a railroad man who died last year of fever, the news story said. The widow and kids were living on paltry insurance and the county dole, and now would be homeless except for Catholic Charities.

The mother described herself as "terrified" and the children "hysterical."

"See," Janie said, "that is what your gangsters never consider. They have no feelings and no heart."

"Oh," I said, "I think they have feelings. It's just sometimes, you know, it's a trap. It's like quicksand. Once these guys step in, they can't get out. The more they struggle, the more they sink."

Janie wiped her hands on the dishtowel.

"You can't see the forest for the trees," she said.

"I've never understood that saying."

She squatted to look me square in the eyes while giving Snowflake a rub behind the ears. Hula Girl liked Janie, but Snowflake adored her, and would mewl when he saw her in the parking lot.

Janie spread her hands. "It means the whole picture."

"Okay give me the whole picture."

"Franklin Roosevelt."

"That's the picture?"

"He's got a wave of Wets behind him, and if he makes it to the White House," she snapped her fingers, "poof, no more Prohibition. And then what are all you bootleggers going to do? So go ahead, fight your skirmishes over who's going to be mayor, but you're missing the big battle. It's all about the White House."

I had not expected to receive a wise scolding from a 22-year-old. I sat there with something to think about. And then those thoughts rolled over into a sense of guilt and shame. True, I had not known in advance exactly what I was doing, but still, I had terrified a broke, helpless widow and children. They were frightened out of their skin now, and living in charity beds. The children's toys and clothing had gone up in smoke. The children would have nightmares now, of gangsters knocking on doors. Gangsters who looked like me. Without meaning to, without wanting to, I had graduated from bootlegger to bag man to jug marker to thug.

"You look pale," said Janie. "I think you're getting it. I think you're catching the flu."

CHAPTER TWENTY THREE

Father Mack and I were sitting back to back on a concrete bench. We were in the Garden of Eden. That's what the priests called it anyway. Its formal name was the Archdiocesan Chancery Garden.

"All right now," said Father Mack, over his broad shoulders.

"My last confession was two years ago," I said.

That admission brought not a whisper of condemnation from the giant priest.

"Father, I ... I participated in a criminal activity ... that resulted in harm to an innocent family."

"What manner of harm?"

"They lost their home because of it. Because of what I did."

Silence from Father Mack.

"Father, I..."

"Were they otherwise harmed?"

"I'm afraid the children were pretty badly frightened."

"There are only two commandments," Father Mack said. "Love God, and love thy neighbor."

"I guess I broke both commandments, Father. Especially the neighbor part."

"As far as is possible, you must restore to this family all you have taken from them," he said. "And you must make a firm resolution never to commit this sin again. Then and only then I can offer you absolution."

"How about the Hail Marys?"

Father Mack snorted. "Prayer is a poor substitute for action."

"Father, two months ago, I took job in all good faith. The job was to report on gangland activity for a wealthy man. We both know this wealthy man. Ever since I took that job, I've been entangled something terrible. It's like I'm a fly and two big spiders have trapped me. If one doesn't eat me the other will."

Father Mack turned and rested one huge prizefighter's hand on my shoulder.

"Even if I could find an honest job now, Father, I couldn't take it. Each of these spiders thinks they own me. Each of these spiders is jealous of the other one."

"Let's finish this over a beer," he said. He gave me conditional absolution in the name of the Father, Son and Holy Ghost. He made the sign of the cross over me, and removed the glossy purple stole from around his neck.

Up Selby Avenue we walked, crossing the streetcar tracks and heading for the Portland Pet Shop. There, puppies played in torn-up newspaper in the window. Seeing parakeets in a cage, I contemplated buying a matched pair for Myrtle. Maybe, I thought, Flyboy died of loneliness. Maybe parakeets live longer if they're two together.

A door at the side of that pet shop led down a dark, twisting hallway and into a hidden garden. It bloomed not with plants but beer steins. This was the Barking Dog speakeasy: A garden was surrounded by brick walls eight feet high. The seating was green-painted wooden picnic benches. A menu on the wall offered a long list of German sausages, and the garden smelled vaguely of sauerkraut.

"Altwasser, two," Father Mack told the fraulein, holding up two fingers. We sat at a bench in the corner. Only four other people were in the beer garden, a bit early for the lunch crowd.

Father Mack wore a light tan shirt, open at the collar, that did nothing to hide his pugilist's physique. He had killed a man in the ring back in Cork, or so they said, and guilt had driven him to the seminary.

"What do you think of Over Time?" Father Mack asked.

"You know me, Father, I'm a hedger."

"Whitney-Sande?"

"Good connections, Father, but this isn't your ordinary race. It's chaos, Father. The bet's against the favorite and on chaos."

"Well, you need a good man in the irons in that traffic jam." He adjusted thick glasses over myopic eyes. "I'll never understand racing in America," he said. "Putting fine horse flesh at risk on the dirt."

The beers were delivered in foamy steins. Father Mack ordered a knockwurst. I declined.

"Gout, Father," I explained. "And I can only sip this beer. I'm living on peanut butter sandwiches, poached eggs and toast."

Father Mack sipped at the foam and said, "Otto makes a decent brew. Pale, but honest enough."

"You boosted me for that job, didn't you Father? With Papa Alt."

"It's the task of the Irish to help Irish. Our history demonstrates that no one else will."

I raised my stein. "I appreciate that. Work is hard to come by. But that's where my trouble started, with Papa Alt."

"I'm afraid the poor man will become a recluse," Father Mack said. "He is convinced that kidnappers are stalking him."

"Maybe they are, Father, who knows what's going on out there?" I sipped at that foamy beer. "It's getting to be a real rough game. I'm looking for a way out of the gangs, Father."

"Perhaps I can speak with Otto again," he said. "He employs hundreds. Surely he can use another good man."

"I have the feeling Papa Alt has no use for me, Father." I lowered my voice to a hoarse whisper. "Anyway, if you'll pardon my boldness father, between you and me, I think he might be just another gangster."

Father Mack set both hands on the bench to steady himself.

"Otto Alt is a pillar of the Church," he growled. "There are families in this parish who would starve without his generosity. Saint Patrick's Pence? My entire program would collapse to nothing without Otto Alt. He is technically a criminal, violating the Volstead Act day and night. And you've no doubt heard the rumors about dark dealing at his bank. But Michael, we're all criminals, every last one of us. We should be on our knees thanking God that there is no Justice. Justice for all would be a terrible calamity. The human race thrives on the endless forgiveness and mercy of God. Justice, Michael, is a dream of cruel hearts. God in his infinite wisdom and mercy has spared us from Justice."

That afternoon, I left an envelope containing $200 at the chancery, addressed to Father McCarthy O'Sullivan. Wrapped around the money was a note requesting that it be used exclusively to aid a certain burned-out family residing at Catholic Charities. It amounted to six months' cheap rent, plus a basket full of groceries. When I left the Chancery, on the walk downhill to my apartment, I felt good, until I reflected that those innocent children would have nightmares for a long time, that they'd get a death chill every time someone knocked on the door, every time they saw even so much as a campfire.

That only added to my resolve to free myself from the gangsters. We bootleggers had started as a bunch of friends providing hooch for parties. How exactly we had evolved into arsonists, robbers and murderers I didn't know. It seemed like the longer we stayed in the game, the darker it got.

I took the Randolph streetcar to its terminus, the Ford Motor Plant. It was built alongside the Mississippi, just on the Saint Paul side. It was surrounded by a parking lot containing hundreds of new Model A's waiting to be loaded onto freight trains. At the front end of the great clattering smoking plant, a tacked-on glass office space, none too clean, held a room with desks and pens. Here supplicants might petition Henry Ford for work. If by some miracle I was selected from among the thousands of desperados applying here, I would accept the job and figure out how to deal with the wrath of Harry and Jack later. I filled out both sides of a form, handed it to a brusque female clerk, and stood hands behind my back expecting ... I don't know what, but not the sneering reply:

"Next in line!"

He builds a crappy car, I muttered on my way out.

On the way home I bought Lonely Hearts of the Midwest. I was too embarrassed to read it on the streetcar but perused the ads once I got home. Snowflake and Hula Girl sat, bookends, while I turned the pages and told myself Myrtle was a lost cause. She didn't love me, I doubted she could ever love any man but the Professor. But I think I loved her. She was a thief and a cynic but she was good company and she understood me. We were comfortable together, like an old suit and a ruined dress hanging neglected in a dark closet.

The problem was that Myrtle had rejected Eagle River and the country life. To be with Myrtle was to live in Gangland. So I read the ads, and petted the dogs for comfort as I slowly discovered that all my potential sweethearts wanted a man with a steady job.

I looked Hula Girl in the eyes and said: "Divorced, childless, out-of-work, low-level gangster wants fresh start, desperately seeking tender hearted female.

"How do you like that?" I asked Hula Girl. Then I added. "Must have room in her heart for two dogs."

Snowflake yawned. Hula Girl snorted.

I fed them sausage and cornflakes, walked them around the Capitol grounds, and then rode the streetcar down to see Billy McAmbly.

Billy was playing darts, the targets being Saint Paul's most wanted men. Bertillion cards featuring the photos of Tommy Carroll and Harry Dalton were the bulls-eyes. Billy stood back, beer in one hand, darts in the other. One dart missed the corkboard entirely. Another struck the far corner and dropped to the floor. A third speared Tommy Carroll a direct hit in the left eye.

"I've figured out a way to supplement my income," Billy said. "A quarter a throw, and the prize is a buck for a direct hit. Got a quarter?"

I turned my trouser pockets inside out.

"You and everybody else in town," he said.

"Which is why I came to see you, old friend."

"Be alarmed," Billy said, "when an Irishman calls you old friend."

"Looking for work," I said.

"See Harry Sawyer."

"No I mean honest work."

"No such thing," said Billy.

"Maybe a government job," I said.

"Everybody's laying off and cutting pay. Or haven't you heard?"

"I heard a man with friends is a man with friends."

Billy set the darts on the counter.

"Look, Mick, even ditch digger has fifty applicants for every job.

The mayor's cousins can't even get work these days."

"Keep those big ears open, all I ask."

"I thought you were on the gravy train over at Alt Mansion."

"Yeah, well."

"What happened?"

I looked around to be sure no nosy cops lurked in the hallway.

"The Alt gravy train went off the rails. Papa hired me to snoop on the Burned Ladies."

"What did he care about the Burned Ladies?"

"Well, they weren't burned when he first hired me."

"Is that so?"

"That's so. He was afraid they were spies for a kidnap or maybe a bank-heist gang."

"Oh I doubt that," Billy said and swigged beer. "Stool pigeons is all those dames were."

"Stool pigeons?" I said.

"They were in here."

"In the police station?"

"Day before they died," Billy said. "In with Crumley."

"Crumley was giving them the third degree?"

"I wasn't in the room, but the way I hear it, those girls were setting up the Hudson robbers."

"What are you talking about?"

"Look, Mickey, there was a reward for the Hudson robbers, right? Well, those girls came in to collect it. They talked to Crumley, I assume they named names. Crumley let 'em go, next day they were burnt to a crisp."

"When did you find this out?"

McAmbly shrugged. "Hard to keep any secrets. I mean, the girls didn't walk in here invisible."

"Billy! Crumley set those girls up."

"You can't say that. Could have been a dozen cops through that room. No way to prove who it was."

"I know who the Hudson robbers were. They're living over in West Saint Paul. Sadie and Rose ratted them out to the cops, and the cops double-crossed those girls. I know who burned the girls now. I always suspected but now I know it for sure: Little Shorty and Boris Karloff."

"Knowledge and proof ain't the same thing. Besides, Mick, you'll get no indictment out of Irish Kinkead. The Hudson robbers are paying off. Otherwise they'd be living on mustard sandwiches down in the dungeon."

"Mustard sandwiches?"

"The jailers pick the ham off before they deliver 'em."

I pounded the table top. "Billy, we got a double murder here. I was down on the docks. I can still smell it, the fire that cooked those girls."

"Criminals ain't guilty if they pay off," Billy said. "Ask Irish Kinkead, he'll tell you."

"What kind of town is this? You go to the cops and end up dead?"

"Those girls made a bad play. Everybody knows to shut your mouth and look the other way."

"I know you can't trust the cops, but they turn you over to gangsters for execution? That's a new one, Billy."

"Keep your voice down."

"For execution?" I whispered.

"I'm drinking a case a day," Billy said. He waved a bottle of beer. "What does that tell you?"

CHAPTER TWENTY FOUR

"So you really want to solve the mystery of the Burned Ladies."

"Of course I do," Janie said. "Don't tease. Just tell me."

"I'll give you something to feed to Goggles. But you must swear an oath: No Freelancing. No Janie Vetter, girl detective. Okay?"

"Oath," said Janie, and crossed her fingers.

"Straight to Thornton."

"A spoon-feed," said Janie. "That's how he gets every story."

We sat at the top of the Cathedral steps, overlooking the vice district on Seven Corners. It was a glorious shirtsleeve day. Janie held Snowflake's leash and I restrained Hula Girl. Snowflake, whose white coat reflected the sun, lay like the Sphinx. Hula Girl panted and squirmed, lobbying to move on.

"After the Hudson robbery," I said, "the town fathers set a reward. Rose and Sadie tried to collect it by going to the police."

"The Hudson police?"

I shook my head.

"The Saint Paul police?" Janie asked. "Why on earth would they trust the Saint Paul police?"

"They were sixth grade dropouts? The were from Duluth? They were desperate for cash? They had been drinking all weekend?"

"So the Saint Paul cops ratted Sadie and Rose out to the gangsters."

"Probably."

"Oh my God," she said. "Is our police force really that treacherous?"

"You should move to an honest city, like Chicago or Havana."

"Who on the police?"

"I don't know exactly, but Crumley might know."

"The cops signed those girls' death warrants."

"Now you've got it. Which means the Hudson gang either killed Sadie and Rose or had them killed. They stole that Buick in Hudson. By lighting them up in the Buick, the killers destroyed both the informants and the evidence."

Janie handed me Snowflake's leash.

"I'm going."

She took two steps down the wide stone stairway and then turned on me. "Who told you that? Which cop?"

"Janie, you know better than that. I can't say. The man's got a family. People end up dead over stuff like this. Give it to Goggles. See what happens."

She hurried down the stairs, crossed the boulevard, and descended the flowering path alongside the Chancery. She let a streetcar pass as she hustled down to Seven Corners, and I imagined her arriving breathless at her desk.

I worried that she would write the story herself, but told myself no, she's smart enough to let Goggles take the risk. I began to feel that maybe I was a man worth something. Maybe there was something besides muck and quicksand under our feet. I took the dogs for a run, began to sweat, and wondered if I could work myself back into Army shape. I recalled Basic at Fort Dix, the pain of running in boots with full pack, followed by the surge of good feeling that lasted the afternoon.

I bought two rounds at O'Connor's Soft Drink Emporium to soften Sam up. Ginger ales, please, with Sam's whored up and mine virginal. I asked him what Violet was like and he said, "Icy, remote. Very hard to get to know. Fabulous athlete, you know. Friendly when she wants something from you. Could play on the national tennis circuit, and men who play golf with her never ask her to join them again."

"No he-man wants to be bested by a beauty queen," I said.

"I think she was brought up correctly," said Sam. "Her attraction to Jack, it's yin-yang. She's a burning candle, he's the dark mystery. He started as a carnival barker, did you know that? And then a bellboy-pimp. She's what she appears to be, a chilly Scandinavian beauty."

"Sam," I said, "about the Derby."

"I've been meaning to talk to you about that."

"Well vice-versa," I said. "You first."

Sam sipped. Staring down at the bar as if its fine grain revealed the mysteries of life, he said: "I cannot go. They are going. Jack and Violet."

"And you're not driving?"

"They're taking the train with friends. A judge from Minneapolis, and his wife. I'm to watch that Saph doesn't rob the till during Jack's absence." He looked at me with soft eyes.

"So..." he said, "I'm sorry."

I clapped him on the back.

"It might work out," I said. "What we save on travel we can add to our wager."

"I've figured out ..."

I stopped him with a hand on the arm of his tweed jacket.

"New strategy," I said.

"Oh?"

"Plunge."

"No hedge?" He looked down at his hands. "I've worked out the class angles," he said. "We've got it down to five horses."

"You hedge. I'll plunge."

Sam bit his lip, swirled his ginger-and-whiskey.

"Sam, I have to."

"How much?"

"All five hundred."

"On one horse?"

I nodded. "Economic," I said. "If I can get twelve to one."

Sam said, "I'll be back," and walked brisk for the bathroom.

Our hedge strategy had worked for two Derbies in a row. The Kentucky Derby is a vanity race. Many of the horses are entered merely to provide wealthy owners with bragging rights. These poor animals have no chance to win. Also, since there are so many horses in the gate, only the fast starters can avoid the traffic chaos that always develops.

Once you eliminate slow starters and vanity horses, you can match the rest by speed and class. This gives you maybe five true contenders, and you can hedge-bet them all and make a 20 percent return. On a thousand dollar hedge, Sam and I would split $200, and more if we were lucky.

A thousand bucks is barely enough for a decent hedge, and $500 reduces your chances to make the correct spread. When Sam walked back from the men's room, he tossed down his drink.

"Benedict Arnold," he said and slammed the glass on the bar. "Knife in the back."

I was surprised by his sudden anger. He stomped out into the back alley. I followed and when he jumped into Jack's Packard, I stood in front of the car.

"Run me down, go ahead."

"Out of the way!" he shouted, head out the window.

"Please Sam," I said.

I put my foot on the running board.

"I've got to put it all on one horse, Sam," I pleaded. "I need out of this life. Five hundred at twelve to one, Sam, that's retirement money. My aunt owns this ruined potato farm in Wisconsin. I could go there now if I had starter money, raise chickens, grow potatoes, just like my ancestors did in the old country."

"If you don't hedge, you will lose," Sam snarled.

"Then I'm no worse off, because five hundred is not escape money, Sam. We're old friends. I'd hoped you'd understand."

"I don't suppose you've considered anyone but yourself," Sam said. "That is typical of you. But I am a father. I cannot close my eyes without imagining Chinese hordes overrunning Nagasaki. My children are there. If I gamble all or nothing, and lose my entire stake, I may not get home in time. So the answer is all bets are off, Mick. My children come first."

He rolled up the window, nearly crushing my fingers, and drove off in a cloud of exhaust fumes.

I took the streetcar to the Royal, slipped in the back door. Choking on the smoke of cheap cigars, I stood in Pat Reilly's betting line. He glared through the bars of his cage.

"Jeez, I been looking for you."

"Well, I'm standing right in front of you."

"Two minutes to Jamaica Fourth," he said.

"The hell with that," I said. "Future book."

Pat lifted a leather-bound ledger from a drawer.

"Derby," I said.

He flipped pages.

"Economic," I said.

"That nag? Are you nuts? Fourteen to one, it says here. Today." He shrugged. "Tomorrow, who knows?"

I handed him five one hundred dollar bills.

He whistled. "You get a tip or something?"

"Just book it," I said, "split it into two tickets."

He pulled the crank on his ticket machine, punched in numbers, pulled the crank again.

"Should I drop a few bucks on Economic?" he asked.

"You're on your own, Pat."

"I got a feeling you know something. You're a sneaky player."

He handed me two tickets, both marked: Churchill Ninth, number 1006.

"That's Economic, right? Double check."

"Number a thousand and six," said Pat.

I snatched the black pen that was chained to the steel bars of his cage. On the back of one ticket I printed *Pay only to Michael Powers.* On the other I wrote: *Pay only to Sam Tanaka.*

I looked up at Reilly and said: "Now why were you looking for me?"

"Harry business," he said.

"I don't suppose I could conveniently be out of town?"

"Something brewing," he said.

"Besides beer?"

"Simple bag," he said.

A horseplayer in line behind me began grumbling.

"Serious Bobby," Pat said. "Rice Park."

"Right under the nose of the G-men."

"They never look out the windows," Pat said. "They're too busy shining their shoes. See, there's a Colored fellow up on Rondo. See Bobby, Wednesday, sundown, Rice Park."

The gambler behind me rushed toward another teller's cage, and shot me an angry look. The bell rang as a thousand miles away, horses burst from the gate in Jamaica, New York.

"The Colored now?" I said. "I thought they ran their own game."

"Caesar's empire is expanding," said Pat.

CHAPTER TWENTY FIVE

A certain Colored fellow ran a grocery shack on Rondo. He sold boot and ran a Friday night dice game in the side room. That was beneath Harry's notice, but his venture into numbers was not.

The numbers game was to guess the last three digits of yesterday's bank clearings, as printed in the Pioneer Press. I wondered if the editors realized how many "readers" just wanted to check that number.

The grocer's name was Louis, and he did not care to be called Lou, or so Serious Bobby said when he assigned me the job. I wondered if Harry was desperate, moving in on numbers games in the Colored neighborhoods.

I visited Louis at his Smart Variety store, which sold fruits and vegetables, canned goods, cigars, cigarettes, magazines, and his most popular item, popcorn made hot and fresh in a big glassy wagon. He sold a small bag for 2 cents. You'd see kids walking with red-and-white bags of popcorn on Rondo Street, good advertising for Smart Variety. Some of those schoolboys were also running numbers for Louis.

I timed my visit for 2 p.m. to avoid the school kids and the lunch crowd. "Shop Here, Be Smart" said a hand-lettered sign in the window, which listed specials on Libby's Canned Corned Beef, 19 cents, and Ivory Snow, two boxes for a quarter.

Only Louis was in the store. When I walked in, he was at a glass counter, penciling sums on a flattened paper bag. A pressed white shirt and gold cufflinks told me he was a prosperous man. He ignored my entrance. I suppose he figured a white guy could only be here to sell him something.

He was right about that.

I leaned over the counter and said: "Harry sent me."

"Uh huh," said Louis. He finally looked at me. "Popcorn?"

He handed me a bag of popcorn, warm and greasy, and led me through a curtain of beads and to his office. A huge American flag was nailed to the wall above a home-built desk. Battered five-gallon tin cans littered his office. I assumed they had once held bootleg gin. One wall was decorated with photos torn from boxing magazines. Every photo depicted a black prizefighter: Jack Johnson, Kid Chocolate, Panama Al Brown, and some I'd never heard of.

I settled into the chair across from that battered desk. I was there as diplomat, not to make nasty threats. Nasty was what happened if polite failed. Nasty was Swede Fanlund throwing a gasoline bomb through a store window at midnight.

"So you're one of them Green Lantern fellas," said Louis.

"I am."

I munched popcorn. "Fresh," I said. "Very good."

"You can get popcorn downtown," Louis said.

"Harry wants to be your numerical friend," I said.

"I was afraid of that."

"Friend and protector," I said. "Don't forget the protection angle. You're getting something in return. Look, Harry doesn't care how much boot you sell, but the numbers ..." I wagged my finger at him ... "that he takes personally."

"How personally?"

"A hundred to start..."

Louis whistled.

"But only ten percent of the rake," I said.

"Why the hell does he want to bother someone like me?"

"Harry's a fair man. These are the exact terms offered to whites and Chinese. You think the joints downtown are running for free?"

"I don't have a hundred," he said.

A bell rang up front. An old bent lady walked in.

"I'll be back," Louis said.

I tapped my feet. I ate popcorn. I looked past burglar bars, through a smudged window into a sunny alley. Three boys were shooting marbles in the dirt, using cigarettes as money.

Louis walked back through the bead curtain.

"I hear you're the neighborhood ..." I didn't want to say loan shark ... "banker," I said.

"Well you hear a lot of things," said Louis.

I rolled up the empty, greasy popcorn bag, pitched it toward the trash can.

"When Harry's your friend, you have no enemies," I said.

Louis's look of chagrin turned into a reluctant laugh.

"How does that work?" he asked.

"The word goes out. You're safe with Harry. Anybody who tries to rob you, threaten you, or shake you down, will next be seen in a wheelchair."

Louis huffed.

"Also, you'll see a big, note that I said *big*, improvement in the attitude of Rondo cops."

Louis bit his tongue.

"Or," I said. "You can take your chances."

At sundown, I delivered $75 in small bills to Serious Bobby, and kept $25 for myself.

This was the Mick Powers I liked. Nobody hurt, profit made. People could stop into Louis's shack and plunk a dime in hopes of a $70 score. The whole setup was protected by Harry, fair and square. The Rondo cops would get a weekly tip via Harry. The lottery winners would be paid, no welshing. My reputation with Harry would rise. I briefly thought of telling Jack that Harry was moving into Rondo numbers, but no. This job was clean and I wanted to keep it that way. I bought a Coney Dog, a detective magazine and a root beer and saved $24.50 for the future.

I figured I could to take it easy until Derby Day. I ran the dogs over to the Capitol lawn, came home, threw open the windows, took long, deep breaths of spring.

I climbed to the rooftop, sat in a lawn chair, admired the city's new skyline. Down there amid the cluster of apartments, churches, hotels and warehouses, Saint Paul was changing. It wasn't just a gritty steamboat port any more. Skyscrapers were rising in defiance of hard times. A bold new Art-Deco City Hall towered above the banks of Mississippi. Even taller was the First National Bank, topped by a big red-glowing number 1, which could be seen for miles around. It seemed that America, and Saint Paul too, were working on a brighter future.

I imagined the finish at Churchill, as Economic won by seven lengths and freed me from Saint Paul's gangs.

But then I ran out of optimism, like a car runs out of gas. I had to admit it wasn't all peachy. I had made good money this afternoon, but Louis was now trapped in The Deal. He would regret it someday. The gangsters would squeeze all the profits out the numbers game, just as they'd done to bootleggers. Harry's fee would soon jump to 20 percent. Now and then a "special tax" would be levied on guys like Louis. He'd be required to vote a certain way in city elections, and to pressure friends and family to follow. He'd have to nail up posters for gangland's candidates, and recommend them up to his customers. After a while, the Rondo cops would be back in Louis's store with their hands out. The promises of "protection" would prove to be just words.

Welcome to gangland, Louis. May you survive and not be too sorry.

I sat back in that lawn chair, drank a big lemonade and read True Detective Mysteries, April edition. I worked through the main story, about a supposed …

APE MAN WHO TERRORIZED EUROPE

The magazine featured stories about bank robberies in Denver and thrill killings in California. The stories were meant for the entertainment of the rubes, of course. The basic facts might be true but the stories were puffed up with lurid drama. All the women were beautiful, all the men were tough, all the victims bloodied.

I lit my pipe, blew smoke into the breeze, flipped pages until I saw familiar faces. It was a spread of wanted men, headlined:

THE LINEUP

The first two mugs were Little Shorty Gold Teeth and Boris Karloff.

Except their names were Fred Barker and Alvin Karpis.

Their mug shots topped the page because they had killed the sheriff of West Plains, Missouri. Anybody seeing them was to contact Mrs. C.R. Kelly, of West Plains. She was the widow, and now sheriff. The reward was $1200 each.

The true identity of "Pa Anderson" and "Ma Anderson" was anybody's guess. But there was no doubt the "Anderson brothers" were notorious killers from Missouri. I rose from the lawn chair but had a dizzy spell and sat back down. So these guys weren't the bloodless bank robbers I'd imagined them to be. Missouri wanted to hang them, which meant Barker and Karpis had nothing lose by killing anyone they suspected of talking to the cops. Sadie and Rose may have been their first victims in Saint Paul, but wouldn't be the last.

I ran down to my apartment, threw peanuts for the dogs, borrowed a jalopy from Herb's Garage, and drove to Billy McAmbly's house.

Billy lived in South Saint Paul, where the homes were downwind of the stinking stockyards and sold cheap. His house was a tilting yellow pile of clapboards, backed up to freight yards. There were three bedrooms, the smallest for him, one for his four boys and another for his two girls. His wife had been dead two years, from an infection doctors could not identify. Billy had doubled down on his drinking the day after the funeral.

Behind his house clanked railroad cars taking cattle to slaughter. Billy lived in mortal fear that one of his boys would be cut in two by a train. He could not keep them from playing on the tracks.

I found Billy in his back yard, drinking beer and listening to the Saint Louis Cardinals on the radio. Perhaps during pioneer days, this yard sprouted grass, but Billy's kids had trampled it to hard-packed earth.

"Cards losing. You have the Cards?" Billy asked.

"I don't bet baseball," I said. "Remember the Black Sox? It ain't honest."

"What brings you to the South Side?"

He was sitting in a kitchen chair and kicked a milk carton in my direction. I sat on it. His fuzzy-sounding tabletop radio lay in the dirt beside him, connected by extension cord through the kitchen window.

Was that a baseball broadcast, or signals from Mars? I couldn't tell through the static.

"Where's the kids?" I asked.

"Aunt Jo took 'em to the movies. She's a saint. It's the only way I get an afternoon's peace."

Behind us, a locomotive chugged. Freight cars coupled with a heavy clank, and were dragged off with metallic protests from squeaky wheels and loose track.

"Look at this," I said, and folded the magazine back to the photos of Barker and Karpis.

"Yeah, so."

"First two guys."

"I see them."

"Living over on Robert Street."

"Well, well."

"They're the Hudson robbers. For sure. Probably they torched the Burned Ladies, or maybe just set them up. Certainly they held up the North American Bank over in Minneapolis. And they left a dead sheriff in Missouri."

Billy sipped from a bottle of Hamm's and studied the photos.

"These ain't just yeggs, Billy, these are stone-eyed killers."

"Robert Street you said?"

"I've been in the house."

"You what?"

"I haven't seen Barker and Karpis there, but I ate fried chicken at their kitchen table. These guys travel with an old man and an old woman. The woman could be the mother of Fred Barker. They look similar and both talk like Okies."

"These dumb hicks led the North American?"

"I'm sure of it, Billy."

He set the beer bottle on hard packed earth.

"Well, Mickey," he said, "you've got a problem."

"How so?"

"If they robbed the North American, they're connected to Harry Sawyer. I hear that job was laid out by Harry's jug marker.

And if they're connected to Harry Sawyer, they've bought an umbrella from Big Ryan."

He leaned back in the chair.

"And it never rains under Big Ryan's umbrella. So good luck collecting the reward, if that's what was on your mind."

I tapped the magazine. "They'll be hanged. The sheriff's widow wants revenge."

"Sheriff's widow has no powers of arrest here. Her extradition order gets tossed into Big Ryan's wastebasket."

He snapped off the radio. "Cards heading for a lousy year."

I said: "Those women didn't have to burn, Billy. We used to have rules about women. Rose and Sadie could have been slapped around, put on a train bound for the coast, and ordered never to come back under pain of death. That's the way we handled it in the old days."

"But you bootleg fellas," Billy said, "were only facing a couple of months in the workhouse. The hangman's waiting for these guys. That changes the stakes. Oh hell's bells, in Saint Paul, even cop killers are untouchable. Who's going to enforce the law? Big Ryan? Irish Kinkead? Don't make me laugh, I'll end up in tears."

I drove out Robert Street, a dangerous drive, because I was thinking so hard I barely saw the traffic. There was no question of asking Billy to make the arrest. He was a desk cop, this was too dangerous, and his first duty was to those six children. Anyway, uniformed cops often arrested a gangster, only to have detectives free him for a price.

I had a vision of Barker and Karpis, in handcuffs, on a train bound for Missouri. How I would accomplish that I didn't know. But time was short. Soon, Fred Barker would figure out I'd been spying on him and his girlfriend. Alvin Karpis would discover I was a regular visitor at the Saint Paul Police Station, and had a close friend on the force. I hid the jalopy behind a garage a half-block up the alley from the "Andersons." I lay the shiny pistol Jack had given me on the front seat. The windows fogged and I had to roll them down and let in the chill.

I waited for hours, smoking my pipe, worrying about my dogs, wondering whether I'd made a bad bet on the Derby, imagining that widow-sheriff in Missouri handing me the reward. Near midnight I was fighting the sleepy shivers when Alvin Karpis, driving his DeSoto, parked it in the garage, and let himself in to a dark house via the kitchen door.

Maybe twenty minutes later, Pop Anderson stumbled up the alley. He let himself in through the kitchen door and lights flashed on.

I had a longshot chance, but it was the only ticket I had. The Barker-Karpis house was just across the city line, in the town of West Saint Paul. That meant it was in Dakota County, two blocks away from the Big Ryan's jurisdiction.

Saint Paul's epic corruption often caused trouble in border towns, and some of the cops out there resented it. There was a chance that the Dakota County sheriff would raid the Barker house, especially if the tip came Billy McAmbly. But I needed to be certain that both Fred and Karpis were home, and preferably sleeping. The arrest of one, but not the other, would mean certain death for the tipster.

I pocketed the pistol and walked the alley, staying in the night shadows. I flattened against the garage wall, maybe thirty feet from the kitchen windows.

Out those windows came shouts.

"God damn it woman!"

That was Pop's voice.

"Don't curse me, you old goat," Ma Barker said.

"Get up and fix my eggs," Pop demanded.

I heard the sound of something heavy, maybe a frying pan, hitting the wall. Grunts and noises of a struggle followed, then came a long silence.

It was broken by Pop's scream: "You whorry old bitch."

"Fix you own eggs."

That was the Chicago voice, Karpis.

The door opened and Pop Anderson was shoved out.

"Go for a walk," Karpis growled. "Come back sober."

Karpis shut the door, parted the curtain and watched. Pop held a middle finger up to the glass, in front of Karpis' face, then stumbled down the stairs. He threw a rock, but it bounced harmless off the house.

It wasn't hard to follow Pop in those shadowy alleys. He turned in at The Last Roundup speakeasy. I retreated to my car, lit my pipe, and figured my strategy.

I was certain Karpis and Barker were about to blow town. Harry was negotiating the ransom of the stolen securities with Pinkertons who were agents for the North American Bank. Once the bonds had been ransomed for cash, robbers typically beat it and cooled off in Chicago or Reno.

When Barker and Karpis hit the road, they would no longer be under Big Ryan's umbrella. I could have the Wisconsin cops waiting for them as they crossed the Saint Croix.

If the Barker-Karpis gang headed for Reno, getting them arrested would be trickier. But there's only one road out there, Federal Twelve, and I could follow miles behind and check the motor courts. Probably they'd pull over to sleep somewhere in South Dakota. A late night visit to the sheriff, with the magazine in hand, would accomplish my goal. Barker and Karpis would go on trial in Missouri, for murdering the sheriff. The Burned Ladies would take be character witnesses, taking the stand in their corner of Hell.

I wouldn't be a level guy anymore, and that bothered me. I had been on the side of the bootleggers for a dozen years now, and made a decent living . My old man labored a year for the kind of money I made in a few months. But money wasn't the only thing. We bootleggers were the good guys. You paid, we delivered. It was the cops who spit out of both sides of their mouths, taking their salary from the public, and bribes from anyone they could squeeze.

Cops were the enemy, and a stool pigeon the lowest form of life. But in arranging the murder of those hapless prostitutes, Barker and Karpis had violated the code. I owed them nothing.

I made myself wait in that car for shivering half an hour before I crossed the dark street and entered The Last Roundup. Pop Anderson was drunk, and I intended to get him to reveal whether both Fred and Karpis were home.

In the dim light, a back table was filled with stockyards men, playing poker and drinking. The long bar was empty except for Pop. I walked past him as if on the way to the men's room, then faked a surprised halt.

"Why Mister Anderson," I said.

He looked up at me. He was so drunk, I might have been Babe Ruth, Thomas Edison, Albert Einstein.

I held out a friendly hand.

"Patrick Powell," I said. "Remember?"

"Yesh," he managed to say.

His droopy white mustache was wet with beer foam. Before him stood a mug of spiked near-beer and a shallow glass of golden liquor.

"We had a talk, remember?"

"Shertainly," he said, eyes out of focus.

I didn't get a chance to sneak in a question about whether Fred was at home. The speakeasy door opened and in rushed a blast of chill night.

In walked Alvin Karpis, wearing a loose black silk shirt over fishing trousers. A thunderbolt of fear rumbled through me, but Karpis just nodded at me and focused on the old man.

"Drink up," Karpis said to Pop. "Ma wants you home."

"Damn that old Bible-thumping bitch," muttered Pop.

"You know Ma hates bad language," Karpis chided him.

I looked Karpis over. He was a short, very thin man whose clothes hung off him as if he were a coatrack. His black hair was greased straight back. And his eyes! They were dark, the cold merciless eyes of a lizard.

"Come on, Pop," Karpis said, and dug into his pocket for a coin to leave the bartender. He muscled the old fellow off the stool.

"Get your hands off me," shouted Pop.

The poker players looked up, went back to their game.

"He's cantankerous when he drinks," Karpis said to me. "He sobers up good."

Karpis strong-armed Pop toward the front door, and the old fellow turned and pointed at me.

"I remember you," he declared, as Karpis pushed him out the door.

I jammed my hand into my pocket and gripped that pistol, but the door slammed and Karpis walked the old man home.

CHAPTER TWENTY SIX

I was puffing my pipe, staring out the windows at the weaving traffic when a Yellow Cab pulled into the parking lot. Out of it popped Janie. Instead of descending to her cellar entrance, she pushed into the lobby. The dogs yipped as she climbed the stairs. I held the door open.

"So, mister smarty," she said. "I've figured out the Burned Ladies."

"Just like that?"

She snapped her fingers. "Just like that. Apparently your investigation didn't go far enough." She squatted to pet Snowflake.

"Do tell," I said.

"Well," she said, and gave Hula Girl equal petting, "I take a lot of cabs. If you ask enough cab drivers you'll eventually find ..."

She looked proud of herself. " ... that Jack Peifer hustled them into his car."

"When?"

"That Saturday night. Technically, it was Sunday, after two in the morning. My cabbie happened to be on duty, third in line. Jack's Packard entered the circular driveway. Everybody at the Hotel Saint Paul knows that Packard convertible, there's only one like it in town. Rose and Sadie were waiting in the lobby. Boom, they got in and he drove away."

"How can you be sure it was Peifer driving?"

"The Packard. Olive Green. With light pin-striping, a custom job, right?"

"So you're not sure it was Peifer driving."

"Oh yes I am sure."

"He didn't get out? He sat in the car and the women walked out of the lobby?"

"Ran out of the lobby."

"Did your cabbie get a look at the Packard's driver? How sure is he it was Peifer?"

"Pretty sure."

"Not good enough. It was cold, it was snowing, the windows were probably frosted."

"You're not going to talk me out of it," Janie said and stood tall. "Jack Peifer picked them up…"

"Or his driver did."

"Oh, hogwash. His driver's Japanese, shorter and huskier, with a crew-cut. Jack is bigger, paler, and has long greasy hair. They don't look alike."

"At two in the morning? Was your cabbie sober?"

"Powers, you are starting to make me angry."

"You see how hard it is, Janie, to prove anything?"

"I'm leaving."

"Wait," I said. "Coffee."

I boiled water. Janie stood fuming at the big windows that overlooked the crazy intersection at Seven Corners. Neither of us said a thing for maybe five minutes. Snowflake lay on his viewing stand, and Janie absently stroked his regal white head. Hula Girl stayed in the kitchen with me, vigilant in case a speck of food might fall from the counter.

I was experimenting with a French Press. I brought that frothing carafe into the living room, along with shortbread cookies and chocolate crackers. When I lay the tray down, Janie wandered over. She glanced at the wounded speaker of my radio and said:

"When are you going to get that fixed?"

"Now a tube's out."

"They sell tubes," she said.

She sat across from me in one of my grandmother's elegant dining room chairs. I sipped coffee.

"I think this is the answer," I said.

"I'm glad you agree," said Janie.

"No, I mean the French press, it's the coffee answer. The Burned Ladies, you've got a motivation problem. That's what's missing. Motivation for Jack to take that kind of risk. It's bright at the hotel's entrance. There are bound to be witnesses."

"That's where you come in," she said. "You know gangland, I don't."

"What doesn't make sense," I said, "is that the women went to the police station for the purpose of ratting out the Hudson robbers. But those are Harry's boys. Harry and Jack are rivals. So Jack was in no danger, and had zero motivation to burn those girls."

She picked up a shortbread cookie. She asked: "Wouldn't Jack's driver know if Jack had taken the Packard out at two in the morning? Sam. Doesn't he live at the Hollyhocks?"

"Sam and I are on the outs now. Gambling quarrel. Even so, Janie, he'd never betray his boss, innocent or guilty. I know Sam. He wouldn't do it."

"I think I'm being lied to, Powers."

"Assume that. Always."

Janie bit into that cookie, then looked at it, as if some stranger had put it in her hand.

"I'm being lied to, all right," she said. "By you."

"There are things I can't tell you."

"Damn you."

"Besides," I said, "your news about Jack messes up my theory.

The Hudson gang. I need them to be guilty of arranging the murder of the Burned Ladies."

"Now who's building a shoddy case. Based on what did you say? You *need* them to be guilty?"

"Jack has no motive," I said.

"The Packard was there. They got into it. Period."

"What have you told Goggles?"

"Nothing. This is my story. Mine. I'm pitching it to the detective mags."

"Oh boy."

"Powers, it was my story from Day One. I was down on the levee before you were. Me, I smelled the stench, the kind of stench that gets into your bloodstream. I saw them drag the corpses from the car when it was still smoking. I'm the one who found out Peifer paid for the funeral."

She sipped coffee. "That's why he paid for the funeral. Because he killed them. He feels guilty. All I need is one gang source and one cop source."

"People like you get a bullet in the head."

"Goggles has been doing it ten years." She stood up. "I suppose that's okay because Goggles is a man."

Hula Girl stood alarmed at the door.

"I like you, Janie. That's why I'm not going to help you. Go do something else. Go find the Lindbergh baby. Or learn to fly, it worked for Amelia Earhart."

"You know, Powers," she said. "You're irritating sometimes."

At the doorway she turned and said, "Thank you for the coffee, and you're right, it's better from a French press. But that's all you're right about."

There were two dirty words I wasn't ready to say in front of Janie: Barker and Karpis. Sure, I wanted to help her get off the damn women's pages. If someday Barker and Karpis were arrested, I would give Janie an inside tip, and she could break the news. But I couldn't risk her barging into the police station with those names on her lips, not while Barker and Karpis were loose.

Her news about Jack Peifer wrapped up my theory. Rose and Sadie show up at the police station, trying to collect the reward; the cops tell Harry; he tells Barker and Karpis; they hire Swede and Rico to do their dirty work.

No way would Rose and Sadie get into a car with thugs they didn't know.

However, they would get into a car with Jack. As the city's whoremaster, he was a man they needed to trust. Jack delivered them to Swede and Rico on the dark cold levee, with the blizzard moving in from the Dakotas.

But why would Jack take the risk of a double murder rap? That question I couldn't answer.

At the Portland Pet Shop, I bought a shiny new cage and two matched parakeets. I drove them over to Myrtle's apartment and knocked, but she wasn't home. I set their covered cage at the landing nearest her door. The birds squawked and fussed, and I got them a tin cup of water from the backyard spigot.

I tracked down Myrtle at a speakeasy on Grand Avenue, its specialty being fried walleye and beer. This was Myrtle's hangout with her Free Love Group. They were women of independent spirit, who planned trips together, and occasionally even embarked on them. At a smoky corner table filled with eight women, Myrtle and her best friend Loretta were leading a debate: should they cruise to the boozy Bahamas or tavern-crawl through sleazy Tijuana? I slipped into the hallway and phoned the Hollyhocks, but found that Saph the bouncer, and not Sam, was in charge of the house.

Myrtle, on her way to the ladies room, bumped into me in that dark hallway. She hadn't noticed me walk in, so feverish was her dream of a tropical vacation.

"What are you doing here?"

"Looking for you."

"Well aren't you the swell detective."

"Question," I said.

"Answer," she said.

"Outside," I said.

We stepped out into the vague sunshine. Myrtle wore a dark dress that showed off her soft, fleshy shoulders. She leaned against the brick wall and lit a cigarette.

"Go ahead," she said. "Bite my head off."

"For what?"

"For letting the phone ring."

"Wasn't me," I said. "Haven't called you."

She blew smoke into the wind. "Why did you track me down?"

"What if Jack Peifer called for the Burned Ladies the night they were killed?"

She glanced up and down the alley. "Sure," she said. "I could see it."

"Why?"

She whispered: "Denver … Mint."

And then in full voice she said: "Let's not speak those unholy words ever again. It was ten years ago, but those words are still trouble in this town. The Federals are like elephants, they never forget."

"Okay, but…"

"Rose's husband was one of the stickup guys. Jack did the laundry. So that's the connection. Maybe Jack picked Rose up for old time's sake. What more do you need from me?"

"Jack did the laundry?" I said. "Jack had two hundred grand

sitting around in the bottom drawer?"

"A piece of the laundry," Myrtle said.

"Still…"

"That's where our favorite beer-brewing banker comes in," said Myrtle. "You know the name. Don't make me say it. The old banker had the cash, Jack was a pimp with all the right connections. How do you think Jack ended up buying a mansion and turning it into a casino? How do you think the old banker bought an entire brewery, including the trucks and barrels?"

I kissed her on the cheek. "You're going home after this meeting right? I left a present at your door."

"What kind of present?"

"The kind with wings."

She cocked her head at me, almost like a bird does.

I said: "I bought you a matched set of parakeets."

"Oh no you didn't."

"I did."

"Take 'em away. I can't use a pet right now."

"Two. One bird gets lonely, and dies sooner, don't you know?"

"Mick, I'm going on vacation soon. I can't have a bird."

"I'll take care of 'em when you're gone."

Her face flushed. "Mick, take them away, I mean it. No more birds. All they do is die on you. No birds. Final."

"All right, all right. I'll take 'em back."

She sighed. "Thank you."

"Maybe sometime before you leave on vacation, we'll have dinner at the Lowry."

"Sure, maybe. Call me."

"You're not answering the phone."

"That's right," she said.

CHAPTER TWENTY SEVEN

"Some citizens in our Land of Opportunity," said Agent Roland Heater, "loathe the notion of a federal police force."

A blunt cheroot waggled in his teeth.

"So for us to go out of jurisdiction, stepping on toes, the Director would frown. Nix on these local hijinks. Bring me a federal crime."

"The Denver Mint. How much more federal can it get?"

He sputtered. "Ancient history."

"I heard the Mint dough was laundered in Saint Paul. Through a certain nightclub operator."

"Tell me something I don't know."

I sat with a detective magazine in my lap, flicked its pages.

"Rose Perry," I said. "Her husband robbed the Mint."

Heater plucked the cheroot out of his mouth and yawned. "Now you'll try to drag Papa Alt into this."

I played innocent. "Oh? Papa Alt? Denver Mint?"

"Where were you in 1922?"

"Making runs from Winnipeg. Heater, I've got something big for you."

"Oh sure." He swung his boots off the desk and stood in front of the Stars and Stripes. Nailed to the wall beside that flag was a photo of a stern J. Edgar Hoover.

"Okay, hell, it's all over town," Heater said. "Papa Alt's River

State Bank. They say that's where the Mint money was laundered. Jack Peifer was a middle man. He didn't have enough soap to do the laundry."

I played dumb. "This is known?"

"Rumored," said Heater. "And we can't build a case on rumors. Look, the Director doesn't care about the Denver Mint, no more than he cares about the Civil War. It's the Lindbergh Kidnapping now, and I'm glad we're a thousand miles from New Jersey. If the Director rescues the Lindbergh baby, he'll be splashed on magazine covers around the world."

"So," I said, "Papa Alt laundered Mint money. Using those profits, bought a ruined brewery for dimes on the dollar. He bribed the cops, made a fortune on illegal beer. Now he's a big political donor, buddies with Franklin Roosevelt. And the Justice Department is afraid to piss him off."

"Behind every fortune is a crime, Powers. Bring me strong evidence of a federal crime, and I'll take it to the Grand Jury."

He stared me down. "You didn't come here for a history lesson."

I flipped the magazine onto his desk. "There's two sheriff killers," I said. "Ten blocks away. Their wanted posters are in that magazine."

"I've heard the Irish were thick skulled. Is it the whiskey or the potatoes? No juris-dick-shun. Is that word too long for you? We're not bounty hunters, we're bound by the law here, Powers."

He sighed. "Day like today, a man ought to be fishing. Do you fish?"

"I'm fishing right now," I said. "Tug on the line. Make the bobber sink."

Heater walked to the sunny window, his back turned to me. The only eyes I could see belonged to J. Edgar Hoover.

Heater lit a cheroot and said: "Call me if you find the Lindbergh

Baby."

I went home to see how my dogs liked their new pets, Charles and Amelia. I knocked at Little Elmer's door. The boy, on crutches, said he couldn't get upstairs to feed the birds.

"Elmer," I said, "you've been getting up stairs like a champ."

"I'm not feeling that good anymore, Mr. Powers," he said. Tears rimmed his eyes but he was too proud to shed them.

What can you say to a ten-year-old boy facing a dark, crippled future? He might never make love to a woman, have children, find a job, drive a car. He might die gasping for air in an iron lung.

"Your mama is a good woman," I said, stupid, groping for anything. "She'll always take care of you."

"Can I play with your gun?" Elmer asked.

"My what?"

"Mama says you're a dirty low-down gangster. She says I should watch out, because you shoot little children with your tommygun."

"No," I said, "No tommygun."

"Aw shit," said Little Elmer.

"I'll tell you what," I said. I pulled my pocket pistol, opened the cylinder, dropped four brass rounds into my palm. Four. I counted them twice. I spun the cylinder and looked: five empty chambers. I handed Elmer the pistol.

"Now you're a dirty low-down gangster too," I said.

He twirled the cylinders. His eyes glowed.

"Can I rob a bank with this?" he asked.

"No, but I'll pay you a twenty-five cent ransom for it," I said.

He was a pouty little boy when he handed back the revolver.

Upstairs, I phoned an ad in to the Daily News, two parakeets for a dollar. The birds could have been stuffed animals for all Snowflake cared. Hula Girl resented their intrusion and stalked them whenever she was bored. I liked their cheerful chirping, but my schedule was too dicey to keep birds without Elmer's help.

It was the loveliest of spring days, with seven months of fine weather ahead. Anticipating the season's first thunderstorms, I threw the windows wide open. The caged birds chirped, happy for parakeet weather at last. Snowflake gazed out the windows, mesmerized by the traffic at Seven Corners. Did the dodging cars looked like sheep to him? I lit the flame under the kettle and waited for the whistle.

Four stories down there, Mrs. Strutz pushed her dirty tin garbage can to the curb. She tossed a sour look toward my windows. The poor woman could hear my every footfall. I was sure she'd be pleased if I died and lay rotting for years in blessed silence. She hated me, but we were Midwesterners after all. I gave her a friendly wave.

The Derby was only ten days away, so I sat on the sunny couch and worked on fractional times. I was so absorbed I heard no one mounting the stairs, and the knock on the door turned out to be Janie.

She clutched the afternoon Dispatch under her arm and a sheaf of papers in her hand.

She shoved the newspaper at me.

"Mahoney wins the primary," she said.

"That red communist bastard," I said. "If he's mayor, throw the cards up in the air."

"What are you talking about?"

"Mahoney will name gangster names."

"I like him," said Janie. "He's progressive. He's for the working girl."

"Oh really."

"Yes, we newsies are in unions too, you know."

"He'll be the death of me."

"How so?"

"Janie, did you see the crowd that turned our for Roosevelt?"

"I was at work. On my weddings. For your information, women reporters don't cover presidential candidates. That's for the Old Boys Club."

"No mayor is going to clean up this dirty town," I said. "But Mahoney is the, he's like the watch-a-call of change. The watchdog of change, no offense to my dogs."

I drew my finger across my throat.

"Oh," said Janie, skeptical.

"If there's a repeal, the river of money doesn't flow here anymore."

"The repeal of a constitutional amendment? That's never been done."

"Yeah, well, nobody flew the Atlantic before Lindbergh, either."

"Oh Powers," she said. She sat at the kitchen table while I rescued the whistling tea kettle. With a pencil, she began correcting what she had typed.

Her headline said:

TRAGEDY OF THE BURNED LADIES

"You're publishing this under your own name?"

She nodded.

"Where?" I asked.

"In whatever magazine buys it."

"Go anonymous and I'll help you."

"Anonymous? I'm trying to build a career."

"Who's going to supply the lurid photos?"

"Croaker," she said.

"Who's Croaker?"

"He took photos of the Sadie and Rose death car. If you think the pictures we publish are gruesome, you should see the ones in

Croaker's darkroom. He's a ghoul."

I started to read over Janie's shoulder. Hula Girl nudged me for dinner and I fed both dogs in the kitchen. Janie followed me.

"That's not good for dogs, is it? Sausage?"

"Oh I don't know, it seems to have the canine seal of approval."

Janie frowned. "Please read and stop putting it off, Powers."

I sat at the kitchen table, sunlight streaming in over the Cathedral's dome, and read Janie's story.

"Inspector Crumley?" I said. "You called Crumley for comment? Janie, jeez."

"Jeez what?"

"You can't trust the police."

"It's only a quote," she said.

I put the manuscript down. "Sadie and Rose trusted the police. Janie, this is hopelessly naive."

She glared at me. "Fuck you, Powers."

She snatched the manuscript out of my hands and stumbled toward the door.

"Janie!" I shouted.

"Crumley put those girls on the spot," she said. "I can't prove it, but…"

"Yes, somebody at the police station double-crossed those women. But we'll never know who. It could have been Big Ryan, it could have been any cop in the station. It could have been a gossip who saw them walking down the steps."

"But only the cops knew Sadie and Rose were ratting out the Hudson gang. I'm putting Crumley on the record, Powers. That's how it's done. You don't know the first thing about reporting. I don't know why I bothered to come up here."

"Because I'm your only source in gangland, that's why."

She slammed the door and stomped down the stairs.

The next morning I started my loaner jalopy but idled in the parking lot, unable to get going. It was a dark, cloudy day, and I was sunk in my own personal fog. I stared at Janie's basement apartment, at the chipped brick facade, the barred windows that made it look like a prison, the chintz curtains she'd put up for spring. She was an earnest kid, and she didn't have a chance.

Inspector James Crumley. I couldn't shake him out of my mind. Crumley, a glutton for food, booze and gossip. Gangsters would soon hear that Janie was poking around. She was defenseless in that basement apartment. Two kicks on the door, and the killers would be in there.

I had to get Barker and Karpis out of town before they realized Janie was on to them. So I drove my loaner jalopy over to Billy McAmbly's. The clouds had turned black and blue, threatening rain. Billy was in back, on a wobbly, paint-spattered wood ladder. His son Kevin, a tall muscular teenager, held the ladder steady, his foot shod in baseball cleats. Kevin wore basketball shorts and a red sweatshirt that said SACRED HEART in gold letters.

"Uncle Mick," Kevin said.

"Take a break," I said.

"I'm doing all the work up here," Billy shouted down.

"You've got a driver's license?" I asked Kevin.

"Yup."

I palmed him a dollar. "Take my car. Get donuts."

Billy, his white painters outfit splashed with yellow, climbed down the ladder.

"That kid," said Billy. "Any excuse to drive a car."

As Kevin bounded down the alley, I pulled the detective magazine out of my back pocket. I showed Billy the photos to remind him who Barker and Karpis were.

He wiped his hands with a paint rag.

"Do you have friends in Dakota County?" I asked.

"You mean the sheriff?"

"Anybody who could pull off a raid. These are bad, bad guys Billy."

"I'd see Sharkey first."

"Who's Sharkey?"

"West Saint Paul cops."

"There's how many cops in that burg, five?"

"Still, you don't go over their heads."

"Sharkey's honest?"

Billy shrugged. "He'll walk past a speakeasy. But basically, he's solid."

"Then I'll see Sharkey. I can use your name?"

"If you've got to."

I rolled the magazine into my pocket and backed away.

"Hey, the donuts?" Billy said.

"Gotta go," I said. "No time."

Only then did I realize that Kevin McAmbly had taken off in my car.

The wait for Kevin delayed me by a half hour, but finally I tossed a wax-paper bag of crullers into the passenger seat and zoomed off. My purpose was to see Sergeant Sharkey at the West Saint Paul police station. It was an uphill drive over the long steep banks of the Mississippi. When I crested that bank, I was surprised to see six police cars, parked at odd angles, near the Barker-Karpis house.

I circled the block. Two Dakota County sheriff's cars had cut off the alleyway. I parked and hustled to the barber shop across the street. It wasn't open yet and I huddled in the doorway. The West Saint Paul cops were represented by both their squad cars. Other marked cars belonged to the Saint Paul Police. I also recognized Bulldog McMullen's battered Dodge.

When I realized nobody would be brought out in handcuffs, I joined a crowd of neighbors in front of the house. Bulldog McMullen hustled down the stairs, ignoring us, and ran back into the house with a crowbar.

The neighbors told me that just after dawn the "Andersons" had packed two cars with suitcases, a console radio and a few pieces of furniture. Karpis drove the DeSoto, with Ma Barker, mink-wrapped, in the passenger seat. Pop followed solo, driving the old Essex. The neighbors knew Fred as the wiry little guy with red hair and gold teeth. Nobody had seen him in days. That meant, I figured, he was staying with Paula.

Huge raindrops began to fall from dark, dark clouds. I could hear the cops in the house, tearing up the floorboards. I wandered back to my car and sat there, depressed, as rain bombs spattered the windshield.

When I arrived home, Pat Reilly was sitting in his truck in my parking space. I had the exact same feeling as when I'd come home, back in my married days, to see a debt collector at my door. It was pouring rain, so I talked to him from my car.

"Downtown," said Pat. "You're a wanted man."

He sneered. "Cheer up. The Sea Lion is flapping his flippers. Work is hard to find."

He started the truck.

"Save gas," he said. "Ride with me."

I hustled through the rain and into the passenger seat. Pat ground that truck downhill and through the flood at Seven Corners. It seemed the whole mess of gin joints, dice rooms and bordellos might be washed into the Mississippi.

"Who you got in the Derby?" he asked.

"You know my money's on Economic. But I'm starting to wish I'd backed Burgoo King."

I wanted to throw Pat off. Burgoo King was a good horse but the odds would be down in sucker territory.

"That nag?" Pat said. "That's what your magic numbers say?"

"A winner in every race," I said.

"I heard you and Sam was going to Louisville."

I shrugged.

He said: "I might see you down there, where you staying?"

"That's up to Sam," I said.

"You guys ought to set up a syndicate. See Harry about that. I told him you guys win all the time. I keep telling him, you got a head for numbers, you're a horse genius."

I grunted.

We arrived at the Green Lantern's muddy parking lot and pushed in through the back door. Bess took my dripping jacket and avoided my eyes. Pat slipped behind the bar and tied on his white apron. I passed into the dark hallway that led to Harry's office. I heard men talking.

I opened the door with sweaty palms.

Alvin Karpis stared at me. Around his greasy hair was a halo provided by a single glaring bulb. Everything else was in shadow.

"This is the guy?" said Karpis out of the side of his mouth.

Harry said: "Yep."

Karpis shot me a nasty look. "How do you know the old man?" he demanded.

"What old man?"

"It's okay," Harry said. "We're all level here."

"I'll ask one last time," said Karpis. "How do you know old Pop?"

"Met him in a barber shop," I said.

"Yeah, and then what?"

"Went for a drink," I said.

"And then what?"

"I asked if he wanted to partner on a whiskey deal. He dressed good, like he had money, that was all."

"You always get your hair cut in West Saint Paul?" Karpis asked. "What's wrong with the barbers downtown?"

"I'm looking to move out there. I've got dogs. I'd like to get out of the apartment. They need a yard."

"You sound full of shit to me, but if Harry says you're level…" Karpis shrugged. He dug into his pocket for a key and threw it to me.

"Blue Chevy," he said. "Parked out back. Take orders from Harry. Don't screw up."

Karpis, in straw hat and shirtsleeves, brushed past me and closed the door.

"I don't need that guy around," said Harry, and nipped from a pint bottle. He sat slovenly at his desk, wrinkled shirt, smelly bare feet, as if he'd been there all night.

"What am I doing?" I said.

"You know the place I use over there?"

"What place?"

"Over there. The hospital."

"You mean the Jung Sanitarium."

"Yeah, that place. Over there."

"Okay."

"Take the old man over for a checkup. He needs to get sober."

"I see."

"He'll stay a few days. We're stashing him, that's all."

"Where's the old man now?"

"Tommy's shop. Drive him across the river in the blue Chevy. I doubt the cops will stop you, but if they do, have 'em call …" he drank … "You're under Big Ryan's umbrella. It ain't raining a drop."

I started up the blue Chevy. It purred like it had just been tuned up. I felt like I had been knocked cold and left in a dark alley. I'd hoped Saint Paul had gotten rid of Karpis but there he was brazen, within a block of the police station. Janie was safe in the newsroom for now, but I promised myself that I'd soon hustle her out of town. She was too deep in it. Damn her for calling Crumley.

I drove four rain-slicked blocks to Emerald Radio, wedged that Chevy down the alley and parked in front of Filben's magic self-rising door. I stumbled into the dark warehouse, tripping over a slot machine, and found Pop Anderson drunk and cowering in Filben's office.

"Old man," I said. "It's all right. We got you set up in a hospital. You're going to be Arthur Smiley for a few days. Come on, think of all those pretty nurses."

He was so drunk he could hardly stand. Filben appeared behind me and together we manned Pop through the warehouse. Pop, bent double, threw up in the alley.

"He'll be all right," I said to Filben. "He's going for the cure at Harry's Sanitarium."

"I was never here," said Filben. He retreated into his warehouse as I pushed Pop through the rain. "I don't know anybody named Harry," Filben called. His magic door closed.

As the rain retreated to a miserable drizzle, I drove Pop out Federal Twelve and across the Hudson Bridge. He slumped, sick, silent and stinky, in the passenger seat.

This errand made sense to me. Karpis had stashed Ma Barker somewhere. Since the cops would be looking for Ma and Pop together, Karpis had separated them, arranging with Harry to cool out the old man at the Jung. Those Jung doctors dried out people all the time, and to them, Pop Anderson was just another Saint Paul drunk.

I settled it all in my head. In an hour I would be idling this

Chevy outside the Daily News, waiting for Janie. I began to calm down. The Chevy had no radio, so I mentally worked Churchill fractionals to pass the time. I imagined that I would somehow, despite it all, make it to Louisville for the Derby. Harry had not mentioned the fee I would earn for today's mission, but he could be a generous guy.

Or, he could forget to pay you at all.

I drove past Hudson and up the face of the riverbank. The landscape turned to farms and I drove down a rough county road, swerving around deep puddles.

On a hill ahead of us, the Jung Sanitarium was set like a jewel amid the muddy, stubbly, black-earth fields. Up the winding road I drove and reached out to shake Pop's shoulder.

"Time to get well," I said.

Eyes closed, he belched.

The Sanitarium was like a castle behind stone pillars and a black iron gate. In front of that gate idled a long dark Lincoln. I stopped and honked, expecting it to move.

Two guys emerged: Swede Fanlund and his buddy Rico.

Rico carried a sawed-off, double barrel shotgun.

I sat stone paralyzed.

Swede had the sleeves of his blue mechanic's uniform rolled up to reveal a snake tattoo. Swede yanked open the passenger door, dragged Pop out. Rico twisted the old man's arm. They marched him over the muddy driveway to the Lincoln, locked him in the back seat.

Swede turned to me and shouted: "Scram, Shaky."

Rico leaped in behind the Lincoln's steering wheel. Swede slammed himself into the passenger side. With that big V8 rumbling, they sped away from the Jung Sanitarium and toward the dark horizon.

CHAPTER TWENTY EIGHT

I hid in my apartment for two days. Feeding the pets was my only contact with living beings, except for a phone call to the radio repairman. On the third day I ventured up Selby to purchase newspapers and bread.

SLAYING VICTIM IDENTIFIED

said the Dispatch, in type spread across the front page.

WEST SAINT PAUL VICTIM
FRIEND OF MISSING PAIR

I sat on a bench at the streetcar stop and read, the newspaper shaking in my hands.

```
Melvin E. Passolt, head of the Minnesota Bureau of
Criminal Apprehension, said today the man slain at
Webster, Wis. Tuesday has been tentatively identified as
George E. Anderson, alias George Cooper, 1031 Robert St.,
West St. Paul.
    Anderson had been living at the West St. Paul address
with Fred Barker and Alvin Karpis, and Karpis moved from
that address days before the slaying.
```

Pop Anderson had been stripped of his clothes, shot three times, and dumped at a muddy lakeshore. The story noted that Barker and Karpis were wanted for killing a Missouri sheriff. It said that William Mahoney, mayoral candidate, was using the Anderson murder to illustrate his charge that Saint Paul was infested by gangsters, and that police were doing nothing to stop them.

I quit reading. I stumbled into a drugstore for a pack of Camels, and lit one up at the counter. It was my first cigarette since high school. I ordered coffee but it had no flavor.

I turned, lightheaded, to the sports page. The writers were giving the main Derby chance to Top Flight, a filly who would be odds-on at the Wood Memorial Stakes in New York. Gut churning so much that it was making noise, I could not concentrate on reading.

I wandered out of the drugstore, trashed the newspaper and caught the streetcar three stops to the Barking Dog speakeasy. From its bar phone I called Billy McAmbly and said I would be buying.

He bumped through the back door, in uniform, ten minutes later.

He slapped me on the shoulders.

"Back on the sauce," he said.

He belched. "Altwasser with a bomb," he told the fraulein, a woman in her 40s with bleached, ragged hair.

He watched her walk off.

"She'd be a catch, Billy," I said. "She owns the joint."

"Aye Christ," said Billy, "she's got five children of her own. You can barely elbow through the crowd in my house as it is."

We took our drinks to the shady part of the brick wall. Mine was a stein of Altwasser and a glass of absinth, guaranteeing a hangover and maybe a throbbing attack of gout.

"You hear the mayor-to-be bloviating last night?" Billy asked.

"Trying to get my radio fixed," I said.

"He's a true Irishman, talks five times as big as he really is. But I tell you, Mahoney has got them frightened out of their shoes downtown. The Fox and Hounds took all their slot machines and hid them in Filben's garage. A couple of joints closed outright. They're taking no chances. You'd think Mahoney would bring on the end of the world."

He drank.

"What'll it mean for you, Billy?"

"Mahoney? A blessing, by Christ. Big Ryan will shrink so much they'll be calling him Midget Ryan. I'll get a bump to sergeant."

"You sure?"

"Oh, Dahill's my man. And Dahill is Mahoney's man. It's all about the factions. How are you doing Mickey? You look like somebody run over your dogs."

"No," I said. The last of the absinth burned down my throat, and I gargled the beer chaser.

"Well," Billy said, "you didn't invite me here to talk about the Derby."

"No."

"And I ain't seen you drunk since Peggy ... I shouldn't have mentioned her, Mick."

"I'm in deep, Billy. You read the papers?"

"What else do I have to do all day?"

"Passolt's case."

"The corpse in Wisconsin?"

"That one."

"It's sure to be bungled in the hands of Commander Passolt."

"See, Billy, I set a certain fellow up."

"Who?"

"The guy."

"The dead man?"

I nodded. "Put him on the spot."

"By Christ," he said, and drank off his boilermaker, stomped to the bar and ordered another. This left me in the dappled shade of a just budding elm tree. A drunken foursome at an umbrella table were laughing the afternoon away. They had barely noticed that Billy in full uniform had entered the speakeasy. Billy lifted his glass to them as he plodded across the courtyard.

He brought another stein of beer for me.

"Put on the spot," he said, "what does that mean in the Irish language?"

"Irish?"

"Yes, true speaking, not this bullshit of the king's English. Speak plain Irish, will you?"

"In plain Irish Billy, I drove the man to meet his killers."

"What the Christ did you do that for?"

"I didn't know they were going to kill him," I said.

"Ah for the love of Jesus," Billy said.

"Is that plain Irish enough?"

"Too much," Billy said. "Go away and forget it, Mick."

He leaned in, red faced, as if to tell me a secret. "With these murdering thugs, there's nothing you can do. Big Ryan has this town locked down like a fortress. Go away, man. I'd miss you for sure but it's go away or this town will ruin you."

"They tricked me, Billy."

"I have no doubt."

"Thirty pieces of silver."

"Oh, Christ, the Catholic schools, the ruination of us all."

He fixed me with a heartfelt look in those bloodshot blue eyes. "Mickey, don't be swimming in the sea of guilt now, you'll only drown."

He sat back.

"Who's your horse in the Derby?" he asked.

"Economic."

"Why?"

"The stopwatch doesn't lie, Billy."

"Are you down on that colt?"

"Big," I said.

He leaned in toward me. "I heard the fix is in for the filly."

"Only one filly ever won this thing, Regret, and she was a freak of nature."

"Ah Christ, I leave the figuring to you. I've no head for the higher math. Throw darts and play longshots, that's my game."

He raised his glass to me.

"Send me a post-card Mick."

"After the Derby," I said. "Economic wins, and you can come visit me in Eagle River. I'll be running a potato farm, like me sainted ancestors in West Cork."

"Potatoes?" said Billy. "It was potatoes ruined our people."

Billy dropped me off at my apartment, and I opened the door to barking dogs, tweeting parakeets, and a dirty envelope that had been slipped under. In it were two fifty-dollar bills. Not a scribble of explanation was given.

I replenished the water for Charles and Amelia, and let them out of their cages for a flight. Charles lit fluttering at the Cathedral windowsill. Amelia perched on the curtain rod at the city windows.

Snowflake, jealous creature, barked to let me know he should have been first in my attentions. Hula Girl eyed the birds. I doubt she wanted to eat them but to enforce her dominance of all the apartment's surfaces. After she made one rush at Charles, both birds kept to high perches.

I sat down and fell briefly into a drunken nap, then woke up remembering I had to walk the dogs. I put those fifties in my jacket pocket and hooked up Snowflake and Hula Girl. Uphill we walked, past the Chancery and across Summit to the mighty Cathedral. I brought them inside with me.

Dogs know God, and so observe no pieties. It's we humans who have lost touch and need to build Cathedrals. Anyway, the Blessed Sacrament was not in residence, the little golden door open to let all know there was no need to genuflect.

I walked the dogs in front of the altar, earning a horrified look from an Italian widow dressed in black. I stuffed the two fifties into the poor-box. I knew this was emptied daily by Father Mack, otherwise I wouldn't have trusted that the cash would actually get to the poor.

I walked the dogs up and down Selby, feeling loose-limbed now, stoked on alcohol that had not quite worn off. A couple of blocks to Myrtle's, and I walked the dogs over, a harassed referee in their eternal contest to lead the pack.

In the backyard of Myrtle's apartment, Hula Girl sniffed at Flyboy's popsicle stick grave. I followed the dogs up the stairs and when I knocked on Myrtle's door she shouted:

"Who is it?"

"Powers."

"Oh for Pete's sake," she said.

She opened the door on the security chain.

"I'm entertaining," she said.

"You certainly are," I joked.

She looked me over. "You smell like a brewery."

"You smell delicious," I said.

"Look at how drunk you are."

"I should hope I'm drunk, after all the liquor I've consumed."

"I'm on a date," she whispered.

"Well ditch the bastard," I said.

"I can't," she said. "Call me tonight, slugger."

And then she closed the door on me.

To hell with that, I told myself, and waited at the picnic bench in the yard. It had a tiny black-steel barbecue oven, and the leftover aromas kept Hula Girl and Snowflake entertained for a while.

I began to desire a beer, but the only place that would serve you with dogs along was the Barking Dog, blocks away. I stuck it out. I smoked my pipe. I walked the dogs here and there, never out of sight of Myrtle's back door.

I was half a block away when Bulldog McMullen emerged from the back door, in fine spring threads. He walked the opposite way, and around the block to, I presumed, his squad car.

I bounded up the stairs behind Hula Girl and Snowflake.

Myrtle was waiting for me at the door, barring the entrance. She wore strands of pearls over her parrot-green dress. Her lipstick was smeared.

I said: "Slumming, I see."

"No, you don't see, buster. That's your problem, you're blind drunk and you don't see."

Hula Girl and Snowflake, wary, were picking up bad feelings.

"Myrtle…"

"Aw, come in. Don't stand blurting my business in the hallway."

The dogs, unleashed, settled on her Persian rug as if born there.

"I'm giving notice," I said, hardly able to catch my breath. "I'm moving out to the farm."

"Good for you," she said, hands on hips.

"I'd love your company out there," I said.

"Keeping chickens?" she said.

"I'd marry you, Myrtle."

"Fat chance," she said.

She raised, for the first time I'd ever seen, the window shades in her luxurious living room. Her back turned to me she said, "Mick …"

And then she turned around, looking like a saint, in a halo of sudden sunlight.

"I'm a rotten hopeless case."

"No you're not Myrtle."

"I'm bad, and I need to live bad."

She fingered those pearls. She smiled with only one side of her mouth.

"I ain't got what it takes to be the farmer's wife. I never baked a pie."

I sank in her sultan's chair.

"This town is getting under my skin," I said. "It's too dangerous. It's full of double-crossers."

"So? Your dogs are loyal."

"Maybe."

"You need love too bad."

"Maybe I do."

"But I got no love inside of me, Mick. I had the love whipped out of me as a girl. My old man done it to me with a razor strap. And that's the truth about Myrtle."

She sat, sighed, played with her pearls. She seemed defeated by her own words.

"Stick around, Mick, I like you. Don't go chicken farming. There ain't enough decent men in this town."

"Like Bulldog McMullen?" I said.

"Well ain't you bitter?"

"He's kind of an asshole."

"Don't you realize these cops can slam a girl into jail just for fun? Why I know a girl they stuck in there and never put her on the books. Her family had to bribe that fat tub of guts."

"Crumley."

"I don't even say his name no more. You got to keep the cops happy in this town, Mick, what's the matter with you?"

She approached the chair, caressed my face with her rough hands.

"Come on, buy a girl dinner, it'll do you good."

CHAPTER TWENTY NINE

I saw the omens everywhere. Mahoney won for mayor of Saint Paul. Big Ryan, the gangsters' choice for police chief, would soon be a traffic cop. Roosevelt was gaining for president. Al Capone, cursing and fuming, was slapped into prison on tax charges. Myrtle and Loretta's Free Love Group rented a room at the Lowry so they could organize an all-women Beer Parade.

Janie was wrong about the political odds against repeal: Prohibition was dead.

Maybe, I told myself, Mahoney can clean up this town. Repeal might break the hold the gangsters had on this city. Maybe Franklin Roosevelt could pull off his economic miracle. Jobs would come back, and if nothing else, I could drive a truck.

As I speculated on the future, Hula Girl watched the parakeets and Snowflake stared at me. Snowflake was a simple opportunist, devoid of judgment, awaiting the next meal or the next adventure. I looked into his brown eyes and they asked the dogs' eternal question: "Now what?"

I wondered that myself. The Kentucky Derby was next, then with any luck, off to Eagle River. Maybe there was a lonely widow out in Wisconsin who wanted to bake pies, raise chickens, dig potatoes. The dogs' world would expand from 1200 square feet to

40 acres, including lakeside bathing.

I looked over the Unholy City. Seven Corners itself was a double-cross: of trolleys, trucks and autos cutting each other off and quite often, slamming into one another. With an absinthe hangover, I felt like I was bursting at my painful skin. Head movements made me dizzy. I dosed myself with milk and chocolate crackers. I fell into a chill, restless sleep in the sunshine.

In the afternoon, I knocked at Janie's dungeon with the Form folded under my arm. In the shade of the big oak, I lit my pipe. She said: "Aren't we going upstairs?"

"Change of plan," I said. "My radio repairman never showed up. We'll hear the Derby under blessed circumstances."

"Under what?"

"At the Chancery."

"With the Bishop?"

I shook my head. "He's an invalid who detests horse racing."

"Do they allow women in the Chancery?"

"Of course they do. You know Father Mack. No? Well, you've met him. Believe me he is a great influence in this town. He puts in words for people."

"Oh," she said. "I've got to change, then."

She let herself into her apartment. She disappeared wearing a pink blouse over rough white canvas trousers. She reappeared in a dark business suit, jacket over blouse over skirt accented with green pinstripes. Her pale legs were hidden in dark stockings.

"Bishop clothes," she said.

"Archbishop," I said. "And if the old fart is wheeled out of his sick room, his title is Excellency."

Janie's lips pursed, and she mock curtsied.

With that we crossed the street and climbed the steps to the Chancery.

The Kentucky Derby, in the last few days, had begun falling apart. The great filly Top Flight had lost the Wood Memorial Stakes in New York, had arrived lame at Churchill, and was scratched. Now the panicked players were backing Tick On, unbettable at 2-1, a horse who had lost five of his seven races.

At the top of the steps, I showed Janie the cover of the Racing Form. It featured a cartoon drawing of Tick On.

"Never bet the Racing Form's choice."

"Oh is that the key?" she said, laughing at me.

"Truth," I said. "In a pari-mutuel game, you *must* avoid following the crowd. A million people will see this Form today, and by power of suggestion, they'll bet Tick On to insane levels. You can't win every race, but you must get paid fairly when you do win."

We arrived breathless at the sunny Garden of Eden, knocked at the Chancery door, and were admitted by a hefty, pale grandmother, Mrs. Bold.

"This good lady runs the place," I told Janie.

"Oh not quite," said Mrs. Bold with a laugh. "He's in the Library. You know the way."

The Chancery was furnished for nobility, and we zigzagged over plush rugs. The place was like a museum of the Middle Ages, its walls hung with paintings of virgins, saints and cherubs. In the sunny library, Father Mack stood before the windows, hands at his back, listening to a radio announcer babbling to fill time between races.

"Janie Vetter," I said. "Father McCarthy O'Sullivan."

Her freckled hand disappeared into his giant meat-hook. She performed a small curtsy, without the mock in it this time.

"Janie," I said, "works at the Daily News."

Father Mack's eye fluttered, not with flirtation, but as the result of a wicked punch during his bare-knuckle days in Ireland.

"Who's your horse?" asked Father Mack.

"She doesn't have one," I said.

"I asked the young lady," Father Mack scolded me.

"I've never," said Janie, "… well I've never bet on anything."

Father Mack smiled. "Don't let this Powers fellow lead you astray. There's one sure path to salvation, and it doesn't begin in the paddock."

The ghostly Mrs. Bold, moving under a cloud of curly white hair, served us almost immediately. We sat to tea and fancy cakes at a sunny table. The chatter from Louisville filtered through the radio speakers, but we ignored it. We talked of Mayor Mahoney's victory, of Roosevelt's momentum. We lamented the weak showing of Roosevelt's primary rival, Al Smith, the only Catholic who had ever come close to the presidency.

Janie said the newspaper brass were terrified of Mahoney because his election dealt the unions a strong hand.

"And the gangsters a weak one," said Father Mack. He wiped his lips with a napkin and said, "So Powers, name your animal."

"Economic," I said.

"Rationale," he demanded.

"He lost the Wood Memorial by a neck."

"What of the horse who beat him?"

"Universe? The public over-bets winners. Economic proved himself the equal of Universe, and will pay much better odds. The only rivals to my horse are the duo sent by Colonel Bradley."

"How much of your money is Economic carrying to the finish line."

"Five hundred, Father."

He whistled. "Lord save us."

Janie said: "That's crazy."

"I've split it up," I told Janie. "Half for me, half for Sam Tanaka. I'm sure Father Mack knows, but Sam is desperate to get back to his family in Nagasaki."

"A good Catholic city if there ever was one," said Father Mack.

"Really?" Janie said. "Catholics in Japan?"

"Jesuits," said Father Mack. "Those fellas can establish a beachhead for Christ anywhere."

On the radio, the crowd was singing My Old Kentucky Home.

"For me," I said, "I need to get out of these rackets. I've got my eye on my aunt's old potato farm. But I need startup money. I've bet Economic on the future books at 14-1."

I dug into my pocket for the tickets.

"See? Suppose I move out to that farm. If all I have is a couple of hundred, I'm broke and snowbound by Christmas. But with three or four thousand, I can keep chickens and plant potatoes and have a cushion of cash underneath me. When the potatoes are in the cellar, and the snows arrive, I can bolt for Havana."

"Why Havana?" Janie asked.

"Never been there. Heard fabulous tales."

"What happens to the chickens?"

"I sell them. In spring I start again. Chicks and potato cuttings. With a cushion of cash, I'll have years to make it pay."

"I don't know." Janie said. "Farming is hard, hard work."

I held up one hand to ask for silence. I walked to the radio and listened as the announcer ran down the odds. Economic was at 9-1 on the board, so I'd made a great play to get 14-1. My only regret was that Sam refused my phone calls, so I'd had no access to his study of class. I had only my speed numbers and whatever wisdom came from taking a thousand beatings at the betting windows.

When I turned away from the radio and began paying attention to the life around me again, Father Mack was asking Janie about her duties at the Daily News. She said she hoped to break out of the society pages by writing an article about the Burned Ladies.

Those murders had occurred only two months ago, but there

was so much gangster crime in Saint Paul that Father Mack's memory had to be nudged. I must have missed the first mention, because suddenly Father Mack said: "And what does this have to do with Otto Alt?"

"Well, Father," Janie said, and spread her skirt primly over her knees. "You do know about the Denver Mint Robbery of 1922?"

"What of it?"

"Papa Alt's River State Bank apparently handled the stolen money. One of the Burned Ladies, Rose, was the wife of one of the Mint robbers. So at the very least there's a connection."

Turning from the radio, where I'd crouched listening, I made frantic hand signals at Janie.

Father Mack snorted. "And what, young lady, is your source for this accusation?"

Janie pointed at me.

"Spoiling this girl, are you?" said Father Mack. He turned rosy with anger. "Otto Alt," he thundered, "is a fine friend of the poor."

But his scolding was halted by events in Louisville, where the horses were approaching the starting gate. Hoping to steer the conversation back to the Derby, I said: "Bradley's horse? Burgoo King? He's number 13. Bad number and an outside post. He'll be swallowed up in the pack."

The anxiety grew both in Louisville and at the Chancery when the favored Tick On refused to load. The starter led him into the gate, but Tick On backed out. The starters ganged up to force him into the gate, and he reared and threw the jockey. All the horses, wild with energy in the starting gate, had to be backed out and reloaded.

"They're off," screeched the announcer. "Economic takes the lead with Burgoo King right behind…"

I dreamed of fuzzy baby chicks and potato cuttings and summers swimming in the quiet of Snipe Lake. Of fresh eggs in the morning and hash-browns made from my own potato cellar and fried crisp on a wood-fired stove.

"Economic in the clubhouse turn, still in the lead."

No more strangling the dogs on a leash, you just opened the farmhouse door and let them out for a day of romping in the woods. I'd stoke the barrel stove on a cool evening with the wood Uncle Joe had stored in the barn.

"Economic by two in the backstretch…"

And when the snow flew in Eagle River, a train would take me to Miami for the boat to Cuba. I would roam Havana's warm streets at night, when everyone in the Midwest was freezing. Of course I would meet a Cuban sweetheart, why else have the dream?

I circled the library, Janie staring at her hands and Father Mack leaning forward, listening to the race intently.

"In the stretch now, Economic, Burgoo King, Stepenfetchit. Everyone else far behind…"

I stood at the big globe and spun it. With one hand I beat my thigh as if a race horse were under me.

"Economic!" I shouted. "Economic!"

The announcer screeched. "A stalking Burgoo King makes his move. Economic fights back by a head. They're even now. Economic weakening."

"Christ no!" I screamed.

"Burgoo King by a neck. It's just these two now for the roses. Burgoo King by a half, he's pulling away, Economic fading badly, it's Burgoo King by a length on the outside, moving toward the rail, gaining with every stride, Burgoo King by two, a widening two, by three, here comes Stepenfetchit but it's too late…."

"No! No! No!"

"It's a runaway! Burgoo King by five lengths. Number Thirteen Burgoo King under the wire to win the 58th Run for the Roses."

I stopped spinning the globe. Janie made a feint toward the

library door. Father Mack held his head in his hands. I stepped over to the radio and stared in disbelief.

I kicked the radio. I looked out the window to the Cathedral, the home, I once believed, of a merciful God.

"Economic! You bum! I've lost it all!"

###

A SHORT HISTORY
OF THE REAL CRIMES

Rose Perry and Sadie Carmacher were killed on March 7, 1932. Their faces were eaten away by nitric acid and their bodies were burned in a stolen Buick. The crime occurred in Turtle Lake, Wisconsin, but was commonly attributed to Saint Paul gangsters The FBI was told, in an account they could never corroborate, that the women were last seen at a Saint Paul hotel, getting into a car driven by Jack Peifer. No one was ever charged for these double murders.

The North American bank robbery took place in Minneapolis on March 29, 1932. The robbers netted $50,000 in cash, roughly equal to $1 million in today's currency. Also stolen were bonds valued at more than $100,000 in 1932 dollars. In his autobiography, Alvin Karpis described this robbery as the Barker gang's "first major score." No one was ever convicted of this crime.

Arthur Dunlop, aka Pop Anderson, was killed on the day the Barker gang was rousted from its Saint Paul hideout. Dunlop was the last known consort of Kate "Ma" Barker. His body was discovered at a Wisconsin lakeshore on April 25, 1932. This crime may have tilted the Saint Paul mayoral election in favor of William Mahoney, whose campaign promise was to rid Saint Paul of gangsters. Mahoney won, but never fulfilled that promise. His term as mayor would be marked by the most sensational crimes in the city's history.

The murder of Arthur Dunlop was never solved.

THE NEXT MICK POWERS ADVENTURE:

DEAD
A LONG TIME

The boys are back in town. The Barker-Karpis boys, that is.

Mick Powers, desperate to pay the rent, embarks on a gamble of his own. But the stakes are raised to the house maximum when Ma Barker and her murderous brood return to Saint Paul. They need a local "jug marker" to help them plan their crime, and see Mick as perfect for the job.

Meanwhile, Janie Vetter, cub reporter, is determined to solve the case of the Burned Ladies by writing an article for True Detective magazine. And Myrtle, the Midwest's most notorious shoplifter, sinks into a funk, lovelorn for her locked-up Professor. She spurns Mick's earnest proposals, taking up with a well-connected swell.

Inspector Crumley and his partner the Bulldog are doing an awful job of policing, as usual, and Tricky Tom Filben plays the gangster game for laughs. In the last days of Prohibition, the once-innocent game of bootlegging has turned vicious. Come along for a rollicking bad time …

Available as a paperback or e-book on Amazon.

MICK POWERS, BOOK #3

DEAD
LIKE LAZARUS

It was a simple request from Jack Peifer, owner of the most stylish speakeasy in town. Jack asked Mick to put him in touch with Alvin Karpis or Fred Barker. Both those gangsters had beat it out of town after a deadly bank robbery. And Mick Powers had connections deep enough to coax them out of hiding.

What could go wrong?

Plenty, as Barker and Karpis return to Saint Paul with a more powerful and deadly gang than ever. They have bribed prison officials and secured the release of Doc Barker, who'd been serving life for murder. And now, Jack Peifer was introducing the Barker-Karpis gang to Chicago criminals who'd been involved in the Saint Valentine's Day Massacre.

The Barker-Karpis gang then begins its transformation from bank robbers to kidnappers. As they plan the snatch of a wealthy man, they also have to figure out what to do with the notoriously cranky Ma Barker.

Meanwhile, Mick's got his own troubles with his sworn enemies, Swede Fanlund and Ralph Tallerico. These partners in assassination are always skulking around, waiting for their chance to take Mick on his final ride.

And Mick's substitute wife Myrtle, and substitute daughter Janie, each wrestle with their deepening problems.

Available on Amazon in the summer of 2015

MICK POWERS, BOOK #4

DEAD MESSENGER

It's frozen, it's isolated, but Mick's Eagle River retreat offers him protection from the gangsters who want him dead. But his splendid isolation is violated by a series of phone calls and hang-ups.

It's not long before a big sedan slides down Mick's icy driveway. Out of it pops the entire Barker-Karpis gang, dragging a bleeding man. Alvin Karpis tells Mick the gang needs to hide out in his cabin for a few days.

This is the Barker-Karpis gang's final crime, a kidnapping that earns them the wrath of J. Edgar Hoover and puts them on the Public Enemies list. Mick is forced to become the gang's messenger boy, shuttling to and from the city as ransom negotiations go horribly wrong. In Saint Paul, Mick works with the opera-loving gangster Shotgun George Ziegler to wrest the ransom from the wealthy brewer Papa Alt.

Meanwhile, one of the darker figures of the Barker-Karpis gang, Lapland Willie Weaver, has latched on to Mick's former girlfriend Myrtle. Weaver is bruising and abusing Myrtle, and nobody can seem to do anything about it.

Mick's young friend Janie, once a crusading news reporter, has a new focus in life, but is still working to expose the underworld.

In the end, Mick faces the dilemma, and the temptation, of his life and is forced to make a final choice between good and evil.

This final book in the Mick Powers series is available on Amazon in late 2015

THE RESURRECTION OF JOHN DILLINGER

Mick Powers has fled the gangster city of Saint Paul for good, but some of his friends haven't been so lucky. Pat Reilly, gangland's errand boy, nurses the illusion that he will inherit the role of mob chieftain when his boss Harry Sawyer flees town. Pat's plans to take over Harry's notorious Green Lantern tavern, though, are opposed by shrewd, tough Bessie Green, who thinks she should run the joint.

But all bets are off when John Dillinger and his girlfriend Billie Frechette breeze into town. Dillinger, freshly escaped from an Indiana jail, needs the protection only the Green Lantern and Harry Sawyer can provide. With immunity from arrest purchased, Dillinger reassembles his gang, including the dangerous duo of Homer Van Meter and Baby Face Nelson. From their Saint Paul hideouts, this last version of the Dillinger gang launches bank robberies into Iowa and South Dakota.

Meanwhile, Pat and Bessie are tasked to provide the Dillinger gang with cars and hideouts. But Pat and Bessie have domestic problems of their own. Pat's wife Babe had no patience for his dream of gangster glory. Bessie's husband Eddie, the Midwest's shrewdest bank robber, can't seem to quit while he's ahead.

In the end, Pat can't resist the allure of the Dillinger gang, and follows them to a Northwoods retreat called Little Bohemia. And Bessie can't save Eddie from the violent fate that awaits him on the streets of Saint Paul.

The Resurrection of John Dillinger concludes the "Saint Paul quintet," of novels based on the extraordinary true history of this quiet little city with an uproarious, dangerous past.

Available on Amazon in 2016

www.ingramcontent.com/pod-product-compliance
Lightning Source LLC
Chambersburg PA
CBHW020237180626
46810CB00006B/2236